MAVERICK

A NORTH RIDGE NOVEL

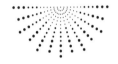

KARINA HALLE

METAL BLONDE BOOKS

For all the first responders - thank you

Dare to reach out your hand into the darkness, to pull
another hand into the light

— NORMAN B. RICE

NOTE TO THE READER

Warning: This is not a Christian romance. This book contains graphic (but fun!) scenes of a sexual nature and enough profanity to make a sailor blush. Please do not read if you are sensitive to sex or swearing. Fucking eh!

PROLOGUE

RILEY

Fuck.

Such a simple word, one-syllable, with harsh intonation, yet it can be used for a multitude of meanings. In fact, I think it might be my favorite word (right behind *Scrumtrulescent*, which, spoiler alert, isn't actually a word).

I love to fuck, I love to get fucked, I love using it instead of the word *really* (I like to get fucking fucked), I like how it can capture every element of surprise, and I really love it when people get creative with it (who can forget "fuck me gently with a chainsaw" from *Heathers*?).

But right now, hovering beside a pine tree with the wind, howling and angry, pushing scratchy snow across my face and obliterating my vision, my limbs dangerously numb, *fuck* seems like the only word possible.

As in I'm fucked, we're all fucked.

We might fucking *die* up here.

And *here* is a place I shouldn't even be. It was supposed to be my day off, Levi's too. We were going to drive to Denver,

1

hope to score tickets to a Bronco's game. Instead, there was a call this morning. One of our team members called in sick, which didn't help, and then the alert was sounded.

Two heli-skiers were dropped off yesterday afternoon on one of the more challenging peaks (though, yes, all heli-skiing is challenging, I mean you're being dropped on a wild mountain face by a helicopter). They never returned to the ski lodge and the helicopter company only reported them missing this morning.

It doesn't help that a wicked front whipped up overnight, causing white-out conditions that cancelled all the runs. Right now, all the skiers and snowboarders are holed up in their fancy châteaux, drinking hot buttered rum and complaining about how they can't hit the slopes. I really hate that part of my job, the fact that I live in Aspen, and while I'm living with my best friend and two of our colleagues in a damp, shitty house on the outskirts of town, the people I'm usually rescuing are living it up in the lavish chalets and lodges, spending money like it's worth nothing at all.

Not only that, but Levi and I are the ones risking our neck every single time we head out on a call, to rescue the ignorant, spoiled tourists who blatantly ignore the rules and trail markers. Yes, sometimes the unthinkable happens out of the blue and tragedies can strike anyone and everyone, but most of the time, it's because of pure carelessness.

Today, though, I don't think it's the case. When skiers are heading down the side of a mountain without ski runs and basically creating their own path, it's not unheard of for them to get lost, which is bad news. But when the fucking company doesn't report them missing for almost a whole day, that's when things go from bad to worse. It doesn't matter how well someone is equipped and dressed for something like heli-skiing, a night out in the elements has the ability to rob even the most experienced souls.

Like me. Right now, I'm holding onto this tree and waiting for Levi, my eyes trying to scan the endless white in hopes of finding him, finding anyone. My cell has no service but our radios work and, despite my constant communication with Brett, our team leader back at the base, no one can seem to pull up Levi. And I'm not going anywhere without him.

"Riley, come in," my radio crackles as if on cue.

I fumble for it and bring it up to my mouth, my voice shaking as I push the button and say, "Riley here. Over."

"How is the visibility? Over," Brett says.

"Complete shit," I tell him. "And I'm not sure how fast the temperature is dropping, but it's dropping. I can't see Levi, can't reach him, can't see anyone, can't hear anything. His transceiver isn't even coming through. Over." I'm trying not to sound panicked, but just relaying my situation out loud has it hitting home for me.

"Don't worry about, Levi. You know better than anyone that he can take care of himself. Give me your coordinates and stay exactly where you are. Once there's a break in the weather, we'll send the chopper out to get you and find Levi." He pauses. "Then we continue the search for the skiers. But you're our priority. Over."

I sigh and slip the device back in the front pocket of my parka which is crusted over with snow. He's right in that I shouldn't worry. We've been in worse situations before. There was the time I fell down a crevice and had to wait for several hours before they found me. Once, Levi struck a tree while skiing and suffered a concussion that affected his ability to find his way off the mountain. This is just a storm and it's not the first time we've been separated while out on the job.

Still, something in my heart squeezes, a vice of unease. Levi and I have been friends since high school, bonding together over the love of snow and the Washington outdoors. Since I was dirt poor and practically trailer trash back then and couldn't afford a snowboard, let alone lift tickets, Levi, who worked part-time as a lift-operator at Mount Baker, pretty much supported my habit. He gave me his old board, would get me on the lifts for free, and taught me everything about the mountains.

After we graduated, I wanted to get as far away from my family as possible and start a new life somewhere else. When Levi said he wanted to join a search and rescue team, I decided I wanted that too. When he went to Utah to train, I went to Utah. Wherever he got a job, I would follow. That's how we both ended up in Aspen.

I love working for SAR. It gives me a sense of purpose, combined with a love for nature and a great respect for the elements. I'm at once powerless and at the mountain's mercy, and yet I'm able to battle against it in order to save lives.

But the truth is, sometimes I wish I didn't work with someone I love. Because that's the fucking truth. Levi might be my best friend, but I love him more than I'll ever be able to tell him. And in moments just like this one, when his own life is at stake, I'm almost paralyzed by the fear of losing him. It's moments like this that I know I should do what Brett is telling me to do, that I need to stay where I am and wait. But each second that ticks past with the slice of snow across my face feels like a second I could be too late.

I need to find him.

I let go of the tree I've been cowering beside and decide to keep going. My boots sink into the snow, all the way to my knee, as I leave the relative shelter of the pines behind and trudge out across the open slope. Though I can barely see more than a few yards in front of me, I'm somewhat familiar with this terrain. Earlier, the chopper had dropped us just to the northeast of here. Levi and I were together for only twenty minutes before we split up. By the time I reached a dead-end against a cliff face and the storm started to worsen, I lost communication with him.

But knowing Levi, he probably kept going, determined to find the skiers. He probably crossed this section of the mountain that I'm crossing right now, a steep open part of the slope devoid of trees and piled high with snow drifts. With the spring, the snow loosens, making this area an avalanche hazard, not to mention the fact that this faux run breaks off into crevasses and drop-offs at the lower elevation.

When I'm halfway across the slope and can make out the shapes of the trees on the other side—shifting shadows that flicker in and out through the ongoing white—a noise makes me stop in my tracks.

It's not a loud noise, kind of a soft *poof* that is barely heard above the roar of the wind and snow, but then I see it. The sky glows a faint pink with a red-hot ember in the middle of it.

A flare!

Shot from where I just came from, but further to the north, though even as I stand here looking at it, it's already moving over, pushed by the wind. But mentally I'm calculating it, tracking exactly where it could have come from.

I bring up the walkie and speak into it. "Brett, come in. A flare just went up, about a mile northeast of where I am. Permission to investigate? Over."

"Permission granted. Be careful, Riley. Over."

Warmth spreads in my chest, a tiny bit of hope. Whoever sent it was capable of shooting a flare. That means they're alive. Most skiers, especially ones who go "off-piste" or beyond the avalanche-controlled boundaries of the mountain resorts, should always have transceivers on them, as well as an emergency kit. This group didn't have the transceivers, but at least they have a flare. It's possible they even saw the helicopter come by earlier and they're too cold or injured to move. That's actually the smartest thing to do—stay exactly where you are and let us find you.

I start back across the open slope, noting that the wind is starting to die down a bit and the visibility is getting better. I glance up at the sky and see faint light patches amongst the whirling snow, meaning the storm is starting to break apart, at least for the time being. I'm just a few feet from the trees again and I can already see how much calmer it is under the canopies.

"Riley!"

My name sounds like a fragment from a dream but even so, it roots me in place. I turn around to see a shadow behind me, emerging from the trees, looking larger than life with his gear on his back.

Levi!

I want to yell back but I can't do anything but smile. I wave at him, frantically, and point toward where the flare went up, the sky just a faint pink in that spot now.

"Stay there! I'm coming," he says, voice faint, and starts making his way over.

He's moving fairly fast, even with his gear, and he's nearly at the middle of the slope when a loud *whumpf* rings through the air.

He stops and looks at me, wide-eyed.

That noise, that *whumpf*, like someone dropping a sack of potatoes from fifty feet high onto the snow, is all too familiar.

It's the sound of fear.

Of death.

To be more specific, it's the sound of fresh powder that's been sitting on top of a frozen layer compressing, shifting, or sliding downhill.

An avalanche.

"Levi!" I scream. "Hurry!"

There's a roar building now, a haunting, ghostly rumble from high up the mountain where I know the snow is now coming down like a freight train, barreling toward us, sending tremors up my legs.

One thing I know about avalanches, is that you never have time.

I look over to Levi who is hurrying through the snow, the powder flying out behind him as he runs. He's so focused on getting to me that he doesn't look to his left, up the slope, where a wall of snow is building, rushing, ready to consume us.

In my panic and the whirling storm, it's hard to tell how big of an avalanche it is, what kind. It could be powder or wet or a deadly slab. It could level trees and knock us unconscious, or be a soft cloud, just enough to dust us like icing sugar. There's no time to wonder because in seconds it will be here and I only have two thoughts ringing in my head:

I hope the trees will protect us.

I hope Levi gets here in time.

And then it's here.

Time is ripped away.

I stare across at Levi's face, his eyes locked on mine, caught in fear and horror and then everything is white.

Somehow, in that split second before the blast of air hits me, followed by the snow moving at fifty miles an hour, I wrap my arms around the pine's rough trunk and hold on for dear life. It feels like an eternity and my world is just ice, the air knocked out of me.

Everything is a roar.

Everything is white.

Everything is sharp and cold and relentless.

I'm drowning and I'm holding on and I don't know if it

will ever stop, if it will ever stop pummeling me, if I'll ever be free of this torment.

Cold.

So, so cold.

So monstrous.

So real.

This is fucking it.

This is how I'm going to die.

Entombed in ice, lungs full of snow.

And I never got a chance to tell Levi how I really felt.

All those years of pushing the feelings down, of swallowing them whole.

He never knew.

And then, then, it…

Stops.

The world is reduced to a muffle. Everything comes to a still, a hushed calm, with powder hanging in the air. I'm caked head to toe in ice and snow.

My mouth opens, gasping for air, and I cough out white.

I feel like I could stay here forever, stuck to this tree, buried to my waist in snow. I could freeze, a statue, frozen in time.

But then…

Levi.

LEVI!

I manage to bring my arms off the tree, frantically dusting away the snow from my limbs, my face, my eyes.

The snow is still whirling from the storm, lighter now, though the world around me glows a deeper white.

Levi is nowhere to be found.

"Levi!" I scream, spinning around to find him, but all I see is a rough blanket of snow. "Levi!"

I know that standing here and screaming isn't going to do me much good. The avalanche wasn't strong enough to flatten the trees, but it would have knocked him off his feet. He's not swept down the mountain, he hasn't made it to safety.

He's buried.

And he only has minutes to live.

I have no time to think.

I go on auto-pilot, all the years of training rising out of me.

I move through the snow, walking as quickly as I can, even though I'm stumbling, falling, my footing loose and unstable.

I don't give up. I keep going, practically wading, swimming, until I'm at the point where Levi was last standing.

Panic claws up my throat but I ignore it. I have to.

The walkie-talkie crackles, Brett is calling in.

He sounds like a dream.

"Riley! Riley, they're reporting seismic activity on the slope, an avalanche. Can you confirm? Riley, come in. Over."

But I have a job to do.

I bring out the shovel from my pack and start digging, frantically at first, then slowly, methodically, as I plow through the top layers.

I don't even think I'm breathing. My heart is bursting from my ribs.

My eyes sting, my fingers in my gloves burn, my face feels raw and stiff as I realize tears have been running down my cheeks and sticking to my skin.

I keep going.

"Riley. Please come in. Are you okay? Have you found Levi? Over."

I keep shoveling.

And then I see a slice of orange-colored fabric.

His jacket.

"Levi!" I scream and throw the shovel aside, start digging him out with my hands like a dog after a bone.

I touch his shoulder, his arm, his torso, his neck.

His face.

Eyes closed, skin blue.

Not breathing.

I immediately clear the snow from his mouth and try to clear as much of his body free as possible. He might have broken bones, but I can't be too slow, too gentle. I have to be quick and I have to save him now.

Summoning all the strength I have left, I bring his upper body out of the snow and feel for a pulse.

Nothing.

Through tears and blubbering words, I start CPR.

I've done it many times before on dummies.

I've seen it performed on near misses and close calls.

I've never had to perform it myself on a real person before.

I've never had to perform it on someone I know.

I've never had to perform it on my best friend.

The man I love.

And now I am, I'm pumping and breathing into him and counting and crying and my world is falling apart around me. Everything is falling apart, I'm falling apart, how is this world still here?

"Please, please, please," I cry out, sending prayers up with my heart, my heavy, tumbling heart. "Please be okay, please come back, please don't die. Please don't leave me. I love you, I love you, I love you."

I keep trying, I keep breathing, his cold lips to mine, and I keep crying.

"I love you, I love you, I love you."

This can't be it. This can't be it.

But as time rolls on and the snow continues to fall, blanketing us in a cold embrace, I know.

This is it.

This is it.

No more.

CHAPTER ONE

MAVERICK

NORTH RIDGE, BRITISH COLUMBIA

THE TEXTS HAVE BEEN COMING IN ALL NIGHT.

Are you still at work?

When will you be off?

Come to The Bear Trap!

Drinks on me!

Those were all sent from my friend Delilah, who owns and bartends our local watering hole.

Where the fuck are you?

I'm heading to the Bear, should I wait for you?

I'm pretty sure your dog pissed on the floor, btw, I can't tell and I don't want to smell it.

Those were from my older brother, Fox, whom I live with, along with my dog Chewie.

I ignored them. Not to be a dick, but I *was* at work. Maybe a few years ago I would have had the whole day off as I had planned, but the fact is, ever since I'd been put in charge of North Ridge's search and rescue team, days off barely exist. Even though it's early March and in some ways winter is winding down, the mountains and ski slopes are still busy, and there's usually some idiot who decides to go skiing off course who we have to rescue later. Besides, winter is a bitch, and like they say on *Game of Thrones*, she's constantly coming. There's always a few more storms that swoop in before the season is done.

It's eleven o'clock at night and pitch-dark out as I park my truck outside the house I share with Fox and glance at my phone, which is lighting up again. This time the texts are from my father, laying it on thick. You know when he uses my real name I'm in big fucking trouble.

John, come to the bar, everyone is here.

You know this is Shane's big night and he's your brother.

He looks up to you, you need to be here. Now.

God damn it, John!

I sigh, breath frozen in the air, and lean back in my seat, watching the snow slowly gather on the windshield. I don't know why I'm dragging my feet about the whole thing, but I am. I'd known for some time that my younger brother was going to propose to his girlfriend Rachel tonight and while I'm happy as hell for them—if there was ever a star-crossed couple that belonged together, it's those two—I guess it makes me feel a little...*old*.

Maybe that's not the right word. I'm turning thirty-one this year. I'm fit as fuck, in prime shape, and advancing nicely in my career, even though it's a challenge being the boss of my colleagues and friends now. I guess it's just complicated when one of your brothers decides to marry the love of his life. Makes you wonder why that doesn't seem to be happening for yourself.

And of course I can answer that question right away. I live in a small town smack in the mid-south of the province of British Columbia. There are about ten thousand full-time residents in North Ridge, and I know I've dated pretty much every attractive female within a fifty-kilometre radius.

The term *dating* is even a bit of a stretch. There's been less than a dozen I've full-on dated, whether for a few weeks or a few months. The rest are just one-night stands and hook-ups. I'm not exactly proud of my reputation (I believe Rachel called me a man-whore and I didn't correct her) but at the same time, I'm not ashamed of it. I know what I want and it doesn't seem to be changing anytime soon. With my lifestyle and my line of work, relationships just seem to mess everything up. What's the point of getting close to someone if it's just eventually going to end anyway? What woman would not only understand me, but the job that I have to do, how important that is? Not many.

Not that there's anyone I'd even consider getting close with. It's been a few months actually since I last got laid, some French tourists who were in town. Yes, I used the plural. What can I say? They liked to share and I loved to let them.

A pitiful howl snaps me out of my musings. I glance up and see Chewie at the large windows overlooking the deck. She knows I'm home and if I don't go inside and pay her some attention, there will be hell to pay. She's not just named after Chewbacca (I dare you to think her barks, whines, and howls aren't Wookie speak), she will literally chew her way through fucking everything and anything. I'm pretty sure Fox regrets the day I brought that pit bull home from the rescue, especially as she immediately ate one of his girl-friend's bras.

I sigh, suddenly weary from the day, and trudge up to the house where I'm immediately greeted by Chewie who's acting like she hasn't seen me in months, her body wiggling all over the place and nearly knocking over the stack of winter boots by the door.

"Easy, silly girl," I tell her, scratching her behind her ears as she does circles around me before she runs outside into the snow to do her business. As much as Fox gives me hell over her, at least she never expects me to take her on a walk in negative temps.

I look around the house. It's clean, albeit a bit messy. That's natural when you have two guys living together, both of whom are rarely home. In the summer and fall, Fox works as a hot shot, a wildfire fighter and smoke jumper, which takes him away from North Ridge and into little camps across BC and other provinces as he fights the blazes on the ground. In the winter, he works as a ski and snowboard guide at our local ski resort.

Chewie rushes back in from the cold and gives me one of those looks of hers that warms your heart before it breaks.

"I'm sorry," I tell her as I head down the hall to my bedroom, stripping off the layers of work gear as I go. "I'd stay home with you if I could. But you know family. If I don't go, I'll look like an asshole."

She snorts in protest, following me, trying her hardest to win me over with her damn sweet eyes. I've always been a sucker for the ladies.

It doesn't take long for me to throw on a thermal and sweater, then distract Chewie with a Milk-Bone and head back out to the truck before she realizes that I'm gone. The snow is falling even harder than it was earlier and I fishtail in the truck for a bit as I head down the driveway.

The bar isn't too far from our house, so I have barely enough time to put on my game face before I pull into the parking lot.

"You're happy for him," I tell myself as I park the truck.

And I am. Shane deserves all of this and more. As his brother, I couldn't be more proud. I just have to shake off that tinge of self-doubt that's clouding me and let it go. The truth is, and I know this, that I can't even imagine settling down with anyone. And since that's the truth, there's no reason to feel anything but pure joy for my brother. And maybe a bit of relief that it's not me who's making a lifetime commitment.

Inside the pub, the celebration is in full-swing. Normally there's just a few of us in here, ordering drinks to keep Delilah busy and in business while shooting the shit, flicking peanut shells on the floor, fucking around. Now it seems like half the town is crammed inside. Music from the jukebox is blaring Willie Nelson, people are dancing, drinking, yelling.

Some of them are yelling at me.

"Holy fuck, you finally showed up!" Fox yells, coming over to me with two bottles of beer in his hands, immediately handing me one. He's drunk, which is a surprise since I don't see him like this too often.

"I told you I was coming," I tell him, taking the beer and having a tepid sip, knowing I'll have to take it easy tonight since I'll be the one taking his drunk ass back home.

"Actually, you didn't," he says, throwing his arm around my shoulder like he didn't just see me this morning. Guess he forgot about the dog piss.

"John," my father says, appearing at my side. My father isn't a tall man, though all his sons tower over him, including me. I'm 6'3", Fox is 6'2" and Shane is 6' even. Even so, the man wrote the book on tough love and can side-eye you into retreating with your tail between your legs. For all my height and brawn, my father will always be able to put me in my place.

"About time," he says gruffly.

I try to give him my most appeasing smile. Lately it's been working on him, though I think it has more to do with him finding love again than it does with me.

"I worked late," I explain, "not much I can do about that."

My father narrows his eyes at me, seeking the truth.

"What?" I say.

"I know you've got a lot more on your plate now and the government keeps you on a short leash, but don't forget that family is family. Now go give your younger brother a damn hug."

He stalks off to the bathroom and I catch the eye of Vernalee, Rachel's mother, waving me over to her stool at the bar.

Fox is already distracted by the dart board so I head toward her.

"Maverick, you came," she says happily, a glass of sparkling wine in her hand. I know it's sparkling wine because Del would never stock real champagne for the bar. This ain't that kind of place.

I give her a quick hug. "Wouldn't miss it for the world. You must be thrilled."

She gives me a wry grin. "I am. Though I know it's a little weird."

"Weird is good."

Last year Vernalee was diagnosed with lung cancer (she's fine now), which prompted Rachel to come back to North Ridge for the first time in six years. Their relationship was pretty rocky but they managed to repair it, while Rachel also found herself repairing her relationship with Shane. Obviously that worked too, a little too well.

But what was also happening at the same time was that my father and Rachel's mother were falling for each other. I don't like to dwell on the sappy shit too much, but the two of them are obviously happy. And while it is a little weird that our families are connected now in two different ways, this is the first time I've seen my dad with someone other than my mother. She died just after Shane was born and I was only five years old. As much as I can't forget my mother, my dad deserves to find love again more than anyone.

I look over my shoulder and spot Shane, his arm around Rachel, both of them drinking and smiling with some of the locals. When I catch their eye, Rachel grins at me and Shane raises his drink. I raise my beer.

"So when do you think you'll settle down?" Vernalee asks, not so innocently.

I give her a wry smile and raise my brow. "When I find a good reason to."

She shakes her head. "All playboy types eventually settle. Even George Clooney. If you stopped being so damn picky, perhaps you'd end up married with babies one day too."

I laugh. "I don't know, I think being picky worked in Clooney's favor. His wife is not only insanely hot, she's a lawyer too."

"Well we both know you lack his looks, charm, and money, but it doesn't hurt to try, does it?"

"Vernalee, are you picking on Mav again?" Delilah asks from the bar as she pops open a few beers for customers.

"Thank you, Del," I tell her. "Always looking out for me."

Fox laughs, appearing behind me. "Yeah, she'll have you believe that but she's the first one to throw you under a bus."

Del shrugs, popping limes into the neck of the Coronas and sliding them down the bar. "Maybe you deserve to be thrown under a bus. All you Nelson brothers are obstinate. Shane is the only one with half a brain, marrying someone as lovely as Rachel."

"Oh, Rachel was just the first girl he saw," Vernalee jokes.

"Hey," Rachel chides her mother, pulling Shane over to us. Apparently she has superhuman hearing. I think all women do.

I give Rachel a hug and kiss on the cheek and Shane a loud whack on the back. "Sorry I'm late," I tell them.

"It doesn't matter," Shane says, his voice rock steady. "You're here now."

"And missing most of the party, it seems." I look around. "You're so composed," I point out, nudging him with my elbow. "I would have thought after the proposal and committing yourself to one woman for life, you'd be drunk off your ass."

"It's an illusion," he says with a wink but I know that's a lie. Shane's always had a good head on his shoulders, barely anything rattles him. By contrast, Fox is short-tempered and impulsive. Me, I'm somewhere in between.

"Aren't you going to ask to see the ring?" Rachel asks, fluttering her fingers in my direction.

"Hate to break it to you, but I've already seen it. The rest of us knew about this way before you did."

"You're so good at keeping secrets," Rachel says to Shane, leaning into him. Then she looks at me with bright blue eyes. "I'm not though. Guess who we saw tonight."

I frown. "George Clooney?"

She frowns right back. "No," she says slowly. "Your new employee."

"Riley Clarke?" I ask.

She nods, a teasing smile on her lips.

"How did you know it was her?" I ask. "I haven't even seen her picture."

Shane bites back a smile. "You haven't even seen her picture? I thought you hired her yourself."

"You don't submit photographs when you apply for a job, we're not a fucking modelling agency." I pause. "And I've searched for her all over social media. She's practically a ghost."

The moment I took over as head of the North Ridge Search and Rescue (or SAR), I was immediately tasked with help in hiring new talent. The BC government specifically wanted me to hire a woman or minority so they could meet their quota. So I looked through the resumes and applications that had been sent in over the last year or so when we last put out a job ad and Riley was pretty much the only qualified woman who applied.

On paper, she was almost perfect. Born in Washington state, then working at resorts and volunteering at SARs in Utah, Wyoming, and Colorado, Riley was twenty-five years old and had dual citizenship, which meant she could legally work in Canada and expressed interest in relocating to North Ridge. Why, I have no idea.

The only problem I found was that she was involved in a rather traumatic event at her last position in Aspen, an avalanche that left one of her colleagues in a coma. But if she was still wanting to work in SAR, then I wasn't going to stop her. I passed her information onto the government higher ups and through a series of emails and phone call interviews they conducted, she was hired.

Now she's here in town, and though I have yet to officially meet the woman I'll be working beside, I do have a meeting with her tomorrow to get her oriented before she starts and break the ice.

But how *they* knew about her, I have no idea.

"It was Del," Rachel tells me, raising her voice to be heard above the music which had suddenly gotten louder. "She said she's come into the bar a few times and they got to talking."

"You really haven't seen her?" Shane asks again.

"No. Why? Does she look like sasquatch?"

"Only if sasquatch's mother was Kim Basinger."

"Interesting," I say, getting a strange picture of sasquatch with a blonde wig in my head.

"She's a fucking *babe*," she says emphatically. "Shane couldn't stop drooling."

"Oh come off it," Shane says, rolling his eyes. Then he

KARINA HALLE

looks to me. "But she's right. She's hot. You're going to go crazy, Mav, I'm calling it now."

I shrug and take a sip of my beer. "I'm sure I'll be able to handle myself. We have a rule about screwing around anyway."

"Yeah, you say that," he says. "But just you wait."

I roll my eyes. I appreciate a gorgeous female as much as the next guy, but I'm pretty good at keeping it in my pants when I have to. And I'm not about to fuck up my new position by getting involved with someone I work with. Besides, how hot can she be? I couldn't find a single Facebook, Twitter, or Instagram page for her. All I found was her LinkedIn, and that didn't have a photo. Most hot chicks have their pictures floating all over the damn internet for the world to fawn over.

"We'll see about that," I tell him. "Enough about me anyway, let's talk you and wedding plans."

Rachel levels me with her gaze. "Do you really want to talk about our wedding plans?"

"Nah, I'm just bullshitting you guys. How about we all just get drunk instead." I raise my beer to them. "Cheers, brother. Future sister. Here's to you. Here's to family. Here's to what's next."

"Here's to what's next," they say in unison.

But as we clink our drinks against each other, I can't help but think about what's next for me.

Tomorrow.

I'll meet this now infamous Riley Clarke.

2

CHAPTER TWO

RILEY

"UGH," I MOAN OUT LOUD TO MYSELF. THE ALARM BESIDE ME has been going on and off for the last hour as I've pressed snooze again and again, trying in vain to stave off my hangover and slip away into blissful sleep where pain doesn't exist and bright lights can't hurt me.

But it's by the billionth ring that I realize that if I don't eventually get up and face the day, I'm going to miss out on orientation at the new job. And even though going out last night was regretful in more than a few ways, I don't want to further that feeling by not showing up at North Ridge Search and Rescue at all. Even though I don't start officially until later in the week, I still haven't met my boss or been formally introduced to the team.

"Riley, you're an idiot," I tell myself. Yes, out loud. Again. Hey, when you live by yourself and don't know anyone in a new town, talking to yourself becomes more and more comforting. I don't even know why there's such a stigma anyway, I dare anyone to tell me they've never done it themselves. You're often your own best listener, even if you ignore most of your advice.

And today I'm listening. Because honestly, I *am* an idiot. I should have gone home last night right after I left The Bear Trap Pub, but instead I headed over to Altitudes bar, which I know is the hookup place in town. I'm not sure what I was thinking, other than that The Bear Trap seemed full of couples and cliquey friends and I think it started to get to me. What better way to waste a night than to head to a bar and suck face with the first guy I see?

But it was more than just sucking face. I got drunk, fast, and ended up bringing the guy back here to my place for a late night roll in the hay. God, I'm so fucking needy. I have no problems with casual sex, not in the slightest, but I did it last night because I was feeling lonely, and that's usually the worst reason of all. You should get laid because you're aching for dick and not because you feel you've lost your place in the world.

What the hell was even his name? Ned? Nate? All I remember about him is he was fairly cute, at least harmless looking, and was trying to talk me up the moment I stepped into the bar. You'd think that I'd get attention and pick up lines all the time, but the truth is, most guys stay the hell away from me. I've been told time and time again that they're intimidated, but no matter the reason, it doesn't really help me. When I meet a guy "brave" enough to say hello, it means a lot.

Apparently, in the town of North Ridge, it means enough for me to sleep with the damn guy. I didn't even call it off when I discovered he had a micropenis, but dammit I should have.

I manage to turn off the alarm for good and swing my legs out of bed, taking in a deep breath and ignoring the throbbing in my temples. My mouth tastes acidic, my tongue rough. I know I'm supposed to be at North Ridge SAR in about an hour and yet I can't seem to get my body in motion. Luckily, the basement suite I'm renting isn't too far from the office. Then again, everything in this town seems within arm's reach, a quintessential hamlet.

I wonder if Nate/Ned/whatever his name was already talked about me. If there's something I know very well it's how fast gossip spreads in a small town. I won't be surprised if everyone already knows that he screwed the new girl.

Again, you're an idiot.

It doesn't help that I'm supposedly the only women on the SAR team here. I've had more than my fair share of misogyny being a woman in this field and the last thing I need is for word to spread that I'm sleeping around. I mean, I'm twenty-five years old and way past all that high school bullshit but like I said, I know small towns and most of them operate like an extension of high school.

Despite my brain having turned to mush and my body moving at a drunken snail's pace, I manage to get ready and out the door. The bracing air automatically sobers me up, the temperatures below freezing and making my nose dry out, my eyelashes stick together. I haven't a lick of makeup on my face because I know it doesn't make a difference when I'm going to be completely red-nosed from the cold.

I head down the town's main street, glad that I'm completely bundled under my faux-fur lined parka, my boots trudging in the fresh snowfall. The crispness in the air does a great job of clearing the cobwebs and making me feel excited about this job for the first time since I moved here last week. In some ways I've been dreading this new beginning and everything it means, but in other ways I know it's exactly what I need in order to move on.

The North Ridge Search and Rescue office is a rather boxy and drab-looking building located near the edge of town that totally screams "government run!" Which it is. I've heard working for the government can be a bit of a no-fun zone with people who do things by the book. That's not exactly me, but I was ready for a change when I applied. Plus, unlike so many SAR operations, they actually pay you a salary, with benefits to boot.

I walk up past a truck with the North Ridge SAR logo on the side and stop in front of the door, suddenly hit with a wave of nausea and a case of nerves. I know I have the job, but I've yet to meet the boss, John Nelson, or anyone else from the team. What if they don't like me? Scratch that, I don't care if they don't like me, but what if they don't *need* me? What if I'm not ready for this job again? What happens if it's just all too soon—or that this cements the fact that there's no starting over for me at all?

What if the past...hasn't passed?

Somehow though I find the courage to put my gloved hand on the door and open it, stepping inside.

There are three things I immediately notice about the office; one is that the room is dimly lit with some pretty horrible, flickering lighting that gives the area a sickly glow. Two, it's messy, printed photos and maps and papers scattered across several desks, coffee cups acting like paperweights and leaving stains, Cliff bar wrappers and crumbs dotted everywhere.

Three, there's only one person in here. And the guy sitting behind a desk, leaning back in his chair like he's waiting for an old friend to show up, is disturbingly handsome. Like, the kind of handsome that you know is dangerous and should be outlawed because it's apt to make the world bend over for you, every woman to fall on their knees. The kind of handsome that's beyond handsome, because it's not just a masculine face with gorgeous baby-blue eyes and a jaw that can cut paper, it's everything else that it's attached to, a giant hulk of a man that can probably bench press a bear.

And he's staring right at me. Not saying a word.

"Uh," I stammer awkwardly as I close the door behind me, "Hi. Are you John Nelson?"

My boss.

I mean, this guy can't be my boss.

This guy can't be anyone's boss, except if he was a model for Hugo Boss. And, shit, he could be, if he was trying to sell some rugged new cologne that smells like testosterone and whisky.

"I am," he says after a moment. "But you can call me Mav."

"Mav?"

"Short for Maverick," he says. He still hasn't moved, his big beastly body is just leaning back in his chair and looking me over. I can't read his expression at all, so I can't tell if he's joking.

"Really? Maverick? Like the Mel Gibson movie? Or like *Top Gun*?"

"Actually, the original Maverick was James Garner," he says smoothly. "And Maverick, as in that's my name. John Maverick Nelson. The one and only." He pauses, narrowing his eyes. "And who are you, sweetheart?"

Shit. Does he not realize who I am?

"Riley," I tell him. "Riley Clarke."

What I should do is walk across the room, stick out my hand, and hope he shakes it. But instead I stay where I am. I'm not usually intimidated, but this guy has my panties all twisted and being close to the door seems like a good strategy.

He arches a dark brow and slowly nods. "*You're* Riley…"

And here it comes. I'm going to get the "You don't look like you'd be a search and rescue worker" bit or something similar. I decide to nip it in the bud.

"Reporting for duty, *sir*," I tell him robotically, straightening up and giving him a mock salute.

Again, what I should have done is, well, anything but *that*.

But his full lips are quirking up into a smile, his eyes dancing with amusement.

"I think we're going to get along just fine," he says after a few beats, and with one fluid movement he gets out of his seat and to his feet.

I feel like the wind is knocked out of me.

This man—Maverick—is built like a fucking bear. No, he's more than that, like if someone used a grizzly bear as the prototype for the next Robocop. He's a beastly machine, tall, with hulking wide shoulders, and biceps I could see myself swinging off of. Who am I kidding, I could climb his whole damn body like Mount Everest and there's more than enough tempting places to hold base camp for a few days.

And, of course, while I'm standing here practically drooling, Maverick comes over, striding across the room with his hand out to me.

"Nice to finally meet you, Riley," he says.

I snap out of it and quickly take his hand. His grip is firm, his hand large, his skin warm. I know I'm probably imagining it, but I swear there's a mild current of electricity running from his skin to mine. It's either that or the fact that my wool sweater generates enough static to power a city.

"Nice to meet you, too."

Despite my hormones going crazy inside and my nerves all frazzled, I put on my stone face and try to sound as professional as possible. This is my problem, always has been. Because I'm tall, curvy, slim, blonde, and I have tattoos, everyone I meet makes a snap judgment about me. They don't take me seriously.

Then when you factor in that I'm kind of a goofball at heart and choose to laugh my way through life, it only makes it worse. So I have to remind myself, more often than not, that I need to work extra hard to rein myself in.

That said, Maverick holds onto my hand for what I know is a second too long, then he goes back over to his desk, which, at closer inspection, looks like a tornado hit it. "Take a seat," he says, nodding at the chair across from it.

I walk across the room and sit down, noting that his eyes don't leave me the entire time. Even though he's just observing me, there's something infinitely carnal about his gaze. I bet he gives great eye contact while fucking.

Not appropriate, rein it in, Riley.

"So," Maverick says, picking up a piece of paper. "I've been looking at your resume here."

"Hold up," I say, showing him my palm. "I *am* already hired, aren't I? I signed the contract."

"Yes. You are officially an employee of the BC government and North Ridge Search and Rescue. You wouldn't have had to come all this way if that wasn't the case."

I relax slightly.

"Back to the resume," he says, "I just wanted to touch on something with you that might be a sensitive subject. I probably don't have to, since you're here and ready, but it would give me peace of mind...your last job was nearly two years ago in Aspen. I know you and your partner were caught in an avalanche."

I swallow hard and feel my features grow harder, a cold stone building in my stomach. My defences go up automatically and everything inside me gets switched off.

"Yes, that's right."

He clears his throat and frowns, leaning back in his chair. "I don't mean to pry, but I can only imagine how traumatizing it must have been."

"It was just a class two slab avalanche."

"I see. Well, your partner—"

29

"Yes, he was buried. I got him out but it was too late to prevent any damage. He's still in a coma, in a hospital in Denver." He opens his mouth to say something but I plow on. "No disrespect, but if you're concerned on whether I can do my job properly or not, the fact is I'm here and that means I can. It was two years ago. I've gone through grief counselling. I've worked through things. I want to push it past me and move on. This is the only way how. I'm ready."

He stares at me for a moment and a flash of something, maybe respect, comes through. "All right," he says after a moment. "I trust you."

"Good," I tell him, still looking him steadily in the eye. I can't let him think for a second that I'm not ready for this, otherwise he's going to be handling me with kid gloves from this point forward.

"Also, you haven't put anything down on your resume with regards to where you've been working since then…you had to have survived somehow."

I always survive. "I was doing a lot of waitressing jobs in small towns. Nothing relative to the position or worth putting down on the resume." I pause. "Is that a problem?"

"No," he says quickly. "I was just curious. Well, now that that's all out of the way," he says, scratching at the scruffy stubble on his jaw, "how are you settling into North Ridge. Not a thing like Aspen, is it?"

If only he knew I grew up in a trailer park. I smile. "It's charming. And the people are way less pretentious. I was never a fan of Aspen…" *I was only there because of Levi.* I push the image of his face out of my head. "And since my father was Canadian, I thought maybe I should make the switch and move up north. It's a great country for starting over."

He studies me, so I in turn study him. He's not just handsome, he has the face of someone who loves getting rough and dirty. I can see a few faint scars on his cheek, one across his nose, a little slice at his bottom lip. He wasn't built to be a pretty boy. The only thing that's remotely beautiful about him are his eyes. His penetrating gaze aside, they're the color of shadowed ice, that deep bright impossible blue that exists only in nature, at the heart of glaciers. They contrast against the sharp, rugged masculine planes of his nose, chin, and jaw.

I'm not sure how long we stare at each other like this, nor am I sure how appropriate it is. After Levi, I learned my lesson when it comes to getting close to the people I work with. Hell, with people in general. I've gone through enough loss in my life, in all different ways. The last thing I need is to be attracted to my boss.

Even though, let's face it, I fucking am. Especially when he rolls up the sleeves of his navy-blue sweater and I see the dark swathes of intricate tattoos on his strong forearms. My panties melt a little bit more.

He clears his throat, as if he knows what I'm thinking, and then looks away, eyes scanning my resume as if he's hoping to get some new information off of it. "So, tomorrow come in at nine and we'll ease you into the week, do some orientation of the mountains. I'll have Neil take you on the helicopter, show you around the terrain so you get a feel for the place from up high."

"Neil?" I ask, my mind tripping over itself for some reason.

"One of your new colleagues. There's also Tim, Jace, and Tony. Bunch of loons, but good eggs all around, once you get used to them. And you will. Tim's up at the resort right now, doing controlled avalanche blasts. I'm here. Everyone else is on call." The sound of a car parking outside the building has Maverick straightening up, peering over my shoulder at the window. "Oh, and speak of the devil, Neil's here now."

I turn around in my chair to see the door open and a guy step in.

Neil.

Fucking Neil.

Not Ned, not Nate, but *Neil*.

As in the fucking guy I had stupid drunken sex with last night.

Micropenis Neil, my new colleague.

"Hey," he says and stops short when he sees me. He gives me an odd look, but manages to compose himself. He's wearing light jeans and a taxi-yellow ribbed puffer jacket that makes his head look disproportionately small. What the fuck is wrong with me? What was I thinking? *This* is the guy?

But if Maverick notices Neil's look, he doesn't show it. "Neil, I'd like you to meet Riley. She's the new hire."

"Riley," he says slowly. I would have thought he'd avoid looking at me, but instead he's looking extra smug. "Nice name, *Riley*."

And that's a jab at me. Because last night I lied and said my name was Candace. I don't know, it's just a thing I do in bars, though of course it's pointless in a small town, and especially pointless when you end up *working with the fucking dude you fucked*.

"Thanks," I say, trying to sound breezy. I turn my attention to Maverick because his face is a sight for sore eyes compared to Neil's. It's not that Neil isn't cute, it's that he's not as cute as my drunken brain thought last night, and that lame-ass cocky look in his eyes, like he thinks he owns me because he stuck his tiny dick in me, isn't doing him any favors.

"New in town?" Neil asks, obviously prying now. "I could show you around. The locals are real friendly, especially when you get to know them *really* well."

I get to my feet and glance at him. "A little too friendly," I tell him before I look at Maverick. "So, it was nice meeting you. I'll come here tomorrow at nine."

Maverick raises his brows, surprised at my abruptness. "Uh, yes. Of course. See you then."

I give him a tight smile, avoid Neil's eyes, and then leave before my face can grow any redder.

Fucking hell.

CHAPTER THREE

MAVERICK

Jesus.

When Shane and Rachel told me that Riley was a babe, I honestly didn't believe them. Thought that maybe they were either being generous about a run-of-the-mill pretty girl, or just joking about some heinous beast. I mean, I'm not picky. I love all types of girls. But it's rare that I get to set my eyes on someone like her.

Riley Clarke is probably the most gorgeous woman I've ever seen in real life. More than that, she's *real*. I get that I don't know the girl at all, but just talking with her for a half hour has cemented the fact that she has zero pretensions. Yeah, she's a bit rough around the edges with certain subjects and that's totally my fault for prying and pushing, but she comes across as someone who'll be as upfront with you as you need.

Which is a rarity these days. It seems everyone is always saying one thing and doing another. Everyone wants to save face, no one wants to follow through. Words become meaningless after a while. When you find someone who is a straight shooter, you want to hold onto them.

And…fuck. Could I fucking hold onto her. Her skin is like rich cream I just want to lap up, her lips are so perfectly lush and plump, they'd be a dream to sink my dick into. Her eyes are a sweet blue, girl-next-door innocent with a naughty twinkle to them that just hints at her layers underneath. And then there's her hair. Usually men don't give a rat's ass about a girl's hair but hers is big and blonde, the kind I want to twist around my hand and tug until I'm coming.

But of course all of this is a big fucking problem since I'm her new boss and getting involved with an employee is all sorts of trouble. Though I'm always a sucker for trouble, especially when it has a nice pair of tits.

"Is she seriously going to work here?" Neil asks. It takes me a moment to realize I've been staring dumbly at the door ever since Riley abruptly got up and walked away.

I manage to look at him, trying to shake some sense into me and ignore the erection in my jeans. Damn it, that was just from talking to her. How the fuck am I going to survive everything else?

"Yes. She's Riley Clarke," I tell him, doing my fucking hardest to act like the boss. Neil is a bit of a loser and always trying to undermine what I'm doing. It was always there in the past but ever since I was promoted to head of the department, he's gotten shittier. He's the type of guy who would throw me under every bus if he could and then brag about it.

He nods, biting his lip. There's something about his expression I don't like and I'm afraid to ask. So I don't. I wait. Neil also has a bad habit of sharing too much information.

"Damn," he eventually says to himself, flopping down in the seat where she just was. "Damn, damn, damn."

"Something the matter?"

"Have you seen her, Mav?"

"I have eyes, dipshit."

He shakes his head. "Oh man. Oh…fuck. I shouldn't tell you this because I don't want to get in trouble but…"

I sit up in my chair. "What?"

"Nah," he says, squeezing the bridge of his nose while smiling at nothing. "Nah, forget it."

I fight the urge to roll my eyes. "What the fuck is it, Neil?"

He takes in a deep breath, completely over dramatic, which already makes me want to punch him, so it's not starting out good. "Okay. Okay. Dude. Okay. So…"

"I swear to God, Neil…"

He grins. "That girl? That fucking hot piece of ass we just saw stroll out of here. Well…guess what?"

I stare at him.

He slaps his hand on the desk, making my coffee cup jump. "Guess!"

"*What?*"

"I met her last night."

I jerk my chin back. "What? Where? How?"

"At Altitudes. She came in, drunk and smiling and she came straight over to me. Out of everyone in the bar, she came to *me*."

I shouldn't feel anything as he's telling me this except the annoyance I get every time he speaks, but I am. Jealousy. The red-hot kind that hits your gut like a poker. The kind I rarely feel.

I don't want him to go on.

But he does.

"Before you lecture me, she told me her name was Candace. I believed her. More than that, I didn't care. Soon she was all over me and she took me back to her place."

You fucking asshole.

"I've never been one to kiss and tell," he says, flashing me an overly smug smile as he tugs at the collar of his jacket.

"But I fucked that pussy all night long. She couldn't stop moaning."

I manage to swallow, my jaw tense, everything inside me wanting to rise up and kill him. "You didn't."

"Oh, I did. Didn't you just see the way she looked at me? She wants me. Bad. And I'll give that blondie whatever she wants."

"Fucking hell you will."

Neil rolls his eyes as he gets to his feet. "You jealous, Mav? The town's lady-killer can't bear to share, huh? Can't stand that I got the hottest chick North Ridge has ever seen, while you didn't."

I give him an acidic smile. "What do you think this is, a pissing contest on the playground?"

He shrugs, his hands on the back of the chair and leaning over me. "Maybe. I'm just saying, I've never seen you look so bothered before. Everything usually rolls right off you."

"It's because I am bothered, Neil. I'm bothered that I have such a fucking douchebag on my team. And yeah, I'm talking about you. You know that you absolutely cannot touch her again."

"Yeah, sure. Stop me." He scoffs, completely playing the part like he's in some sort of bad 80s movie.

I get up and cross my arms, knowing I'm more than intimidating when standing next to him. "I have a million ways of stopping you, believe me. But the only one worse than my fist is the fact that it's against the goddamn rules."

"What rules?"

"The rules, assface. I'm your boss, I think I'd know them."

"Pretty sure it's against the rules for my boss to call me assface," he mumbles.

"I'll call you whatever the fuck I want to until you listen to me. She is off-limits, you got it? Not that I think she would dare touch you again, but regardless, she's just your colleague from now on."

"What are you going to do, fire me for that?"

I take in a deep breath. "No. I wish I could. But I would have to report it to the higher ups and then what? Fraternizing with colleagues is against the rules. Maybe at an office job you could let it fly, who the hell knows, but when it comes to what we do, when we put our lives on the line as well as the lives of the people we rescue, we can't afford to get involved with each other."

He looks me over, thinking with that stupid expression still on his face. "Didn't you get in shit for something like this once before?"

"It doesn't matter. What matters is, right now, going forward, if you touch her, I have to report you. It's the government man, you know how they operate. You'll be gone."

Now he's full-on glaring which has the same intensity of a mouse trying to stare down a cat. "And if she touches me? Is this a personal thing, Mav? What happens to her?"

"She'd be fired too. But I'll make sure she knows the rules in case she doesn't."

He makes a growling sound as he pushes back from the chair and points at me. "This is all because you hate me, isn't it?"

"I don't hate you. I tolerate you. And these are just the rules. If you were in my position—"

"Yeah, if I were in your position. We both know I should have gotten the promotion, not you."

"Right. Well, them's the breaks, ain't it, kid?"

He shrugs, throwing his arms out and heads toward the door. "I don't even know why I came here today."

"Me neither, but as long as you know why you're leaving."

He opens the door and pauses at it, cold air rushing in.

"Fine. She's off-limits to me, which means she's off-limits to you. Don't think I didn't notice how you were looking at her, what you were thinking. I doubt you'd want my sloppy seconds anyway, but even so, if you're watching me, I'm watching *you*."

"Fine with me."

"I guess the only thing I have over you, *boss*, is that I know what it's like to be inside a fine specimen like that. And you never will. Hope that eats you up inside every day you end up working beside her."

And with that he leaves, slamming the door behind him.

I exhale loudly, trying to dispel the bad energy inside, and run my hand over my face. Jesus, that all escalated fast. I'm pretty sure I scared him off from trying anything with Riley, but now I have to stick to my own fucking word. And it doesn't change the fact that Riley will be starting here in a bit of a sticky situation.

After that morning, I have no urge to stick around the office anymore so I lock up and head to the resort to hit the slopes. You'd think when I work in the mountains most of the time I'd end up going elsewhere for stress relief, but the truth is the mountains always have a way of bringing me down to earth. It's not even that it's the wild, there's something about being high up and looking down that helps you look down on your own problems. When you're on the ground, you don't know what's above. When you're above, you know everything—where you've come from, where you're going.

I snowboard for a few hours, alone, just whipping along the snow until I'm numb on the outside and alive on the inside.

It's ridiculous, really, for me to get worked up over Neil. We never see eye-to-eye and honestly, now that I'm his boss, I shouldn't let him get to me at all. We're no longer on the same playing field and in order to lead my team, I can't be seen as a friend anymore. Not that I ever was with Neil, but I had gotten close to Tony, Tim, and Jace over the years. I still don't think they see me as a leader or someone in charge, just good ol' Mav, always up for a laugh and a good time. I need to work harder at being taken seriously and that's only going to happen when I stop thinking of these guys as my friends. We have a job to do and it's a serious one.

But, damn it. Riley. I know there was never any reason to think she'd even be interested in me. I mean, I know I'm a good fuck, I know I've got the tattoos and muscles and I can both clean-up and dirty-down real well. But my ego isn't so out of control as to think every woman wants me. Usually they do, but sometimes there's a wild card out there who throws me for a loop. Riley might have been that.

Not with the way she was looking at you, a voice says. This is the voice that continuously gets me in trouble, the one that tells me I can do things like hit on a married woman or try and date two sisters at once. *You know she liked what she saw.*

And while that may be true, it doesn't mean a thing. The last thing I need is to complicate shit as a new boss by sleeping with the new hire. That ship has sailed and I should thank Neil for that one. He probably, and inadvertently, saved me from making a big mistake.

I just wish *he* hadn't slept with her. It's not that I've lost any respect for Riley—after all, I just met her—and a woman's body is her own business. If she wants to get some, good for her. But I don't think Riley has any idea what kind of a tool Neil is. She seems too smart and good for that.

Plus, Neil did say she was drunk. For all I know, it was a colossal mistake on her behalf. Even so, I know I have to talk to her about it. The last thing I want is to bring it up, but if she is under the impression that any of that is okay, I have to tell her before things get worse.

I have to cockblock her against Neil—ironically, I'll also end up cockblocking myself.

Later that evening, after I'm spent from boarding and have watched an obscene amount of Netflix with Chewie, I convince Fox to go with me to The Bear Trap. Not that he needs much convincing, it's practically his second home. My theory isn't because there's beer there, it's the company.

Over the years I've become increasingly convinced that he has it bad for Delilah. He denies it when I bring it up, of course. The girl is practically a sister to us and it's her mother, Jeanine, that raised us boys after our mother died. But even so, I swear there's something there. It's none of my business, but sometimes I think that Fox would calm down a bit if he finally let it all out.

Compared to Shane's celebrations last night, the pub tonight is quiet. There's only old-timer Joe—the pub's drunk —and a few other locals that Fox knows from the resort, Del behind the bar, and…

Riley.

Sitting right there on the bar stool, sipping on a beer and tossing peanut shells to the ground.

And fuck me.

She's even hotter than before. Now I can see more of her body and skin and I'm floored to find her arms have tattoos. I see some vibrant colors, a rose and a heart peeking out underneath the three-quarter length sleeve of her white sweater, bright reds that match the bright red stain on her lips.

She looks over at me and her eyes widen for a second, gorgeous baby-blue saucers that drink me in, before she gives me a quick smile and looks back to Del.

Del is loving this a little too much.

"Hey boys," she says with a big smile. "What are you having?"

Fox returns the grin as he sidles up to the bar. "Why do you even ask?"

Del shrugs. "Bad habits die hard." She jerks her head at Riley. "Fox, have you met Riley before?"

He nods at her. "You're the newcomer."

"Word travels fast in small towns, doesn't it," she says, though she looks at me as she says it.

"Why are you standing over there?" Del asks, waving me over. "She doesn't bite."

"Not usually," Riley says under her breath, holding the top of her beer bottle loosely between her fingers.

I come over, feeling strangely awkward about this whole thing. "I didn't know you'd be here," I told her, hoping she doesn't think I'm stalking her.

"Well I figured you might be here," she says, nodding at the stool beside her. "Are you going to sit down or what?"

She's a fucking firecracker.

"Actually," I tell her, leaning in close enough that I can smell her, a faint lemon and sugar scent that courses through me, "now that you're here, there's something I'd like to talk to you about. In private."

Fox clears his throat and nods at the dart board. "Think I'll do better tonight. Del, you're not serving anyone, have a game."

I don't have to look at Del to know that the last thing she wants to do is leave her post and throw darts when she can just eavesdrop on us, but as usual, Fox wins her over.

Riley watches as they go, chewing on her lip momentarily and looking as if she wishes she could be anywhere else but here. Not me though. I'm more than enjoying being this close to her. I could fucking smell her all day. Up close, her skin looks even more tempting than before.

"I hate to ask," she says slowly as she brings her eyes back to meet mine. "But am I in trouble?"

I take the seat next to her, one arm leaning against the bar. "No. It's nothing like that." I pause. "Not really."

"Oh shit," she says and then slams down the rest of her beer.

"Look, I know we only met each other today and we're going to be working alongside each other for hopefully a long time. So I want to start things off on the right foot. I want this to be a good working environment for you. We have an important job to do. It's taxing. It's stressful. I get that you need as much support from the people you work with as possible."

She stares at me and I have to ignore the heat that's building inside me, that pure primal urge that makes me want to stop talking and kiss her. I think her mouth would taste like cherries, it looks like cherries. Sweet and red and shiny.

"But," I go on, tearing my eyes away from them, "I have to set something straight. I don't want you to think that you can't talk to me about anything and vice versa. So, well, as awkward as this is for me to tell you, I know what, uh, happened between you and Neil last night."

She pinches her eyes shut with a heavy sigh. "I knew it."

"And it's fine. I don't want you to think I'm judging. Okay, I am a little. Neil, if you haven't realized it by now, is a complete shitburger and you can do a million times better. But it happened and I get that."

"This is so embarrassing," she moans, pressing the tip of her beer bottle repeatedly against her forehead, her blonde hair falling across her face.

"I get that too. As your boss, this is the last thing I want to talk to you about. But it has to be said. You're not in trouble for what happened, but just know that there are rules. Unfortunately in some cases, maybe not so unfortunately in yours. But we're not allowed to date each other."

She looks at me through the strands of hair. "You mean, we can't date each other?"

That catches me off guard. "Uh, well yeah. We can't. But I meant you and anyone you work with. Same goes for me. I'm not sure if you had plans for Neil again, but I have to tell you that would be against the rules. It's a fireable offence. I just gave him this lecture so it was only fair I deliver the same one to you."

"God, I'm such a mess," she says and I still can't see her face through her lion's mane.

Without thinking, I reach out and tuck her hair behind her ear.

Her hair is soft, like silk, her skin even softer.

I should not have just done that. That's way too inappropriate of a gesture considering what we're currently talking about.

And damn it, now she's looking at me in a way I can't read.

"You're not a mess," I say quickly, taking my hand away. "Shit happens."

"I was so drunk last night."

"It's fine. You don't have to explain anything to me."

"And lonely," she adds.

Hell. That one goes straight to my heart. A girl like her should never be lonely.

I swallow. "Oh, well—"

"And he was there and I don't remember much of it. I was just frustrated, you know. I didn't even give him my real name. The whole thing was a giant mistake. One big fucking mistake."

The thing is, I can see the remorse in her eyes. Selfishly, it brings me a lot of relief. She regrets the whole thing, as she should. As anyone should.

"As I said, shit happens. Just don't let shit happen again."

She shakes her head, tapping her slender fingers anxiously along the bar. "I won't. God, you probably think I'm such an idiot."

I laugh. "I may not know you well, but I definitely don't think you're an idiot. You obviously had beer goggles on."

"Did I ever."

"And didn't realize you were sleeping with the biggest tool in town."

Now she bursts out laughing.

"What?"

"Nothing," she says, shaking her head. "Nothing at all. Anyway, don't worry. It will never ever happen again. I just… oh man, if I had only known."

"Well you probably knew a little, otherwise you wouldn't have given him a fake name. Which, by the way, doesn't get you very far in this town. Believe me, I've tried."

"Why, do you have a reputation?"

I give her a curious look. "Why would you think I have a reputation?"

Her eyes dart over to Del and back.

"What did she say?" It figures Del would say something. I guess as a bartender she hears more than her fair share of sob stories from some of the women in this town.

"Oh, not much," she says. "She just asked how today went and I told her that I met you and then she told me to watch out."

"Watch out?"

"You're a lady's man, apparently."

"Not when it comes to the people I work with," I point out.

Riley's mouth curves into a wicked smile before she covers it with her beer. "But you've never worked with me before."

Damn. She just threw that out there.

"You know, Riley, it sounds like I should be the one watching out for you."

You hot little minx.

"Maybe you should," she says, finishing the rest of her beer and pushing it away from her. "I probably shouldn't have another beer. I probably should go home. My boss expects me at work tomorrow morning early, and I hear he can be a hardass."

"I heard he has a hard ass. And it's spectacular."

She laughs again, a deep throaty laugh that's beyond sexy. "Del also said you were full of yourself."

"Did she tell you I have good reason to be?"

Subtly, she looks me up and down and gives me a slow smile. "No, she left that part out."

Okay man, pull back. Now you're on thin ice here.

I'm not sure how this conversation went from me telling her that hooking up with each other is a fireable offence, to us actually flirting with each other, but I have a feeling if I don't put a stop to it soon, things are going to get complicated really fast.

I reach over and push her beer further out of reach. "Well, if I were you I would play it safe. Your boss might have a nice ass, but he's still your boss. And after everything that just happened with Neil, you probably need to start your week out on the right foot. It's better for everyone."

She watches me for a second and it looks like disappointment flashes across her eyes. I wish I hadn't seen that look. I wish I didn't have to tell her otherwise, because if I wasn't her boss and I hadn't just cockblocked myself, I could have easily spent the rest of the night drinking with her and talking to her and looking at her. Fuck, the places it could lead.

"Got it," she says, clearing her throat and getting off the stool. She places her hand on my shoulder and gives me a quick smile. "Thanks for the warning. Really. I'll see you in the morning. Off on the right foot, this time."

And then just as she left earlier from the office, she's off again with her abrupt exit, heading over to the hooks by the door where she grabs her parka and pulls it on. She's gone before I can even find the words to say anything at all.

"What did you do?" Del says accusingly, rushing over with a dart in hand.

"First of all, put the dart away," I tell her, plucking it from her fingers and tossing it over her shoulder toward the board. It hits the wall, sticking into the wood. Not even close. "Second of all, I didn't do anything."

"Mav," she whines. "She's a nice girl. Have you seen her tattoos? She's a million times cooler than me and I want to be her friend. I don't have any cool friends."

I snort. "You're cute, Del."

"I'm serious. I love Rachel but she's in the loved-up zone right now and if I hear one more thing about how wonderful Shane is, I think I'll start hating him."

I chuckle at her dramatics. "Well, I'm sure you will be friends with Riley. I just told her about our company policy, that's all."

"Company policy?" She scrunches up her nose. "And what's that?"

"Just that team members are forbidden from sleeping with each other."

Her brows go to the ceiling. "Why are you having this conversation already?"

"It's none of your business," I say with a sigh, not about to tell her what Riley did. She doesn't need the further humiliation, though I am positive Neil has already told half the town. "It just had to be said."

"So that means you can't sleep with her."

"That's exactly what it means."

"Huh," she muses as she goes around the bar and starts wiping down the counter. "It feels redundant now that I warned her about you."

"Yeah, thanks for that," I say dryly. "Since when have you taken an active interest in the women I do or do not sleep with?"

"Since so many of them end up crying in my bar."

Ah, just as I suspected.

"Well, anyway, that's not going to happen."

"That's a fucking shame," Fox says as he saunters over, having grown bored of darts. Del passes him a beer. "She's unbelievably gorgeous."

I glance slyly over at Del for her reaction. She doesn't look too pleased.

"But," he adds, "there's no way she would have slept with you, brother."

"And what makes you say that?"

"I don't know, she seems kind of smart."

"Fuck off."

"I'm just saying. Even if you didn't have a company policy, you'd just end up jerking off alone every night thinking of her."

"Ew, I do not need that mental image, thank you very much," Del says in disgust.

But Fox isn't too far off with that one. All work and no play makes Mav go crazy with sexual frustration. The real question begins tomorrow: just how bad is this going to get?

CHAPTER FOUR

RILEY

Snow.

Endless white as far as the eye can see.

There are no trees here, no mountains, nothing but white snow and white sky.

And somewhere in this desolation is Levi.

I can't hear him, can't see him, but I can feel him. In my bones.

The cold takes my breath away.

I start running, but quickly slow as my feet sink deeper and deeper. He's so close and yet so far away. I might reach out and touch him, if only I could keep going.

The snow is at my neck now and someone is pulling me under. I know from the grip around my legs that it's my mother and my father. Trying to pull me to the life I once knew, the person I once was. The person I've been running from. The person Levi saved me from.

I kick and I fight but the fear crawls up me, icy tentacles that wrap and wrap and wrap. Somewhere out there is Levi, the man I once loved, the only friend I really had. He walks somewhere into the snow and I'm too scared to save him. Too afraid to follow.

If I was stronger, better, I would be able to break free.

But I can't.

So I let the past pull me under, I let the snow fill my lungs.

And I fail once again.

The world drifts away.

White to black.

Black to white.

Dream to reality.

FUCK.

My eyes fly open.

I'm lying in bed, staring up at the ceiling and trying to breathe. The room looks unfamiliar, everything is cold and foreign and strange. My lungs feel like they're filled with ice, my heart is hammering many miles a minute.

It was a dream, I remind myself. *Just a dream. Just another stupid dream.*

I used to dream about Levi a lot after the accident, but they slowly started to taper off after a year. My counsellor said it was completely normal. But they've appeared again after I decided to take the job in North Ridge, and my parents being in them is something else entirely new.

I don't like it. I don't want to dwell on the past, not when I've got my future at my feet. And I especially don't want to think about any of that today, my first official day on the job.

I groan and rub my hand across my eyes, trying to get the courage to get up. I might have been nervous yesterday because I didn't know what to expect, but today is even worse because I have some idea.

And the idea is that this whole thing is going to be awkward as fuck.

I mean, leave it to me to do something so royally stupid as

to have a one-night stand with a loser right before she's set to work alongside him. And Micropenis Neil is even worse than my nickname suggests. The guy seems like a total jerk and I now know that if Maverick had to talk to me about him, then Neil had to have told him what happened. I can just imagine, he was probably bragging. Who knows what intimate details came out, details my fucking boss now knows.

Ugh. I've gone through life trying not to berate myself for bad choices. I've owned most of them, I've made mistakes and learned to look at them as learning tools more than anything else. There are some words I wish I never said, there are things I wish I never did and yes, sometimes there's a guy I wish I didn't get involved with in one way or another.

But I am regretting every single second of Micropenis Neil, and what makes it all that much worse is that my new boss, that giant hunk of a man, had to lecture me about it. I felt like I was teenager being scolded by her parents (not that they ever gave a rat's ass what I did).

To top it all off, despite how embarrassed and ashamed I was last night over the whole thing, my body kept on running like nothing was said at all. Every look that Maverick gave me set my skin on fire. The way his eyes trailed over me, like I was the dessert he'd been saving up for. Then when he pushed the hair behind my ear, I nearly lost it.

Or maybe I did lose it, because then I started flirting with him. I had only had three beers so I know I wasn't out of control, but my fucking hormones were definitely acting like it. After everything he had just told me about being my boss, I still had to slip into seductress mode.

Which he promptly shut down. Yet again, embarrassing. I've become really fucking good at exiting the scene though lately. I just have to wonder what I'm going to do today and how I'll get out of it. I'm supposed to be going for a helicopter ride. Will I be bailing out the door the moment I put my foot in my mouth again? I should probably pack a parachute.

All my hemming and hawing over the day has me running a bit late, so I walk to the office as quickly as I can, nearly eating shit a few times on the sidewalks. Even though I work a job that's physically taxing and I have to be in excellent shape and health, I'm surprisingly klutzy. There's something about me and ice that ironically don't mix.

There's barely anytime to compose myself though before I'm at the office. I try to take a second outside the door to get my thoughts in order but it's swung open, Maverick on the other side.

"I was worried you wouldn't show," he says to me, keeping his voice low. He's got such a distinctive voice, gravely and rough, these whisky-soaked words every time he speaks. There are a few things that really get me raring when it comes to men, and a good, panty-soaking voice is one of them, along with tattoos, large forearms, wide shoulders, a firm ass, and a big dick. So far Maverick is five out of six, though the way things are, I don't think I'll ever figure out the truth about number six.

Damn it, why did it have to be Micropenis Neil at the bar?

"I was running a bit late," I tell him, "the sidewalks are icy and I'm such a huge klutz when it comes to that sort of thing. I can't tell you the amount of times I've publicly face-planted. I've turned it into an art form."

He purses his lips, squinting at me. "Are you sure you're cut out for this job?"

I sigh. "I'm sorry. Sometimes I don't know when to shut up. It's early. I—"

"I'm just fucking with you." He grins and puts his hand on my shoulder. I can't help but stare at it, so big and meaty and

52

strong. In seconds I'm already imagining what it would be like to have it skirt over my naked body, the feel of it rough and wild on my skin. I wonder how hard his grip would be on my hips.

Focus, focus.

"Come on in, meet the team." He opens the door wider, ushering me in as he leans in close and whispers in my ear, "aside from the one you've already met."

And there he is, sitting down at a desk with his feet up on it, still wearing that ridiculous Big Bird jacket and that smug look on his face, beady eyes taking me all in.

I ignore Neil and look to the rest of them.

"This is Tim," Maverick says, gesturing to a lanky man of Asian descent. "He's been here longer than me and technically he should be the boss, but I try not to tell him that."

"Responsibility is overrated," Tim says in a soft accent. "Nice to meet you, Riley."

I nod my thanks and then Maverick introduces the short but spry Italian guy next to him, looking to be in his late forties. "This is Tony. Don't let his size fool you. He's seen *Cliffhanger* enough times to brainwash him into thinking he's Sly Stallone."

"But better looking," Tony says.

I laugh, grateful that so far everyone here seems nice and completely normal.

Maverick then introduces me to Jace, who looks to be the youngest out of all of us, even me. He's got a stocky build and a quiet demeanor, with dark, watchful eyes.

"Jace is our go-getter," Maverick says. "Day or night, if you need him, he's there. I don't even think you take a fucking break, do you man?"

Jace doesn't say anything, just manages a small smile that doesn't reach his eyes. Okay, so maybe he's not as friendly as everyone else, but he's still better than Neil.

Speaking of. Maverick is nodding in his direction. "And you met Neil yesterday. So that's that. That's the team. I won't further embarrass you by making you make a speech about yourself and telling us all what your favorite color is. Or food. I already gave them the rundown on your background before you got here."

I meet Maverick's eyes, hoping he didn't tell them everything. And by everything, I mean what happened with Levi. I don't want everyone to know about that, to treat me any different. But from the way his eyes stare back at mine, soft, and then his slight nod, I know he didn't.

Relieved, I give everyone an awkward wave. "Hi. Nice to meet you all and I look forward to us working together. And for the record, my favorite color is red and my favorite food is cheeseburgers."

"Any kind of cheeseburgers?" Tony asks.

I nod. "Any kind. McDonald's are classic, but I'll take the fancy ones too, though the less toppings the better."

"Then you have to check out Smitty's," Maverick tells me with a smile.

"Absolutely," Tony adds. "It's a cheap little diner but they do the best greasy, old-fashioned burgers in town."

"I'm sure I will then." I'm so close to turning to Maverick and asking if he'll go with me one day, but again, *inappropriate*. The funny thing is, I've never been like this in a working environment before. Even with Levi, we were so ingrained as friends and co-workers having worked together so often, that I'd learned to bury everything mildly inappropriate deep down. It always took a back seat, even though sometimes I have my regrets.

When it comes to Maverick though, I can't seem to keep my head on straight. I need to be less distracted by him. Especially now, since today he's showing me the ropes.

He explains the office, what everyone does, our schedule, what our average week looks like during each month, the most common rescue scenarios, how we're basically on call all the time at all hours of the night but we still have to put in a set number of hours. Sometimes it's preventative work, like the avalanche triggering that Tim was doing the other day, sometimes it's patrols, sometimes it's hanging out at the resorts and doing safety talks and watching over the hills, sometimes it's checking in with the tour and heli-skiing operators, or heading over to other areas and helping out there in emergencies. Sometimes it's just doing the boring paperwork in the office. And that's just all in the winter. The rest of the year is a whole different ballgame.

All in all, it seems pretty much on par with what I was doing in Aspen, except the provincial government is controlling this operation.

"Which can be a pain in the fucking ass sometimes," Maverick says, as we head outside to his truck to get my tour started. "They like to have their eyes on everything, to make sure resources are being allocated properly. AKA, see if there's any reason to let anyone go."

I head over to the passenger side but he beats me to it, opening the door for me like a gentleman.

I raise my brows. "Do you do this for everyone else?"

"Fuck no," he says. "Get in."

I oblige, even though I hope the rest of the crew aren't watching us through the windows. The last thing I want is for them to think I'm getting special treatment.

I take a quick look around his truck as I buckle up and he gets in. It's relatively clean, though there's what I assume is dog hair absolutely everywhere.

"Do you have a dog or do you just shed a lot?"

He laughs as he starts reversing down the driveway, looking behind him. He's got a good laugh, loud and heartwarming. "I have a dog," he explains with a sentimental grin. "Chewie."

"What kind?"

"She's a pit bull. A rescue. Sweet as pie, even though she chews through everything."

"So it's not just a clever name."

"Wayne's World fan?" he notes. "You can't be old enough to remember that movie."

I shrug. "I'm a fan of everything. You don't have to grow up with a cult comedy to find it funny. If it's funny, I'll find it funny, no matter my age."

"And how old are you?"

I give him a funny look.

"What?" he says. "Your age isn't on your resume."

"Twenty-five," I tell him. "How old are you?"

"Thirty-one."

"That seems about right."

"That age where you look like an adult but you can still get away with a lot of shit?"

"I don't know," I say, feeling a teasing smile slowly turn my lips, "what kind of stuff can you get away with?"

He stares at me for a moment, trying to suss me out, before turning his attention back to the road. "I think you just might be trouble, you know that?"

"I know." I pause, looking out the window. "So where are we going anyway? I thought that Neil was supposed to take me up in a chopper for a bird's eye view."

"You really think I'd let you be alone with him now?"

"Let me?" I repeat.

"Look, as your boss, I'm looking out for you."

"You've only been my boss for like a day, and I think I can take care of myself. No need for you to act like a caveman."

"I'm not acting like a caveman," he scoffs.

"Hey, I'm not complaining," I tell him, softening my

stance. "I like that you care. But don't worry about leaving me with Neil. I don't think he would dare try anything, especially if he knows what's on the line, and if he did, I could hand his ass to him, no problems."

"You're impressing me more and more."

"Good. You should be impressed. Anyway, thank you for taking me instead. I'm sure I'll be working with him alone at some point but until then, it's nice to have things be as awkward-free as possible. I'd like to forget all that shit ever happened."

"Problem is, he's not the type to let you forget it."

I sigh and run my fingers down the cool of the window pane, the town flying past. "Can I pick them, or what?"

Maverick lapses into silence. I look over at him. His jaw wiggles back and forth, tense, his eyes now have laser focus on the road. Since he's not looking at me, I take the opportunity to let all of him soak in. His large hands on the steering wheel, his thick dark hair, like a buzz-cut that's grown out for a few months that showcases his strong neck, the way it slopes into powerful shoulders. I swear to God, every single part of this man is pure perfection.

Finally, his eyes flit toward me and he smiles. "Get a good look?"

"It's hard to say...it's a shame you're wearing clothes."

He's gobsmacked for a moment before he bursts out laughing. I know I need to shut up, but I honestly can't help it and I know I wouldn't say a word if I knew things were getting dicey.

Oh God, I hope things aren't getting dicey now. That's my problem sometimes. I'll push and push and push to see what I can get away with and then everything blows up in my face. It's probably why I've been so attracted to the adrenaline junkie jobs to begin with.

He shakes his head, staring at me with a disbelieving

smile on his face, like he's trying to find the right things to say. I don't even know what I want him to say, I just want him to keep reacting to me. I want to shock him, make him laugh. It's addicting.

"What I said earlier about trouble," he says. He clears his throat and tries to put on a serious face. "You keep throwing me for a loop, Riley Clarke. I'm honestly not sure what to do with you."

Another sly smile comes over me, emboldened by how comfortable I am with this man already. "I can think of a few things."

I have to wonder when he's going to put his foot down and put a stop to this. I know flirting is pretty harmless but there's going to be a point where he'll play the boss card. He will because he has to, especially after what happened with me and Neil.

"You're a little minx, you know that?"

I grin, feeling exceedingly charmed by that. "Maverick's minx. I like it."

"It's Mav," he says imploringly. "Not Maverick. Not John. Mav."

"Alright, Mav. I can be your minx if you want me to."

He tugs at the edge of his jacket, a firmness coming back to his face as he looks back to the road and takes us toward the small regional airport situated alongside the river. "But in all seriousness, as much as I appreciate how, uh, friendly you're being..."

"You want me to knock it off? I can do that. I'm just having a bit of fun."

"Yeah, well," he clears his throat, "the thing is, I'm your boss, right. And we just met..."

"You don't strike me as the kind of man who has a problem with that."

"Okay, so then let's go back to the whole I'm your boss

thing. As much as I know you're having a bit of fun, I just… we have a job to do, a serious one, we have to work together and I don't want things to get complicated. You understand?"

I'm a little bit embarrassed he shot me down so fast, but not so surprised. It's one thing to keep flirting with him as I am if he's actually down for it, it's another if he's only mildly flattered and wish I'd behave myself.

"I understand."

He sighs. "Not that I don't appreciate it. It just makes things—"

"Complicated," I fill in. "Like you said. I get it. Most people don't know what the hell to do with me, I'm used to it."

"You know…" he starts, those glacier eyes trailing over my nose, my lips, my chest. "If our situation were different…"

"If you weren't my boss and there weren't rules in place that you just lectured me on last night and I hadn't just started this job…"

"Then things would be different."

Or it could be that he's just not interested in me in that way. But I don't know, the way he's looking at me right now is both remorseful *and* wild, like he's this close to pulling the truck over to the side of the road and having his way with me in the backseat.

And fuck, he could have his way all day long, anyway he wants it.

"Anyway," he says, pulling the truck to a stop in the parking lot. "That's the helicopter."

I look across to the pad at a small building. "Do you have a usual pilot?"

"I'm the pilot," he says, matter-of-factly.

"You know how to fly a helicopter?" Can he get any fucking hotter?

"I do," he says. "Tony has his licence too and he does most of the flying around here, but it's good to have two just in case. Otherwise we have to rely too much on local pilots, and they're not always willing to take the risk."

I think back to all the helicopter drop-offs I've done. Sometimes it gets pretty nasty with the pilots lives in more danger than our own. We're ready to bail, the pilots aren't always.

"Plus," he says, opening the door, "it's cheaper for them this way."

"From the way you talk about the government cutting corners and saving money, I'm actually surprised I was hired," I tell him as I get out and join him at the hood of the truck. I'm pretty tall—five-foot-eight—but once again I'm struck by the difference between us. He's just all brawn and beast, making me feel impossibly dainty and small.

At that, he looks away toward the chopper, rubbing his lips together.

"What? I was hired, right?"

"Yeah," he eventually says, looking sheepish and rubbing the back of his neck. "But the reason was because we needed to hire either a woman or a minority to keep everyone happy."

"I was only hired because I'm a woman?" I exclaim.

He nods. "The only woman who applied and as far as I could tell, the only minority as well."

"Oh." I'm deflating fast, like a pin to a balloon. "And here I was thinking that I was hired because of my awesome skills and resume."

"Hey," he says, briefly touching my arm. "That's why you got the job. You wouldn't have been hired if you didn't have what it takes. Okay?"

I cross my arms and kick feebly at the snow. "Now I just feel like a token."

"You're not a token, Riley," he tells me, leaning over until he catches my eyes. "You're here because I want you to be here. And you want to be here too. Now come on, let me show you the best part of the job."

I try not to let things get to me, and I'm usually quick to shake things off (with the exception of Micropenis Neil because, let's be honest, that's sticking with me for a while), but I can't help but feel the sting of that one. Obviously you don't always know why you're getting the jobs you do, and you usually assume it's because you're the right person for it, but now that I know the truth here—that it was about meeting a quota to seem politically correct or something—it makes me wonder if that's how I've gotten jobs before. On one hand I have to work extra hard for people to take me seriously, on the other hand I might not have to work hard at all. Just show up and have a vagina.

But the moment I get into that helicopter with Mav and we lift off from the landing pad, snow blowing in all directions beneath us, I feel like all my worries drop away too. One minute I'm fretting over not being good enough for the job, the next I'm in awe at the beauty around us, Mav confidently piloting the craft like it's second nature.

"So this is North Ridge from the raven's point of view," he says to me as I stare down at the town. Even though there's about ten thousand full-time residents, from the air, the town is much larger than I thought. It's nestled in a river valley between mountain peaks, and the town spreads out in brick and pretty colored buildings along the main street and other arteries until the houses and roads back up onto the lower mountain slopes. With snow covering everything, it looks absolutely magical.

"Does it always snow here?"

"Not always, it's mild here in BC compared to out east. But February and March are notorious for that last blast of winter before spring comes along. See that right there," he nods to the tallest mountain rising along the edge of town, "that's the start of the Selkirk Mountain range. And that's the ski resort there. That's where we'll be spending a lot of our time."

I stare down at the tiny skiers and snowboarders slicing down perfectly groomed powder, the lifts in full operation. "It looks nice. Reminds me of a place I worked at in Wyoming. Not as big as Aspen or Whistler, but still fun."

"It is fun," he says, adjusting his big headphones. "We get a lot of powder here and it's reliable, so we get lots of locals from the coast coming here when their snow isn't cutting it. Most winters, the BC coast doesn't get enough snow. Problem is, a lot of those locals are young and by the time they get here, they tend to not listen to the rules. Hence why we're always busy."

He takes the helicopter away from the mountain, skirting along the edge of a lake on the other side. "And over there, that's the Kokanee Glacier. That's another thing that keeps us busy. I blame the beer."

"Beer?"

"We have Kokanee beer and the commercials are always about the glacier and sasquatch. Sounds crazy, but a lot of people seem to think they'll find sasquatch out there. Or beer." He sighs. "It is a beautiful place though, when it's not being trampled by morons."

The helicopter swings even further around until we're flying back toward town. "And now," he says, "on that side of the river, you'll see Cherry Peak and Ravenswood Ranch. That's my home."

I stare down at the picturesque ranch houses and barns nestled beneath a photogenic mountain. "You live there?"

"Well, I was born there. My father lives there, my younger

brother Shane and his fiancée too. The ranch is still in full operation."

"Wow," I whisper. "I've always loved ranches, horses, cows, the whole package."

"What about cowboys?" Mav asks.

I grimace. "No thanks."

"So you wouldn't like me in a cowboy hat and chaps?"

I let out a small laugh, happy that he's playing along again. "If it's just chaps and a hat, you can be whatever you want to be. I'll be there for it."

"Well, hey," he says with a shrug. "I'm sure one day you'll see the place. It's a beautiful ranch, all seven hundred acres of it."

"Will you be taking me there?" I ask pointedly.

"Or Del," he says. "She practically grew up there too. And she really likes you."

And I like you, I think to myself. But for once I keep it to myself.

"At least someone is charmed by me," I say, before I quickly add, "other than he who shall not be named."

Mav stares at me for a moment, studying me with a softness I haven't seen yet. "I'm utterly charmed by you, Riley."

My heart flutters, just for a second.

"You find me amusing," I point out. "And confusing."

"No, not confusing. You're nothing if not straight forward. But yes, I find you amusing. I find you a lot of things that I probably shouldn't."

"Such as?" Now I'm intrigued.

"Nothing I can get into for fear of losing my job," he says. "But just so you know, I'm glad you're here. I'm looking forward to…more of this."

I give him a small smile. "Same."

The only problem is, I'm not sure what more of this *is*. Flirting? Working together? Setting boundaries?

The only thing I do know is that if Mav is already thinking of me in ways he probably shouldn't, and I keep pushing his buttons, we're both going to end up in big trouble.

Bring it on.

CHAPTER FIVE

MAVERICK

It's been one full week since Riley started working at North Ridge Search and Rescue.

Which means it's been one full week of daily blue balls followed by furious bouts of masturbation every waking hour. My hand is cramped, my dick is sore, and I keep going back for seconds.

I can't get her out of my fucking head.

The only saving grace is that it was her first week, which meant there was still a lot of getting to know the terrain and the local processes. I wasn't alone with her often and sometimes I wasn't with her at all. Tim took her out on a controlled avalanche expedition and Tony took her to the resort to get a feel for the scene and give safety talks. She hasn't been on a call yet—none of us have.

Which is usually the calm before the storm. We're almost always rescuing someone weekly, especially since our range and jurisdiction is so large, but this week there hasn't been anything. With the law of averages, when something hits next, it's going to hit hard.

Even the weather seems to be lulling everyone into a false

sense of security. The light snowfall and sub-zero temps of last week have tapered off, bringing fresh, spring-like breezes and slushy streets. So much so that Fox thinks we're in for an early spring.

"Which is a fucking shame in a way," Fox says as he pours himself a cup of coffee. I'm sitting down at the kitchen table, slurping down a protein shake that tastes like ass. And not the good kind of ass.

"Why?" I love winter, the snow, the ice, the boarding, the storms, but it just goes on for far too long here.

"The sooner winter is over, the sooner my winter employment comes to an end," he says, leaning back against the counter. "Then there's a long, penniless window between then and when the forests start burning again."

"Anyone ever tell you you're morbid? You don't get paid until the province is burning."

He takes a sip of his coffee and glares at me over the mug. "I'm not saying I want that, but it's the truth. The forests will burn, every year it's getting worse. Climate change isn't going away. Sad to say, but I think I'll be working more in the future, not less. That said, I hate scrambling for odd jobs."

"You know you don't need those odd jobs, Fox. You live here, we own this place. Mortgage is almost paid off. You've saved up a lot for times like these."

"I've saved for the future. Because I know I won't be able to be a hot shot all my life. It's a young man's job."

"You're not that old," I tell him. "I mean, you're definitely pushing it, but…" Thirty-three is young, but he's the older brother and if I don't do my job and tell him he's over the hill, it's a wasted opportunity.

"Right," he says with a sigh. "But it's a job for single men, really. The guys I know who have wives and kids, they don't stick with it for long. It's too hard. They realize it's not worth it, sacrificing all that time away from their families, not to mention their lives."

I watch him curiously. This is the first time I've ever heard Fox mention marriage or kids. I've always assumed he was a lot like me, no time or need for commitments. I've also assumed that it was Delilah that was holding him back from finding anyone else, whether he realizes it or not.

"So," I begin, "this marriage and kids business…"

He shrugs, looking into his mug like it holds better conversation. "I'm just saying, eventually I'm sure I'll settle down. And when I do, I don't think I'll be a hot shot for much longer."

"Unless you find a woman who completely supports and understands your job," I say carefully, wondering if he'll get the hint.

"Right. Like that's easy to find."

Fuck, he's dense. But I'm not going to go there, he'll just say I'm crazy for thinking so. Now, I can't figure out if he thinks it's crazy that Delilah would be interested in him or that he should have any interest in her. But the denial is very real with those two.

"Maybe you're not looking close enough," I tell him, getting up to put my glass in the sink. "Maybe the right woman is there, right in front of your eyes."

He looks to the ceiling in annoyance. "Please stop leaving dishes in the sink," he says to me as I'm about to raid the cupboards for something else to eat.

I snort and shake my head as I then go and rinse out the glass. "Who needs marriage when you live with your brother?"

"Want to take bets on who will be the first to move out?" he asks, refilling his mug from the coffee pot. He fucking mainlines that shit.

"Seriously?"

"Yeah."

"How much?"

"Five hundred dollars." He says it so confidently, like he's actually been planning this bet.

"You sound so sure of yourself."

"I guess I think you'll be out before I will be."

I eye Chewie, who is snoring loudly from the couch. The couch that Fox says she's not allowed on and yet always is. "Is this your way of telling me you're kicking us out?"

"Us?"

"Me and the doggo."

"Nah. I need you to help with the mortgage. Would be nice if the doggo chipped in, though."

"All right," I tell him, sticking out my hand. "Five hundred dollars. Now what is the bet again?"

He shakes it. "I'm betting you'll move out before I do. So if I'm right, you'll owe me half a grand."

"I'm surprised at your faith in me. Me, of all people."

"Hey, it's people like you that end up surprising everyone. Always the last person you suspect. Anyway, I've seen Riley…"

I frown. "Riley? What does this have to do with her?"

He gives me a steady look. "Oh, come on."

"What?"

"She's your type, Mav."

"*Every* woman is my type."

"Every woman is your type, in bed. I'm talking about more than that."

This is ridiculous. "I don't even know her."

"But you're going to. Don't you know how easy it is to bond with someone when you do the kind of work you do?"

You either bond or do the opposite. Like kick Neil off a cliff.

"There are rules."

"Right. The rules."

"I'm serious. Look, I'm not going to pretend she's not fucking amazing, but as much as she wants it to happen, as much as I want to screw her senseless, that's not going to happen."

"Back up. She wants it to happen?"

I nod, unable to stop from smiling. "She hits on me non-stop."

Fox laughs, shaking his head. "Jesus. Only you would be pursued by someone like her. And you still haven't done anything. You have willpower that I don't have, brother."

"It's only been a week, I'm not an animal."

He gives me a pointed look. Scratch that.

"I mean, I have some brains. I have a good thing going on with my job and I've worked hard for it. She's worked hard too. If we hooked up…that could be the end of it for both of us. And as much as I want to bury my cock in her, it wouldn't be worth it."

He grimaces. "First of all, don't talk about your cock around me. It's enough that I catch you walking around here naked sometimes. And second of all, no one has to know."

I shake my head. "No way. Uh-uh. You know I'm all about leaving it at just sex, but I think in this case, it would royally fuck shit up. Ever since I threatened Neil about her—"

"Why did you threaten Neil?"

I suck at my teeth, debating whether I should tell him what happened or not. "Okay, keep this on the downlow, but she slept with him."

Fox's eyes nearly fall out of his head. "She what?"

"She was drunk," I tell him quickly, feeling defensive on her behalf. "She was drunk and lonely and had just got to town and I'm pretty sure he took advantage of her, something I want to knock his teeth out for. Either way, she didn't realize he was a tool. Now she does and she's beyond ashamed for it, which is why you can't bring it up."

"I won't. Fuck. I bet Neil is running with that one. Fucking hate that guy."

"So does Riley. All week I saw him leering at her. I know she can put him in his place no problem, but I'd still love to do the job for her."

"Getting protective, are we?"

I ignore that. "Anyway, I told Neil that if it happened again, I'd have to report it. And then him being a douche, said the same about me. Said he'd be watching me and he has been. Every time Riley and I are together, he's there, waiting for one of us to slip up."

"What a mess."

"Yeah, it's a mess and it will definitely get messier if anything were to happen between us. So that's why, as hard as it is to say no to her, to resist what she's putting out there, I have to."

"Hmmmm," he muses, finishing his second cup. "I still think the bet will hold."

"Dude, even if I were fucking her, what makes you think it would ever become more than that?"

"Because it's about time."

"That's ridiculous. I have all the time in the world. I like my life. I have a good thing going on. I get laid when I want to, I'm out there saving people's asses day in and day out, I make good money, I have good friends. A great dog. And one annoying roommate. Why fuck all that up just to get laid?"

"Because it's about more than getting laid."

"Okay, why fuck that up just so I can be in a relationship for a while before we both grow sick of each other and it goes up in flames?"

"Fine," he says, leaving the kitchen. "You keep living in denial and I'll be here to collect when you fail."

"You're the one in denial!" I yell after him, but he's already closing the bathroom door. The only one listening to me now is Chewie, sitting up on the couch and giving me the stink-eye for waking her.

* * *

A FEW DAYS later I'm awakened after only a few hours of sleep.

First I hear the wind slamming against the window, driving snow against it in thick spatters, then I'm letting out an "*oof*" as Chewie jumps on the bed, landing on my stomach. She doesn't do well in storms, which is one reason why she'll never be an SAR dog, along with the fact that she'll only use her nose if food is involved. If a medium-rare steak and baked potato ever went missing in the woods, only then would she be the first one to find it.

I should go back to sleep but I can't, because the change in weather has taken me by surprise. I'd been watching the forecast carefully, and while it seemed like there were a few storms brewing in Idaho just below us, North Ridge and the Selkirks didn't look like they'd be hit. In fact, the forecast called for a continuation of the rising temperatures and I was getting ready to be on alert for flooding.

So this is a surprise. The wind is rattling the window panes and as I get out of bed, Chewie hiding under the covers, I look out to see nothing but white. Even the street-light down the road emits only a faint glow, partially obscured by the whirling flakes.

"This isn't good," I say out loud.

Ten minutes later, after I've downed a glass of water from the kitchen, my radio crackles. I keep it in the den next to my bedroom, the door always open so I can hear if anything comes in. Fox hated it at first, but he's gotten used to the calls coming in all hours of the day and night, and he can sleep right through them. We have the same radio down at the office, but when anything happens in the middle of the night, those calls go to me. Perk of being the boss.

"North Ridge SAR, it's Phil at the lodge, come in."

I quickly head to the den and pick it up, pressing the button to talk. "Maverick here, how can I help?"

"We have a skier with us, just came into the lodge for help. She and a buddy earlier came across an ice hiker with a broken leg at about seven thousand feet, below Thompsons Camp. One of the skiers stayed behind with him, the other came here for help. We've got a doctor at the lodge that you can take, if you don't have a medic."

"That's fine, I'll be able to get Tim, do you have the coordinates?" I ask, bringing out a pen and pad of paper and scribbling them down when he gives it to me. I stare at the terrain map on the wall. Thompson's Camp is a popular spot for ice walkers this time of year, situated on the east side of the mountain. At least it's away from the storm, which is blowing in from the west.

"It just started storming down here," I tell Phil. "I have doubts the chopper can fly. Do you have anyone up there who can leave now and be team one?"

"That's a negative. I can ski in, but it sounds like where he's fallen would be inaccessible to someone like me."

"All right, I'll get a team up there whichever way I can. Over and out."

If we can't do a helicopter rescue, and that seems more and more likely given the storm and the location, we're going to have to go up from the lodge. That means setting out for a long hike, up that mountain with our gear, right now. Every second that passes brings that hiker and the other skier closer to death.

I immediately put out the call for everyone on the team,

as well as to a few of our volunteer auxiliary members. Anytime we're going up into the mountains like this, the more searchers we have, the better.

I grab my gear and suit up, then get in the truck and head to Riley's since she's the only one without a car.

She lives in the basement suit of my old high school math teacher and she's already outside, standing on the sidewalk and waiting when I pull up. This is the first time I've seen her in her full gear, head to toe in thick, waterproof material, headlamp on her forehead, and looks completely trans-formed. She's gorgeous without a lick of makeup, but she no longer looks like a young girl. She looks strong now, unstoppable.

Even her expression is determined.

"Hey," she says to me as she buckles up. "Run it all by me again."

No time for chit chat, no smile or teasing words. She's getting right down to business.

And so do I. As we drive up toward the lodge on the winding mountain road, snow already covering the plow's earlier work, I give her the rundown. "Tim and Jace will be sorting out the descent route. It's not an easy area and the hiker will most likely be immobile, so they'll plan where we'll lower and find our anchor spots to match the rescue ropes. The ski lodge has a doctor there, but they won't be able to do much when it comes to getting the guy out. Thankfully we have Tim. Hope you've been practicing your rope skills, because I think it's going to be a long, cold night."

"I'm ready for it," she says, a hardness to her voice. "Do we have plans for the skier who stayed with him?"

"We'll probably have to treat the skier for hypothermia, I've alerted the hospital so they're ready for when we come down."

She shakes her. "Stupid. Brave but stupid."

"The skier?"

"Assuming the skiers that found the injured hiker didn't know them, they went out of their way to help. That puts their lives at risk."

"But if they hadn't, the hiker wouldn't have survived. You break your leg at nearly seven thousand feet, in that terrain, you're dead."

"You don't even know if they're alive right now."

I glance at her, the snow reflecting off the headlights, making her look ghostly. "Not exactly Miss Positive at this time of night."

She manages a tight smile. "I'm nervous," she admits, saying it like she's angry about it.

"We all get a bit nervous," I tell her. "And it's your first time on call since…"

"Yeah," she says quickly. "I know. I just don't want to fuck up."

"Riley, you're not going to fuck up. We've got a big team tonight, I've even called in some of the aux members, including Sam. He retired from the army too early and still thinks he's running a platoon. He also wears hot pink ski pants." Her smile cracks just a little more. I go on. "A few weeks ago, we rescued someone off Kokanee glacier. It took all day to climb up to their spot and all night to get them down. Tim even slipped and it took extra time to get him out. But we did it. We're an odd mix of people, but together we make a well-oiled machine and tonight, you're part of that machine."

She nods, chewing on her lip. After a few beats with the only sounds being the swoosh of snow as we drive further up the black mountain road and the rhythmic *shoop shoop* of the fast-moving wiper blades, she speaks.

"Have you ever lost someone?"

I swallow. I guess we're getting personal. "On the team or

outside of it?"

She considers that for a moment. "Both."

"On the team? No, but we've had a few close calls. One summer, Tony went out marking trails, when he was supposed to be at home with a fever. He got sick, disoriented. Took a few days for us to first realize where he went, since he never told anyone, and then find him. Stupid bastard. Then there was a guy named Heath that used to work for us —this was a couple of years ago. He was a good guy, had a wife and kids. Like Sam, he was also retired from the army, for losing sight in one of his eyes. Took a bullet to the head in Afghanistan, but he was damn good at his job."

"Even with the lack of depth perception?"

"Even so. But one day he went out to get a snowmobiler who had fallen through the ice. As you know, in those cases, the outcome is rarely good, but he went and the snowmobiler was half on the ice, just needed a bit of help to make it. His friends couldn't or wouldn't risk it though. So he went. And he fell in." I sigh, remembering the look on his face when I saw him in the hospital. "He was pulled out by Tim. You know, Tim, he grew up in the mountains of South Korea, he knows his stuff. Anyway, Heath recovered, physically, but I don't know what happened under that ice. He was never the same. He quit a month later."

"I get it," she says quietly, rubbing her hands together as if she's cold, but I have the heat on full blast. "A part of him died inside. You can never get that back."

Her words chill me. I want to ask her about the accident, her partner in the coma, but I don't. I know she'll bring it up if she wants to talk about it, but otherwise I think I'll make things worse.

"So, what about in the life outside of work?" she asks. "Have you lost anyone?"

I nod. "My mother. She died when I was five."

She fixes her eyes on me, curious. They glow blue in the dim light. "Really? How?"

That's usually an insensitive question, but I know she doesn't mean any harm by her bluntness. "She killed herself."

Riley flinches at that. I can be blunt too.

"I'm so sorry," she says. "Did you know at the time, I mean…"

"No. At the time they told me she died by accident. She drowned in the river. Years later I learned the truth. Then I learned about post-partum depression. It gives you answers but it doesn't change anything. If anything, you get angrier. Because there were signs. There were signs and no one did anything."

"So it happened after your…?"

"Younger brother. Shane. Poor guy, I know he still feels responsible for it, even though he was just a baby. The most fucked up thing about it is that Fox, my oldest brother, I swear he still blames him for it." I pause, feeling a wave of shame. While I've always thought this, I've rarely vocalized it like this. When it comes to my brothers and my family, things are often so complicated. "Anyway, they aren't close. And I can't blame either of them for the way they feel. And then there's me, stuck somewhere in the fucking middle, as always."

"I get the feeling you don't talk about that often," she says.

"Well who the hell would I talk to? I can't talk to them. I've tried, but they're both stubborn in their own way and it just opens old wounds. My father would probably backhand me for even mentioning my mother's name, even though he's finally moved on and found someone to love. The only one is my grandfather, but even so, he's getting older and I hate to bother him with something like this. I'm the easygoing one in the family, it would be…out of character for me to say anything."

"And your girlfriends?"

I crack a wry smile. "You and I both know there are no girlfriends."

"Not ever?"

I squint my eyes at her for a moment before focusing back on the road. She's distracting enough as it is and the last thing we need is to end up crashed in a snowbank. "I've had some."

"Unable to commit?"

"Oh, I'm able. I just choose not to. Besides, our jobs aren't exactly cut out for commitment. You should know that."

She taps her delicate fingers along the thick, rough material of her snow pants. "Yeah," she eventually says, her voice soft. "I know."

It sounds like there are so many layers to what she says, a story left untold. I just want to spend all my time talking to her, peeling all those layers back, seeing what this beautiful girl is hiding deep down. Because for all her bluntness and flirting and ballsy behaviour, I know she's keeping some of herself tucked away. Maybe I'll find out in time, maybe I won't. But I want nothing more than to find it for myself.

But she's the one asking me the questions tonight. "Do you miss her?"

"My mother?"

"Yeah."

I feel my throat get thicker and it's harder to swallow. "Yeah. Maybe I shouldn't because I was so young, but I remember her so clearly. I remember the day she died, before she went down to the river. She had made me waffles. Fox was in the living room watching cartoons. X-Men, I think it was. The old kind. She'd just put Shane down in his crib. She said she was going to pick some flowers. But it was October and there were no flowers..." I take in a deep breath, surprised at how shaken up I feel just talking about it. Even

77

more surprised that I'm opening up to her. "So yeah. I missed her from that day forward. We had a nanny after that, Jeanine, who is Del's mother. They lived with us on the property. But as much as I love Jeanine, she's not my mother. No one ever will be. I had her and then she was gone."

My words hang in the air like clouds of breath.

"Do you think that's why you're afraid of commitment?" she asks after a moment. "You know what it's like to lose someone you love?"

I glance at her sharply. "What are you, a shrink?"

"I've been to enough of them…"

"I'm not afraid of commitment, by the way. I've just never met someone that could make me consider having them be a part of my life."

She looks at me, smiling shyly. "I'm the same way. Just wanted to put that out there in case you thought otherwise."

I laugh. "Honestly, I don't know what to think when it comes to you."

Other than how badly I want you.

And how fucking wrong that is.

"As long as I have you thinking," she says, before she abruptly switches the subject and starts asking questions about the possible descent route and the volunteer team.

The problem now is, by the time we get to the ski lodge and meet in the parking lot with the rest of the crew, quickly going over the details before we ski into the endlessly cold, dark, and snow-blasted wilderness, the rescue mission floats somewhere into the back of my thoughts.

I can only think of Riley, about the drive, the ease we have with each other, the conversation, the fact that I opened up to her about things I never talk about with anyone. I think about her and not the mission we're about to embark on.

And for the first time I'm realizing how dangerous that is.

CHAPTER SIX

RILEY

"RILEY, YOU CAN CARRY THE LITTER," SAM SAYS, HANDING IT over. A litter is basically two pieces of backboard. Sometimes there's a modified bike wheel attached to the bottom, made for rolling people out, but when we're dealing with snow and ice, it's not needed. It's heavy enough as it is to carry and will slow me down, but I don't complain, I just take it and strap it on.

This is also the first time I've ever spoken to Sam, the retired army man with a buzz-cut and hot pink snow pants. Even though he's an unpaid volunteer, along with four other people here, he seems to be taking over the operation and Mav steps back, having no problem with it. It must be a lot of pressure having to be in charge of this group of rag-tag SARs. It's something else I want to talk to Mav about, but it will have to wait for another time.

Right now, I'm focused on the rescue. I talked to Mav in the truck on the way up here, wanting something to distract me and he does a pretty damn good job of that. A little too good. But honestly, tonight, I really am nervous and I've been trying hard to seem composed. Maybe a little too hard. All humor has left me, I'm shutting down, becoming a machine. I just hope it gets the job done.

We're standing in a parking lot at the ski lodge. It's late now, past midnight, and the place is quiet. The lower slopes are lit up, but the snow is filtering the light. The chairlifts swing in the wind. It's unbelievably cold and I wished I had put on an extra pair of gloves.

"Everyone set?" Mav asks, eyeing us all. Even though he let Sam take the reins for a bit, it's so obvious that Mav is meant for this job. He exudes confidence and control and because of that, people listen to him. Even Neil, who is usually saying something to undermine him or giving him side-eye, is sober looking and paying attention.

We head out into the snow. I'm at the back with only Tim behind me. Maverick leads, followed by Sam and everyone else. Our headlamps are all shining, casting our path in an eerie blue, our skis sliding rhythmically. At least the freshly fallen snow has made it easier to ski, I had been expecting it hard-packed and icy after the warm weather we've had for the last ten days.

We ski for hours, into the night. We don't stop for a break. I'm in shape, I've spent my afternoons running through the snow, going to the gym down the street. I've never stopped working out, even after the accident. But now my lungs are burning. The lactic acid in my legs is building up. My pack is too heavy. Why the fuck am I carrying the litter? Was that a test, to see if I would do it, the only woman among all these men? Well I fucking passed the test, didn't I? I'm that proud that I took it.

The wind dies down a bit, the only respite, and big, fat flakes illuminate in my lamp, along with the wispy tendrils of my frozen breath.

It's still cold though and despite all my layers and the non-stop skiing, I'm not sweating underneath. I wonder if I'll ever feel warm again. I long to be back in Mav's truck, the heat on, just the two of us. It seemed so safe back then. Now everything is dark and wild and though I'm surrounded by a competent team, fear lurks where I can't see it, only feel it.

Finally, we come to a stop. I can't feel anything. Everyone is talking but I'm not really listening. Headlamps are pointing in all directions, cancelling everyone out.

A hand comes on my shoulder and I look up to see Mav for a split second before his lamp blinds me.

"Sorry," he says, moving it to the side. "How are you?"

I nod. "Cold," I tell him. "But okay."

"We're taking five minutes," he says. "But only five. You need water and you need something to eat."

"I'm fine," I say but my words sound dull. Before I know what he's doing, he's taking the litter off of me.

"I'm carrying this from now on," he says. "You did a good job, but we all share the duties, you got it?"

I'm too tired to argue. I let him take it and my shoulders lift up, immediately feeling lighter. Then he shoves an electrolyte gel pack in my hand and a bottle of water. "Eat that, then drink that, and then we'll go."

I nod, happy to do what I'm told.

But Mav runs a tight ship and I've barely finished the bottle when we start off again. This time though we only go for half an hour, well above the tree line, until we come to the top of a chute between two rock walls. While the snow has been steady during our ski up here, we've rounded the mountainside by now, facing east, which is warmer. There are some exposed rocks on the ridges and our lamps catch trickles of water running down them.

Below us is the chute, the wind having packed it with snow. It's dark and steep and we can't see where it goes.

Maverick, Sam, Tim, and Tony lie down on their stomachs overlooking the drop and talk amongst themselves. And by talk, I mean yell. Even though the wind has died down there's something about being in the dark, on a steep mountain face, that makes you think you need to scream to be heard.

But for all their talking and yelling about what to do next, there are two other voices in the night, far, far below. A faint "help" and "over here."

Maverick yells back for them to not move, that help is on the way. Even if they could move, and we're assuming at least the other skier can, they can't come up. Only we can go down.

And yet, no one is moving.

"Riley," Mav says, waving me over. "Come over here. I want your opinion."

All eyes go to me as I ski forward close to where Mav is lying down, and then carefully and quickly take my skis off.

Slowly, I lower myself to my knees, the cold snow biting through my clothes and then on to my stomach, right up beside Mav. I'm good at climbing and I enjoy it, but the irony is that I'm not a fan of heights. I rarely look down and when I do, I at least feel secure in my harness.

But now, I don't have my harness on yet and even though I'm flat on the ground, I'm not prepared for what I see when I look over.

It just seems to drop away into nothing and the vertigo washes over me so fast that I have to close my eyes and breathe.

"Pretty fucking nuts, huh," Mav says softly. His breath is warm on my cheek.

I can't even nod. I don't want to move an inch.

"What do you think?" he asks and I notice that unlike his earlier conversation with Sam and Tim, he's not yelling at me. He's almost whispering, as if we're having a private conversation on the ledge of a three-hundred-foot chute that ends in blackness.

"What do you mean?"

"Do you think the chute will hold?"

I look back to the dripping water, the change in air temperature on this side of the mountain. The water over time will make the snowpack heavier. The heavier the snowpack on top, the more likely it will slide.

"It might hold for now, but maybe not in an hour. Maybe not even now. And definitely not enough for all of us to go down."

He gives me a smile. "I agree. So the question is, who is going down?"

"Is that innuendo?" It's a feeble joke, but it's the only way for me to deal with how serious this all is. Or maybe it isn't serious at all, maybe they all deal with this all the time. Maybe it's been too long for me and maybe I am still too scarred from what happened with Levi.

"Of course," he says. "But I also want to know what you think." He looks over his shoulder at the others, half who are watching us, the other half arguing over what to do. Tim is the avalanche expert and he seems to think it will hold. Sam and Tony say it won't.

"Is this the kind of thing where my vote decides?" I ask Mav.

He shakes his head, snowflakes falling off his lashes and brows. "No. I'm going down there. Just wondered if you wanted to come. You can stay up here and ski back down the way we came. Or you can hang tight and do radio relay with Tony."

"Isn't there another way?"

"We routed the descent from a slightly different spot so half of the initial descent with the litter is going to be more complicated before it joins up with the original plan. Sam says we could go down further to the east, but that will add an extra two hours and those people are right down there. They're talking, they're alive, but they won't last the night here. We just don't have the time."

"Or you do have the time. You can play it safe and hope they hang on."

"I don't play it safe," he says.

Well, you've been playing it pretty safe with me so far. I don't even know how that thought had the nerve to show up in my brain right now, but there you go.

"Not in these situations, anyway," he adds, as if he knows what I'm thinking. "If you're not in this business to risk your life, why are you in it?"

But I know why so many of the others are hesitant. Because they have families. They have other people they need to take care of in their lives. Mav doesn't. Neither do I.

"I'm in," I tell him. "Let's go."

He stares into my eyes for a moment, searching, and I know he wants to ask me if I'm sure and I also know that if he asks me, I might say no and back out. But he doesn't ask and so now I'm committed.

Shit.

Things just got real.

"Okay," Mav says to the team, inching away from the edge before getting to his feet. "If you're staying, ski back to where we had our break and wait there. If you're coming down with us, let's go."

Carefully, I inch back too. In fact, I inch back until I'm pretty much past the group before I get to my feet, Tony helping me up.

"You okay to do this?" Tony asks.

I dust off my pants and torso. "I think so."

"You could wait a few hours. That's when the chute will slide. Then we could go down."

"But if we wait, they could die."

"It's your first outing with the team," Neil says, coming over.

I manage to stay civil. "Go big or go home."

"Well I'm fucking going home," he says. "Back to my bed. You're welcome to join me." I glare at him so hard until he realizes what he's said. He turns to Tony. "You too, Tony."

"No thanks."

Meanwhile, Mav gets on the radio and calls it in to the local authorities and the lodge to tell them what we're going to do. And I get what we're going to do, I'm just not sure how we're going to do it. The chute looks so steep, I wish I could just ride the litter down like a sled.

But after most of the team leaves, Mav starts explaining it to the brave or stupid ones like myself who have stayed behind. Funny how I was just commenting on the skiers being stupid, risking their neck for the hiker, when now I'm risking my own neck for them.

Tony is one of the ones staying, but his job is to stay where we are right now and do radio relay. He sits among our skis, wraps his legs in an emergency blanket, and waits.

Maverick goes first down the chute, followed by Tim, then Jace, then a guy named Pete, then me. It's steep and slick but we take it slow, one step at a time, moving sideways almost like a crab. My headlamp illuminates my ski boots, a foot of snow, and then blackness beyond until it comes to headlamp after headlamp, little blue dots in the dark.

Once we reach the bottom of the chute in one piece, Mav radios up to Tony who tells us that the base is expecting the temperature to start dropping soon. Which is good, because rain would have ended us.

Mav starts calling for the hiker and skier and they eventually answer back, though their voices are fainter than before.

"Did they move?" I ask him.

"No," he says, the light from his lamp moving in a dizzying arc as he shakes his head. "They're still there, they're just weaker. We have to move fast. Let me do a beacon search."

Mav pulls out the Recco, a handheld detector that locates the tiny reflectors that's sewn in some outdoor gear. We locate one, a couple hundred yards away, though even with Mav's map it's hard to tell what's between us and them. A cliff face? Avalanche debris? A sheet of ice? After all, the hiker was an ice hiker, wearing crampons. If those can't stick to the surface, I don't know what can. According to the other skier, he slid fifty feet and almost went over a cliff face, using his leg to stop him. Unfortunately, he shattered his leg in doing so, right up against a rock.

We work quickly through the basin, ever so aware that the cornices are hanging high above us, waiting to fall. It would be another avalanche and in the middle of the night, with only Tony up there, it's doubtful any of us would survive.

I'm scared. Especially as we come to a section of avalanche debris that I know is unstable but we have no choice but to cross it.

But I can't move. It's like my legs are refusing, cementing me in place. There's terror in going forward and safety where I am, even though I know that safety is only an illusion.

Mav comes back to me as Tim goes first across it. He grabs my hand and gives it a squeeze. "You okay?"

I nod frantically, my voice shaking. "Yes."

"You're scared."

"I'm not."

"You should be."

I give him a sharp look. "What?"

"You should be scared," he says again, voice low and grave. "It's healthy. It protects you. But you have to let it in and you have to deal with it head on. I know this is a lot and I know you're just getting back in the game. So the fear is only natural. But don't push it away. Don't think you can outrun it. Fear will always find you. Better you find it first."

And I don't know how, but Mav's words have an affect on me. Standing there, at the edge of a debris field, with cornices hanging three hundred feet above us, knowing everything can let go right now in the darkness and we'll be buried in seconds, I go after the fear. I let it in.

I let it out.

And we get moving.

Twenty minutes later, after careful walking, sinking into the snow up to our waist in some places, we find the hiker and skier, their backs against an exposed rock.

Both are hypothermic and the hiker has gone into shock, but the skier says it was only recently and he had done a good job of wrapping him up in emergency blankets and garbage bags that act as a bivvy, keeping him dry and warm.

We're all EMTs, but Tim is a medic and tends to the hiker's leg, which is fractured in more than a few places. It's absolutely gruesome to see Tim work, but he gets it done by the light of our headlamps and in the falling snow, setting the leg, bandaging it up, and getting the hiker on the litter we've put together. Mav phones it in to Tony, who will take our skis and meet us along with everyone else.

Mav and Tim hold the litter from each end and we carefully make our way sideways, avoiding the slick slope that the hiker lost control on. Pete and I support the skier, whose name is Garrett, and keep him talking the entire time just to keep him moving and awake and alive.

By the time we meet up with the group at the halfway

point, they take over, letting us have a bit of a rest before following.

Then we ski all the way back down the hill to the lodge.

It's six a.m. The sky is lighting up in the corners, but it will still be a couple of hours until the sun makes an appearance. Then, somehow, we're back in Mav's truck, just the two of us, roaring down the mountain through the pre-dawn.

We don't talk much. I was running on adrenaline that entire ski back to the lodge, but now my brain is numb. My body is numb. I can't even feel the heat from the heater. I can't really feel anything except a faint wash of relief. Relief that I did it. And yeah, we totally saved some lives. But mainly, my relief is selfish. I still have what it takes. Losing Levi didn't break me.

"You did good, kid," Mav says to me as he pulls up outside my house.

I look to him, my eyes skirting over his nose, his lips. The small smile on them. I'm suddenly hit with a wallop of loneliness, an urge to be warm again, to feel something, someone. I want nothing more than to invite him inside. After the night we had, I have a feeling that this time he won't say no. Trauma builds camaraderie. Fear makes bonds. In one night, we've grown closer than before.

Please come inside, I want to say, willing my mouth to open, to say it. I want to grab his hand, hold it. I want him in my bed, deep inside me.

But I don't say a word, not that anyway. I just say, "Thanks. I'll see you later."

And then I get out of his truck and into the house before I do anything that both of us might regret.

CHAPTER SEVEN

RILEY

I SLEEP UNTIL THREE IN THE AFTERNOON. I DON'T GET ANY calls, and when I finally open my eyes and check my phone, I don't have any texts either.

In that small space between waking up and checking my phone, there was a warm sense of peace. A bit of the "yay, I saved a life" running through me and the sticky soft fragments of deep sleep. Plus there's this soft winter light coming through the window. The storm from last night is over.

But after I check my phone and don't see a thing, the warmth is replaced by loneliness. The kind of loneliness that hurts, like something cold and hard and dark is dissolving inside you like a bath bomb. It's a chill in your soul, the type that only a strong embrace can get rid of. Sometimes, I just want to be held.

I don't know what I expected. Maybe a text from Maverick, telling me I was needed into work. Or maybe touching on last night. Maybe just checking up on me.

And that's when it hits me, that realization that, fuck, the only person who might possibly do that is my own boss. I've only known him for ten days or so. Other than him, there's no one. There's been no one for the last two years of my life.

It's by choice. I chose to leave my family back in Washington because they are toxic people. My mother is a drug addict, always choosing pills or whatever she can get her hands on over me, over my father. And my father is a criminal. He's constantly on parole. He's always going in and out of jail. Sometimes I wonder who even raised me since neither of them were ever there.

That's probably why I clung so hard to Levi. Because he understood me. He didn't judge. He saw my parents and he saw the good in me. He took me under his wing. He helped me escape. He helped me be free. How could I not love a man, let alone anyone, who did that for me?

His parents were wonderful too. They loved him so much, they moved to Colorado just so they could be closer to him. I guess they thought he'd work in the state forever, maybe settle down eventually. Not with me though, I was nothing more than a friend. But I was someone to them and that counted.

Of course, now they hate me. They blame me for what happened to Levi and in turn I can't blame them. I blame myself too. I've tried to keep in touch with them, to find out how he is. He's been in a coma for so long and they keep clinging to the hope he'll come back to them. But I had to move out of Colorado and move on, leave it all behind, even though they were really the last real friends I had.

Now I'm here, alone in a basement suite, nearly shivering in my bed with the loneliness rolling through me. I feel like I'm still on that cliff edge, on my stomach, staring down into the black abyss. But instead of Mav by my side, his long, hard body pressed to mine, there's nothing but the dark. It goes and goes and goes, fathomless.

Even going back to sleep doesn't seem like a good idea.

More darkness. My dreams will be unkind. So I get up and get dressed and make pancakes and scarf them all down. Then I watch *Wayne's World* and *Wayne's World 2*, because they always make me laugh.

Then I put on some makeup and make myself go to The Bear Trap, because after a while, even Mike Meyers isn't a good substitute for real people.

It's fairly early when I go, so I'm not expecting it to be busy at all. Delilah waves at me from behind the bar. So far I think I'm the only person in there, except for the old dude who is always at the same booth, trying to sneak a cigarette when she's not looking.

"Hey, how goes it?" she says. "I thought I would have seen you more."

"Been busy," I tell her, taking a seat at the bar. Delilah is super pretty. She's tall, with broad swimmer's shoulders, and she carries herself gracefully. She's got a super sweet face, big big smile, big white teeth, cute cheeks, long brown hair that swings around her face.

"Mav's working you hard, is he?" she says and then smirks. "Sorry. Bad joke."

"It's too early for jokes," I tell her. "I think I'll get a glass of white."

"You got it," she says, fishing out a cheap bottle from the fridge and pouring me a generous glass.

I take a long sip, letting the cold wine slide down my throat, then give her a grateful smile. "This is exactly what I've needed. And the company."

Delilah looks flattered. "Well, thank you. I guess you don't know anyone in town, do you?"

I shrug, trying to make myself look less desperate. "No one other than the people I work with, and I don't think they're the types I'd hang out with or vice versa. I'm still not sure what they think of me. We went on our first call last

91

night." I tell her all about it. When I'm done, she's wide-eyed, clutching the edge of the bar top.

"That's crazy," she says in a hush. "That was your first call here in North Ridge?"

"Yup. Talk about being thrown into the fire."

"Wow. Honestly, I've heard Maverick talk about what he's done and I'll read about it in the paper or hear about it if it's something big, and I don't know how he does it. Or how you do it. Risking your life for people you don't know."

"It's why we do it. It's exciting. And once you start, it's hard to stop."

"I guess," she muses, leaning on her elbows on the bar. "But how many of them have families, you know? It's probably easier to do it if you're alone."

"And that's probably why so many of us are loners," I point out.

She gives me a small smile. "You consider yourself a loner?"

I let out a wry laugh. "Well, yeah. I moved all the way here by myself. Didn't know a soul. Still don't, really."

The door to the bar opens, bringing in a blast of cold. My heart starts beating fast and hot and I find myself hoping that it's Maverick. I want to see him again, talk to him, be near him. It's not just the crazy sexual attraction I feel for him, it's this strange sense of comfort he brings.

But when I turn and look it's not Maverick. It is his younger brother, Shane, and his fiancée, Rachel.

"You guys are here early," Delilah says.

"We just wanted a quick drink before dinner," Rachel says. "We're classy like that." She stops at the bar and gives me a quick smile. "Hello," she says, offering her hand. "I don't believe we've officially met."

"Riley," I tell her, shaking her hand. Like Del, she's also pretty, except in this haunting way, like she stepped out of a gothic painting, all black hair, sharp bone structure and vivid eyes.

"I'm Shane, Mav's brother," Shane says, and I shake his hand too.

"I've heard a lot about you," I tell him teasingly.

"Oh really? I'm always curious on how Mav paints me. The hapless cowpoke?"

"Something like that," I say. I can tell Shane is related to his brothers—they all have the same eye shape and set brow —but he's lighter in eye color and hair color, his face a little prettier than Mav's or Fox's. He definitely takes after one of their parents more than the other. I wonder if he resembles their mother, maybe that's part of the reason why Fox apparently has issues with him?

"Riley was just telling me all about their call last night," Delilah says excitedly.

"I heard about that," Shane says, leaning against the bar. "My grandpa said a hiker broke his leg. He knew one of the skiers who found him, guess he buys cows from us sometimes. Sounded pretty rough."

"It wasn't easy," I say. "But we got it done. In Aspen there were a lot of SARs around, I guess because of the popularity and population. Here it seems like we're going to be working all the time. We're all there is for like, what, one hundred kilometres or something?"

"You were in Aspen before?" Rachel asks. "And now you're here. What made you want to come all the way out to North Ridge? I couldn't wait to blow this popsicle stand."

Shane reaches out and grabs her hand, kissing the back of it. "But you did come back, raven girl."

How cute.

I clear my throat, giving the happy couple one of those sickly-sweet smiles I reserve for those who are sickly sweet. "I needed a change. I'm actually half Canadian and thought it was about time I start living on this side of the border."

"Smart choice," Shane says.

"Riley doesn't really know anyone here, other than your brother and the dudes she works with," Delilah pipes up again.

Rachel and Shane both look at me with pitying looks on their faces.

I raise my glass of wine, which is almost gone. "But hey, that's what your local watering hole is for, right?"

"Well, we're having dinner tomorrow night," Rachel says. "It's Sunday and there's usually a roast that my mother and I make for everyone. Why don't you come over?"

"No, that's okay," I say quickly. I don't want to be anyone's charity case.

"No, seriously," says Shane. "That's a great idea." He looks at Del. "You and Jeanine should come too."

"Sure," Delilah says. "Just make sure Fox and Maverick go."

"I'll try," Rachel says. "Those two are always trying to weasel their way out of things. Fox more so than Mav."

I look at Shane and see a brief tick in his jaw. I think back to what Mav said about his mother and Fox and Shane's relationship.

"Please say you'll come," Rachel goes on to me. "It's super low-key. And you wouldn't be imposing. Having dinner at Ravenswood Ranch is kind of like an initiation into North Ridge. When I was little, the Nelsons were the first family to take my family in, so it's only fair we do the same with you."

She drives a hard bargain, this Rachel. But as much as I hate to impose, being around a family, a group of people who seem to like me well enough, does seem like something I need to do. Something I should do. Anything to get me out of this funk and get me back to my normal self.

"Okay," I tell them. "That would be fun."

"Great!" Delilah exclaims and starts pouring me another glass of wine. "This one is on me."

"Ahem," Shane clears his throat. "And one for your buddy Shane?"

"Do you want to take a look at your bar tab, buddy?"

He rolls his eyes and hands over some bills. She slides them both beers with a smug smile.

I end up having another glass of wine at the bar after Shane and Rachel go on to their dinner plans, just talking with Delilah until it starts getting busy. But even though I stick around, slowly sipping the wine, hoping to see Maverick, he never comes in. I contemplate texting him to tell him I'm here or even just hello, but I never get the nerve. Which is weird, because all week I've had too much nerve. Maybe it was because I didn't really know Mav, I just thought he was a giant hunk of man-meat I wanted to roll around naked with. And while I still don't know him too well, I know him enough that I'm actually starting to like him. As in, want to be around him and talk to him and not just use him for fucking purposes.

Though that would be nice, too.

That would be very nice, indeed.

But, that night he doesn't show up at the bar and I end up walking home through the cold. I get into bed, bring out my vibrator, and end the evening on a high note.

* * *

THE NEXT DAY I'm set to come into work, so I show up at the office and find only Jace there.

Jace is a strange one. Quiet and mopey and emo to the core. He doesn't talk much and I'm still not sure if he likes me or not. I don't need him—or anyone—to like me, but I do get weird when it comes to awkward silences and when we're together there's nothing but awkward silences. So I talk to fill in the gaps. Which means I talk a lot. And when I talk a lot, I get weird and go off on a million different tangents, such as:

Do you like cheese?

I hate shopping for socks.

Michael Keaton is the best Batman.

Gluten is highly underrated.

What do you think is on the dark side of the moon?

So YEAH, who knows if he likes me. He probably doesn't. He probably can't stand me but whatever, I would rather he not like me than me personally have to suffer through the stretches of silence.

Today is no exception. I'm filing paperwork about the rescue we did the other day and he's doing something that looks like updating GPS maps or something like that. Apparently, every time you go over an area you haven't been before, you have to record each coordinate.

There's always something to do.

It's only as I'm done with my shift and am leaving that Jace says, "Can I ask you something?"

I pause at the door and look at him in surprise. "Of course."

I'm prepared for him to tell me that Christian Bale is the best Batman.

He licks his thin lips. "How long have you been doing this for?"

That's a strange question. Not that I haven't been asked that, but it feels strange coming from Tickle Me Emo. "Uh, well, my friend in high school was doing a boy scouts version of it and I started getting involved that way. Just doing what he did. Learning about the mountains, taking first aid classes, learning how to climb, all that stuff. But I've only been paid for this in the last two places I worked at."

He gives me a barely perceptible nod. "Okay. Thank you."

I frown, trying to smile. "Why?"

"No reason. Just curious."

"Well how long have you been doing it?"

"A lot longer than you," is his clipped answer. And then he goes right back to his computer.

Okay then.

I shrug Jace off and head back home where I quickly get ready. Delilah had said she'd come pick me up at five p.m., which gives me twenty minutes to look presentable. Even though I'm tired and usually can't be bothered, I spend some time putting on my makeup and selecting the right outfit. I pick a pair of cheap skinny jeans, a tight-fitting black V-neck sweater, and furry boots that come to my knee.

By the time I slip on my parka and fluff my hair around my shoulders, there's a knock at the basement suite door in the backyard.

Imagine my surprise when I don't see Delilah standing on the other side of it, but Maverick instead.

"Hi," I tell him as I open the door, so glad I put extra care into my appearance, even though he's used to seeing me look ragged.

"Hi," he says, a grin spreading across his face. "You look amazing."

I don't usually blush but I think I'm blushing now. "Thank you. I didn't know you'd be here. I mean, I was expecting Delilah."

He nods, folding his arms across his chest and taking a wide stance. "Well, I only found out you were coming over for dinner the moment Del was leaving to pick you up."

"So you came instead."

"I don't trust her driving," he says. "Come on, the truck's running."

I grab my purse from the coat rack and follow him out. One of the more annoying things about the winter is how much it hides your body. But now, with this quick trip, Mav is dressed in Timberlands, jeans, a thermal, and a leather jacket, and I have a great view of his ass as he walks. He wasn't kidding about it being hard. It makes me think about all his other hard places.

I get in his now familiar truck, immediately relaxing. Even though it's thrown me off guard with him picking me up, I'm glad he did. Just breathing in the same air as him gives me a sense of well-being.

We drive off and I'm already smiling.

CHAPTER EIGHT

MAVERICK

FUCKING *EH*.

I had no idea that Riley was coming over for dinner until Del was literally about to leave the ranch house with her car keys. When Rachel first invited Fox and I over for dinner and was rather insistent that I come, I didn't think much of it. She's often insistent about most things, especially anything related to family matters.

Had I known they'd invited Riley though, fuck. I don't know. After the rescue the other night, I was left feeling nothing but confusion over my feelings for her. On one hand, you can cut the sexual tension with a knife. Which I find almost amusing, considering it's kind of all there on the table. There aren't words unsaid because Riley is saying them, which makes the tension even thicker. All words and, so far, no action.

On the other hand, I feel closer to her, and not in a way I appreciate. If I was protective of her before, I'm more so now. I wish I could keep her all to myself and not share her with anyone else, and that includes co-workers and family. If that makes me a caveman, so be it.

And now she's beside me in my truck, tapping her fingers along the window ledge to Tom Petty playing on the radio. She looks absolutely phenomenal and hot as fuck, her black sweater displaying just the tops of her full breasts. I have to fight to keep my attention on the road.

"It's a shame he died," she says.

"Who? Tom Petty?"

"He seemed immortal. Like Prince and Bowie. I always assumed death couldn't touch them, that it only touched the rest of us." She glances at me, brows raised curiously. "Who are your top three musicians? Like if they died, you'd go into mourning."

"Honestly, I'm still not over Chris Cornell being gone."

She studies me and nods after a moment. "I can see you being a Soundgarden fan."

"I am," I tell her, rolling up my sleeve to show her the band's symbol tattooed on the back of my forearm.

"Nice," she says and reaches over, her finger tracing the outline of the tattoo, as if it's still raised. She's creating goosebumps along my skin but thankfully she pulls her hand away before she notices. "What else do you got?"

"I've got everything, darling." I grin at her. "But unless I'm naked, you won't be able to see them."

Her eyes widen, like she's appreciating the fact that for once I'm the one throwing it out there instead of her.

Even though you shouldn't be, I remind myself. This is a dangerous path and I can't help but think back to what I said the other night, when I told her I didn't play it safe. The more I push and play with this, the riskier it's going to get.

"Well, well, well," she says. "But you didn't answer my question."

Phew. I thought that was going to derail us for a moment, but she put us right back on track. Maybe I'll be able to survive this dinner with her after all.

"Tom Waits, Willie Nelson, and Keith Richards."

"Keith Richards? Really?"

I shrug. "If he died, it would mean he's human, and honestly I'd be a little disappointed to find out otherwise. What about you?"

"Everyone I love is already dead."

I look at her in surprise. "Really? Or are you just being morbid?"

She ticks them off her fingers. "Nina Simone, Ella Fitzgerald, and Muddy Waters."

Okay, now I'm really surprised. "I wouldn't peg you for a jazz or blues lover."

"We all get the blues, baby," she says, voice husky. "Like you say about fear, the blues will find you. It's better you go and find it first."

Good lord. This woman is everything.

I'm so infatuated with her that before I know it, I'm crossing the Queen's River and Cherry Creek and heading up to the main house at Ravenswood Ranch.

"This is it. Where I grew up," I tell her.

She stares out the window, big eyes taking it all in. The sun is setting in the west, making the snow glow pink and purple, the barns and the buildings looking like a winter postcard. "This is magical."

"It's magical on the outside. I can't guarantee the same for the inside. It will be a full house tonight."

"Good," she says, flashing me a wicked smile. "I like a little chaos with my dinner."

Well, chaos it is because we go inside and, even though I thought we were a bit early, everyone is here and apparently waiting for us.

Riley stands beside me in the doorway as my grandpa gets off his chair and barks. "Shut the damn door, John, were you raised in a barn?"

"Pretty much," I tell him, and then gesture to Riley who is smiling broadly at them all and not appearing to be self-conscious or shy in the slightest. "This is my co-worker, Riley, she just moved to North Ridge from Aspen and is the newest member of our search and rescue. Riley, this is," and then I introduce her to my grandpa, my father and Jeanine sitting at the table, Vernalee who pokes her head out of the kitchen, and then Fox who is having a beer with Del on the couch.

When introductions are all done, Rachel comes over to take Riley's coat and then Del brings her a glass of white wine. It warms my heart a little to see these girls being so friendly to her. I know that Riley puts on a tough face some-times and doesn't care what people think, but I remember what she said about loneliness and it'd be good for her to have some girlfriends in this town.

Everything goes smoothly and the only chaos is from having so many different people in the room together, but it's a chaos that works. My grandfather is both the philoso-pher and the joker, alternating between bouts of wisdom and pulling your leg. Vernalee is crass at times and hard to like, but her sense of humor usually puts everyone at ease. My father is tough and perpetually a grumpy old man, and aside from asking Riley the occasional question about working the mountains of Wyoming or Colorado, he doesn't say much, and we're all fine with that.

Jeanine is quiet and soft-spoken and makes you feel like you're the only person in the room when you're talking to her. Del is very similar to her mother, though louder and endlessly curious. She asks the most questions of Riley, and when she asks if she had anyone special in Aspen, Riley is quick to brush that under the table with a smile.

Shane is more of an observer, listening and watching but rarely offering anything up himself. Rachel is more likely to ask questions and she seems just as fascinated by Riley as Del is. I don't know what it is, maybe those girls are getting bored with people in the town, or maybe they secretly harbor dreams of being some adventurous, tattooed tough chick.

We eat really well, roast beef and roasted root vegetables that Rachel and Vernalee probably spent all day on, followed by cherry pie. A lot of wine goes around the table, but I watch what I have since I'll have to take Riley back to her place later.

Then, when everyone seems sufficiently loose for a Sunday evening, music starts playing and the girls all start dancing, while Jeanine and Vernalee wash up in the kitchen.

I can't take my eyes off of Riley. She called herself klutzy at one point but I'm sure it's all in her head. There's a difference between klutzy and goofy and if she's anything, she's the latter. In fact, she's dancing like Mike Meyers in *Austin Powers* and laughing her ass off as she goes.

The feeling I have in my chest is completely unfamiliar. It's like a combination of a warm bath and someone dropping a toaster in it. It's both calming and electrifying and there's no other way to explain it, but I have both those feelings at once when I'm looking at her. And fuck, I don't want to stop.

"She's a real spitfire," my grandfather says as he eases himself into the chair next to me at the table.

"Riley?" I ask, playing dumb, as if my eyes have left her for a second. She's currently holding onto Del's hand and making her twirl around, taking the lead.

"Don't play dumb, boy," he says and then points directly at her. "That one. There. Riley."

I gently grab his finger and push it away. The last thing Riley needs is for us to be pointing at her, though I also think she probably wouldn't care.

"Okay, I get it," I tell him.

"I knew a girl like her once. Before I met your grandmother. I sure did have the biggest darn crush on her, eh? But she couldn't give a pig's snout about me."

Pig's snout?

He goes on. "She was beautiful, long legs. All the boys in the class were always trying to get a look under her skirt."

"Grandpa," I admonish him, teasingly.

"I didn't say I did it," he says defensively, then thinks about it for a moment. "Anyway, trying and doing are two different things. Point is, this girl was a heartbreaker and in the end, she wasn't interested in me and that spared me. I found your grandmother instead. But the boys she did date, oh did she ever break their little hearts."

My eyes are still on Riley, thinking this over as Fox approaches her and asks her to dance. Del looks put out again, but she still smiles and moves out of the way, while Fox dips and twirls Riley around. The music is like 90's R&B, it's not really dancing music, and yet there they are. Both of them seem to be enjoying themselves and I'm sitting here with a hot coal of rage and jealousy slowly building inside me.

"You see," my grandfather says, nudging me on the shoulder. "She's a heartbreaker."

I take in a long, deep breath and look away. If I stared at them any longer, I would have gone up there and broken them apart, and what kind of brother would I be then? I don't have the right, even though every cell in my body is telling me she's mine and mine alone.

I cough and say, "She's my colleague, grandpa. She's part of search and rescue. She's not my girlfriend."

"Baloney," he says. "That doesn't mean a thing."

"There are rules," I say, voice harder. "Rules about that kind of thing."

Now my grandfather is laughing. "Rules? *Rules*? Oh, John boy, you have never been one to follow rules. And you've been better off for it."

He pauses and gets that wise owl look to his weathered face. "Do you remember when you were younger and we told you that the river was off-limits? And you said, 'yes sir,' and pretended to obey us, but you still went down there and you still played by the river. And then one day you saw a fawn that was caught in an eddy, drowning. You went right in and saved that fawn. Next thing I know, you're holding the shivering, wet thing in your arms at the front door. We asked you what happened and you didn't lie. You broke the rules, but if you hadn't, you wouldn't have saved that fawn."

I remember very well. They didn't want me by the river because of my mother, but that's exactly why I went every day after school. I wasn't playing—I was paying respect. It was like visiting her grave. But that one day I did see the fawn and I went into the river to rescue it. I wasn't afraid, I just knew I was at that place for a reason. The damn fawn was orphaned after that, and we took care of it until it was old enough to return to the wild. Sometimes the fawn would follow me into the house, wanting the bottle, and Jeanine would get so fucking mad.

"Anyway, John boy, you're a rule-breaker at heart. No point changing that now."

Except when my career is at stake.

Thankfully, the dance party doesn't last for too much longer with my father complaining of a headache and then it's time to take Riley home.

She's drunk and funny and goofy and leaning on me all the way to the truck.

"Your family is so fun," she says, holding onto my arm. I have to fight the urge to put my arm around her, even though it feels like the most natural thing to do.

"I'm glad they behaved for you," I tell her, opening the passenger door for her and ushering her inside.

She's quiet on the drive back to her place, but not in a bad way. She seems contemplative and she keeps stealing glances at me.

I end up asking, "Penny for your thoughts?"

"I don't think you want to know," she says in a low voice.

I take her word for it.

We pull up to her house and for the first time, things feel awkward. She's drunk on wine and I'm just trying to keep my head on straight. Too many things are rushing up inside me, threatening to erupt like a volcano. That sharp, tangible and irrefutable feeling that she's mine and she needs to know it.

She unbuckles her seat belt and turns to face me and whatever resolve I have inside, that thin one that tells me to play by the rules, to play it safe for once, I feel it weaken.

She is just so beautiful. The full, sex-soaked pout of her gorgeous lips, the way they contrast with her innocent blue eyes. Her hair as it falls softly around her shoulders, begging to be touched. Everything about her is brimming with lust and intensity. Every inch of her is begging to be touched.

I swallow hard, my nostrils flaring as she leans over and puts her palm at my cheek, her skin warm. I freeze, afraid to move. I can only stare at her as she shuffles over, getting closer until her face is right in front of mine.

"What are you so afraid of?" she whispers, staring at my lips.

It takes a moment for me to speak, my heart is beating so hard in my chest it's like a fucking jackhammer. "You," I tell her honestly.

I expect her to smile but she looks dead serious.

"You know I can keep a secret," she says.

Then she climbs on top of me so she's straddling me,

thighs on either side of mine, her crotch pressed against my stomach, her ass into the steering wheel.

Before I can do or say anything, she reaches down and grabs the hem of her sweater and pulls it over her head. Her full breasts are pushed up by a lacey pink bra that matches her lips, her skin like cream, inches away from me.

"I bet you can keep a secret too," she purrs, running her thumb down over my jaw, then my lip. She pushes her thumb in and my mouth opens, sucking gently. Her eyes close and her lips open and the softest moan escapes them and I am so fucking hard I think I'm going to burst right through the fly of my jeans.

She removes her thumb and stares at me, her lids heavy, and I don't know how much longer I can keep it together. I am a fucking weak man in the end.

"You can touch me, you know," she says softly, and she takes both of my hands and places them at her waist. It's so small, so smooth, I feel like I could wrap my fingers all the way around her. I press my palms against her, holding on tight, not because I want to—because I do—but because I'm afraid of moving them elsewhere.

She leans in closer and places her lips at my neck. A small kiss, but a long kiss. I shut my eyes and groan. I can't help it. My grip tightens around her waist. My erection is so hot and tight and hard and I'm just fucking sweating, trying to hold out. "You can do whatever you want to me." Her lips move against my skin as she speaks, wet.

"I can't," I manage to say. My voice breaks with lust as I say it, my blood running hot and loud in my head. "You know we can't. Riley…please."

She pulls back for a moment and smiles. She knows she's wearing me down. God, it's going to feel so fucking good when I finally let go.

"If you could do anything to me, what would you do?" she

whispers in my ear, her breath hot and sweet, her voice dripping with sex. "Pretend there are no rules and tell me everything you'd do to me, right here, right now."

Oh, fuck.

But before I can open my mouth, my phone buzzes.

It's Jace, at the office.

It's a call.

I clear my throat, needing to answer the call, but at the same time, reluctant to move Riley off of me. I'm too terrified to move my hands. I know if I touch another section of bare, soft skin that I'll lose complete control and then I won't need to tell her what I want to do, I'll fucking show her.

But Riley quickly moves off of me, slides her sweater back on and hands me my phone.

I nod my thanks and spend a few seconds clearing my throat, trying to calm my racing heart, before I answer it.

"Mav here."

"They found a backpack on the mountain but no sign of the skier," Jace says. "RCMP wants to do an aerial search in the morning, but figures we can get a head start."

"Might be too late by morning. We'll need everyone," I tell him, adrenaline over the search starting to course through me, competing with my hardened lust for Riley. "Get the team, I'll put out a call for volunteers."

"Will do."

He hangs up and I exhale loudly, trying to get rid of all the sexual frustration.

"Should I get my gear on?" Riley asks, her demeanor back to business.

"We'll get enough volunteers, you don't have to make this one."

Her brows knit together. "Mav, it's my *job*."

"It's your day off. And you've had wine."

"It's your day off, too. And I'm pretty much sober. Are

you trying to keep me safe, or do you think I'm too distracting? Because if it's the latter, you know how I am on the job and if it's the—"

"It's neither," I lie. "I just wanted you to have the night off if you wanted. You had a nice dinner, you shouldn't have to rush out there."

"It's my job," she says again and opens the door. "Now give me a few minutes and I'll be right back."

She runs off around the back of the house to where the basement suite door is. I stare at her for a few moments before I thump the top of the steering wheel with my fist.

"Fuck!" I yell. I need to get it together, but damn it feels good to yell. I do it a few more times, trying to rid myself of all the tension, how close I fucking got to whipping out my cock and impaling her on it.

By the time she comes back out, dressed in her rescue gear and carrying her pack, I've got myself back under control.

We drive off, colleagues again, ready to search and rescue.

CHAPTER NINE

RILEY

"Hey, hot stuff."

I roll my eyes hard and turn away from the map I was studying. Micropenis Neil just walked into the office, which means, oh fucking joy, I'm spending this Wednesday working with both him and Jace. Jace who is sitting in the corner of the room and watching the two of us with a suspicious look on his face. Which, considering he's Dr. Emo, is *extra* suspicious.

"Hi," I say, turning my back to him. I try and play it nice with Neil, but every now and then he starts getting inappropriate and all leering and shit.

Then again, I'm not one to talk. I still don't know what the hell I was thinking the other night after dinner at the Nelsons. I'd had a lot of wine, but my head was still on straight. I just...I saw the way Maverick was watching me as I was dancing and I saw that anger flare in his eyes when Fox came over. I *know* he cares. I know he wants me. And I just want him to fucking give in and fuck me already.

Or hell, kiss me. Touch me. Anything. I'll take anything that man has to give me and I'll take it with gusto.

But no. We got called into a rescue before anything could happen. And maybe that was for the best. I don't know. It definitely sobered me up. We ended up finding the skier in the wee hours of the morning, but there were a lot of us there and Mav and I haven't discussed what happened since. It's been a few days now and we've been working like normal.

Although I don't know what normal is anymore. Is normal wanting to jump someone every waking moment? Is this the normal for the rest of my days here? Me, just continuously hitting on and crushing on my boss? No. Something has to give. We're either going to succumb to what I hope is the inevitable or...fuck. He could tell me to knock it off for good. I don't want to think about that.

"So, what are you doing this weekend?" Neil asks. It's Thursday. We don't always get weekends.

"I'm working," I tell him quickly, hoping he doesn't ask me to do something, because that's what it sounds like.

"I saw your schedule," he says. "You're not working Sunday. Neither am I."

I grumble in response, reading over the same word, "Chairman's Peak," on the map over and over again, waiting for him to give up.

"I thought maybe we could go see a movie," he says.

Jace clears his throat but doesn't interject.

Finally, I turn around and give Neil a look that should make him shrivel up and melt like the Wicked Witch of the West.

He stares back at me with full confidence, as if there's no way I would ever say no. Someone with a micropenis shouldn't be this cocky, especially if he doesn't care to make up for his shortcomings.

"I believe that would be inappropriate," I tell him.

"Going to the movies? Jace and I go all the time."

I look at Jace and he looks confused, which has me doubting it's true.

"Besides," he says, "you went to dinner with Mav to Ravenswood Ranch. That's something."

"He didn't invite me," I point out. "His brother Shane and his fiancée did. I was *their* guest."

The door swings open and Maverick appears, like we conjured him up out of thin air. He's breathless, a dusting of snow on his shoulders, and looking between the two of us with narrowed eyes. "What's going on?" he asks.

My heart flips around in my chest. Not just at the fact that he's here and that's what my heart always does around him, but because he looks so damn bothered that Neil and I are talking about something. I love it when he goes caveman, even if he denies it.

"Neil invited me to the movies and I said no," I say with a smile.

To Neil's credit, he doesn't flinch when Mav fixes a steely, murderous gaze on him. "You what?"

"To be fair," he says, clearing his throat. "She didn't say no. She said it would be inappropriate. So Mav, do you think it would be inappropriate if two colleagues were to see a film together? I mean, Jace and I go all the time."

This time Jace sighs, shaking his head, and he turns around to go back to work.

Mav wiggles his jaw back and forth for a moment before he looks to me. "Riley, it's up to you."

I almost laugh. He's so over-the-top bothered by this I almost decide to push his buttons further. But that would probably mean going out to a movie with Neil and that's the last thing I want. I'd rather lick an electrical socket.

"I'm going nowhere," I tell them. "And nothing good is playing anyway."

Mav seems to calm down and smiles at me. "That's because all the stuff you like has been out for centuries."

"Sometimes they play the classics," Neil says but we both ignore him.

"I thought you had the day off," I say to Mav.

He nods and moves past me, heading to the back room where we keep all the gear. "I do," he says as he opens the door. "But a ranger over in Castlegar said there's a woman who went for a ski and she lost her dog up on the mountains in Valhalla Provincial Park."

"Do we normally rescue dogs?" I ask.

"No," Neil pipes up.

"I do," Mav tells me and disappears into the room. When he comes back out, he's got a sleeping bag and a pack.

"Are you going for a long time?" I ask.

He shrugs. "Valhalla is a beast to traverse and I'm not allowed to take the helicopter for just a dog. There are cabins up there though, it'll be fine." He raises the pack. "And this is the special dog-rescue pack."

"Can I go with you?" I don't want him going off by himself. I mean, I know he could probably survive for weeks out in the mountains because he's a fucking mountain man if nothing else, but even so, I want him near.

He studies me for a moment, head tilted. "If you want," he finally says. His eyes go to Neil. "Take care of things while we're gone, will you? You're in charge."

Neil nods and doesn't say anything, probably happy that he gets to be in charge now. Mav hands me the sleeping bag and then goes back into the room to bring out another one, plus another pack, and a tent, "in case something goes wrong," he says.

Then we're off.

Castlegar is about an hour drive from North Ridge, and Valhalla is another hour north of that, and the two of us

113

don't talk much beyond the basics relating to the rescue. I know Mav has a dog of his own, and it makes my ovaries explode just knowing that he's this big rough and rugged man who is willing to go up a mountain and risk his life to find someone else's lost dog.

The dog in question goes by the name of Charles, and he's a yellow lab who is usually really good in the snow (apparently he's equipped with snow booties and a doggie jacket), but for whatever reason, the owner turned her back and lost track of him.

Now we're standing with the owner in the parking lot at the park and she's crying her eyes out, assuming she'll never see Charles again.

"Not to fear," Maverick says, bringing out a plastic container from his pack. "I have the no-fail rescue tool."

The woman pauses her crying long enough for her to look over as Mav opens the top. Inside there's stinky blue cheese, liverwurst, chorizo sausage, raw ground beef, and hot dogs. "He'll smell this from miles away," Mav says, assuring her.

As we start skiing in, I ask Mav, "If that's what you packed for the dog, what did you pack for us?"

He grins at me over his shoulder. "Had I known you were coming with me tonight, I would have prepared a feast. As it is, you'll have to put up with Maverick's Famous Wild Stew."

"What makes it famous enough for you to talk in third person?" I ask.

"You'll see."

It takes two hours of skiing in complete backcountry, making a gradual ascent, before we get to the area where the woman lost her dog.

We both call out for Charles for a while, and Maverick tries to track the paw prints, which eventually disappear. With the stinky treats container out, wafting the smells into the wind, we do a lot of waiting. Then we keep going until night starts to fall.

In the past, being on the mountain at night would have given me the "okay, time to turn back" feeling. Maybe because in Aspen, we just weren't called for that many night excursions, maybe because darkness falls faster the further north you go. But now, I've accepted it as part of the game, part of the job. And with Maverick by my side, I feel no fear at all.

We ski for another hour, calling for Charles as we go, heading for one of the cabins Maverick was talking about.

It's basically a shanty, four wood walls, ceiling and floor to protect you from the elements. There are no windows, just a door. It looks like someone tried to cook something in the corner with a burner, the wood floor looks a little charred, but other than that, it's totally empty.

But it's dry and relatively clean so there's that. And there's an outhouse just outside, because as comfortable as I am around Mav, I'm not the peeing in your face kind of comfortable. Not yet, anyway.

"All right," he says, dropping the packs and gear in the middle. "How about you set up our beds and I'll get the famous stew going."

I totally pick up on the fact that he said beds, plural. Not that I thought we'd be sharing a sleeping bag or anything like that, but, you know, it wouldn't have been a terrible idea.

So while he starts unpacking the small camping stove, I roll out each sleeping mat and then lie the sleeping bags on top. Then I pull out the rest of the stuff, consisting of a few extra jackets and pants, gloves, toques, scarves, plus drinking water, purification tablets, Cliff bars and beef jerky, bags of powdered tea, milk and sugar, a stick of butter in a Ziploc bag, and a small bottle of whisky.

"What's all this?" I ask.

"Sherpa tea for dinner, whisky for afterward."

"What's Sherpa tea?"

He lights the stove and plunks a small saucepot on top. "Actually, give that to me now and some water; I'll make us some before we eat."

I hand him it all and watch as he puts the water on. When it starts to boil, he adds the powdered tea, milk. and sugar, stirring. I love watching him, his face lit by the lamp by his side, casting half of him in shadow. He looks like he's in his element, like he was born to live in mountain-top shanties, cooking in the near dark.

When he's done, he pours the mixture into two tin mugs and then finishes them off with a dollop of salted butter. "There," he says. "That's Sherpa tea."

The mug is hot, so I wait a while to have a sip but when I do, my taste buds are blown away. I was fairly cold before, not achingly so but that cold that lingers just beyond your clothes, waiting to come in. This heats me up in a minute, plus the salty butter makes it extra satisfying.

I settle down on top of my sleeping bag, sitting down cross-legged, sipping the tea until it's gone. Maverick heads out to clean the pot and comes back in, bringing out a package. He turns his back to me, as if he's trying to keep it from my view. I look around him and peer at the label closer as he rips it open and pours it into the pot.

"Is that...freeze-dried stew?" I ask him. "From Cabela's?"

He hesitates. Then, "Yup."

"But I thought this was Maverick's Famous Wild Stew."

"It is."

Okay, this is cute. "Are you trying to impress me?"

He smiles and, even with his face in profile, it seems to light up all the dark in the room. "Is it working?"

"Depends on what the stew tastes like." I raise the empty

cup of tea. "If it's as good as this, then I'll forgive you for trying to pass off prepackaged food as your own creation."

"Hey, I add a secret ingredient."

"Please don't tell me that it's love."

"You'll see."

It doesn't take long for me to see either. He spoons out the stew into the collapsible bowls, hands me a plastic spoon, and then brings out an eyedropper filled with orangey brown liquid.

"What is that?" I ask as he squirts them in my dish.

"Worcestershire and Cholula hot sauce. It's what makes it Maverick's Famous Wild Stew."

I laugh. "You're unbelievable."

"I know," he says with a wink and sits down cross-legged right across from me, so the tips of our toes are occasionally pressing against each other.

While I do enjoy the stew, it's this close proximity to Mav that my mind is really focused on. There's a light, easy air between us at the moment, but even something as simple as his big toe brushing against mine and I have shivers crawling down my back, this slow-burning lust building inside my core. If I let it get out of control, it could burn down the entire cabin.

And he knows this. I can tell. The way he keeps looking at me and the way he keeps looking away. His gaze is raw, intense, coming from someplace deep. When our eyes meet, I feel something like prey, but prey that wants to be caught. That's dying to be caught.

When we're done, he brings out the whisky and both of us are drinking a little more than we should, taking long swigs out of the bottle and passing them to each other. Each time our fingers touch, and I so clearly remember the way his rough, calloused palms felt around my waist the other night. God, I want that again.

"So what's the plan for tomorrow?" I ask, the cabin feeling extra warm, my head and heart drowsy.

He has the last sip of the bottle and turns it upside down and we watch as a single drop falls out onto the floor. Empty. "Well, providing we're in good shape, we'll get up at dawn and continue the search for Chucky."

"Charles," I correct, lifting up my sleeping bag and slipping inside. It's too cold to get fully undressed (not that he would appreciate it—I had my tits hanging out for him the other night and he did nothing), so I'm in thermal leggings and a long-sleeved shirt.

"Right, Charles. Rather formal name for a dog, don't you think?"

"This is coming from a guy who named his dog Chewie."

"Hey, I told you the name has double meaning. She chews through everything and sounds like a Wookie."

"So when can I come over and meet Chewie?" I ask innocently, as I pull up the edge of the sleeping bag to my chin.

"Anytime you want," he says, getting into his own bag right beside me, nothing but a few inches between us.

I lie on my side and stare at him. "I'll take you up on it, you know."

He smiles back at me. "I have no doubt." He leans over and flicks off the lantern light, plunging the room into black. The silence of the night feels heavier in the darkness. There's only a faint wind that comes and goes, rustling the loose snow outside.

But I can't sleep. I'm warm and somehow comfortable despite where we are, but I can't sleep. Electricity crackles in the air, heavy, like there's an oncoming storm, but the only storm is the one brewing between Mav and me. Hearing him breathing beside me, smelling the fresh yet masculine scent of his soap, the heat of his skin—I'm practically squirming.

I can't handle it.

"Mav," I whisper into the darkness, not wanting to wake him if he's already asleep.

I hear him swallow. "Yeah," he says, his voice hoarse.

"The other night," I say, "in the truck…what were you going to tell me? When I asked you what you wanted to do to me."

He clears his throat. "Riley…"

"Tell me what you were going to say."

I have no idea if he's game, if he'll play along. Like usual, I'm toeing the line here and going out on a limb.

I hear him lick his lips, the sound magnified in the dark. I want to lick his lips too. I want to lick every single inch of him.

"I can't touch you," he finally says.

"Do you at least want to?"

He lets out a dry laugh. "Are you kidding me?"

"I don't know, I had my tits in your face the other night…"

"Riley." He exhales, the sound filling the room. "Do you have any idea how hard this is, to keep my hands off you? How hard I am right now?"

Oh, jeez. Everything inside me ignites, my skin feeling tight, hot and tingly, knowing that he's hard for me, right beside me, so close.

"You keep bringing up the rules," I whisper.

"Because I've worked hard. And you have too. And if I don't have that to keep me in line…fuck, I don't know. I want you like you wouldn't fucking believe, but if we…if we give in, then I don't know where it's going to stop."

Our breaths sound heavier now, filling the space between us. "So then what?"

Pause. "I don't know. I just know…the moment I touch you, that's all I'll ever want."

119

"So don't touch me," I tell him. "Just tell me what you want to do to me."

A low growl comes out of him. "Jesus, you are a little minx, aren't you?"

I wait. I hear his sleeping bag being unzipped, him shuffling around. He doesn't come over though, he doesn't touch me. I think he's just opened his sleeping bag wider. He's breathing heavier. There's a soft sliding sound of skin on skin.

Oh my God. Is he…fuck. Is he jerking off?

I'm about to open my mouth and ask him because if he is, I have the right to know, but he speaks.

"You want to know what I would do, right now, if I could? If we said fuck it to the rules?" he asks, and already his tone is different. His voice is gravely and rough and it makes goosebumps run wild over me.

"Yes," I whisper.

"I'd get out of this sleeping bag and stand right above you. Naked. Cock in my hands."

Oh my God. Oh my God, he's actually going there. And I'm picturing his cock, so big he needs both hands to hold it.

"Can you see me?" he asks, voice thick. "Completely naked and standing above you. My cock is hard as fucking cement, hot against my palm. I stroke it, up and down, feeling it grow in my grip. I see you staring up at me, mouth open, wanting so badly to suck it."

Holy shit.

I don't know what the hell I was expecting, but it was sure as hell not this.

"I want you to suck it, suck my cock all fucking night long. You'll be so good at it too, with those cherry-red lips of yours. So plump and soft and wet, they'll feel like cushions as I slide in your mouth, raze the back of your throat. You're not used to cocks this big, but you're a fucking pro. You'll handle anything I throw your way."

My eyes are so wide in the dark. I half expect Maverick to be standing right above me like he says, naked. Instead it's just empty space and I can sense him beside me. The sound of skin sliding on skin grows louder and now I know for sure he's whacking off. God, I wish I could watch him. It would be such a beautiful sight.

"You're almost begging for it, but you don't want to be greedy. So I tell you to slowly get naked, even though the cabin is cold. But you do." He pauses. "So do it."

With my heart in my throat, I unzip the sleeping bag and start stripping. There's something so thrilling and intoxicating about doing this in the dark, following his every command, knowing he's right beside me, inches away, getting off to this.

"Are you naked?" he whispers.

"Yes."

"Are you touching yourself?"

"Yes." He didn't even have to ask, my fingers have already slid down along my clit, slowly skirting back and forth, building up the pressure.

"Good. Are you wet?"

My words are briefly caught in my throat. "Yes."

"Are you drenched?"

"Tell me what else you're going to do. Then I'll let you know."

He clears his throat and I think he's going to say something but he lapses into a low, guttural moan that makes all my hair stand on end. "I watch you as you play with yourself," he eventually says. "But I know I'm what you really want. You spread your legs for me, begging for me to come inside you. Not yet, little minx, not yet."

He trails off for a moment and then says, "I get down on

my knees, between your legs. My cock is so stiff in my hand, so fucking thick and hard and hot for you. My body is hungry, starving, but I take my time. I drag the tip of my cock over your clit, down below, until it's wet. Back and forth. I move it back and forth. Can you feel me doing that?"

I nod even though he can't see me. My words burn in my throat. I'm touching myself, pretending my fingers are the crown of his cock, imaging what it would feel like, so tight and hot and round. Thick.

"You're such a good little minx," he growls. "So fucking good. I think I'll fuck you slow tonight. There's no rush. I want every single second to keep going. I keep rubbing my cock against your sweet little cunt, dipping it in, feeling how damn tight you are."

Oh my God. I'm pushing my fingers in now, pretending it's him. It's a poor substitute, but I'm so turned on right now it doesn't matter. I'm so wet, I'm drenched.

"I can hear you," he whispers hoarsely. "Hear how wet you are. That slick sound. I want to put my head between your legs, lick it all up. Do you want that?"

Fucking hell, I will take absolutely anything at this point. Even just his hand.

"Can you feel it, my tongue running over your clit, sucking you in my mouth, slowly, gently, until you grow thicker with want, your hands are in my hair, tugging on it, your thighs are squeezing my face. My stubble is rough against your skin. You don't care, you like it rough and hard. You're so fucking ready for me, you want it all, want it now. I run my fingers down, slowly, getting them wet until they're at your ass."

"Mav," I whisper, my fingers working harder now. "I seriously…"

But I trail off, caught in the wave of everything that's

going on, how hot and wild my body is running, needing more.

"I'll fuck you in a million ways, my little minx. But this time, I'll do it with my mouth. I'll plunge my stiff, thick tongue deep inside your tight little cunt, in and out, in and out, just tasting you from the inside. Then I'll push my large, wet fingers in your ass. You'll be surprised at first, but then you'll give in. You want it so fucking bad. It's so wrong it's right. Just like this. Just like we're not supposed to be together, like I'm not supposed to devour your cunt with my lips while fucking your ass with my fingers."

"Jesus," I cry out, pushing myself to the breaking point. "I'm coming soon."

"Fuck yeah," he moans, and I hear his breath become shorter as he gasps for air. "Fucking come for me, Riley," he growls. "Come all over your hand."

But he doesn't have to command me, it's already happening. I'm pulled under the waves, sucked down into the whirling abyss. My voice echoes in the cabin as I call out his name over and over. I don't care. I don't care about anything except the blissful warmth surrounding me, that out-of-body experience that only good sex can bring.

And, fucking hell, that wasn't even sex. I was just getting myself off to his command. That was one of the best orgasms I've ever had and he didn't even lay a finger on me.

Once my breath returns to normal, I listen for him. I hear him groan a little, then the sleeping bag unzipping further.

I smile to myself then say, "Did you make a mess?"

I hear his soft laugh. "I usually have good aim but…" There's a crinkle as he looks in his pack, and then a soft sound as he cleans himself off. "I'm good."

I can't believe we did that, I want to say. But for once, I'm tongue-tied. I'm still swimming on the high of what just happened. How hot that was and yet so fucking crazy. And then I'm thinking, what does it mean? Is that what we are, two people so obviously attracted to each other, yet confined to just jerk off in front of each other?

Not that I have a problem with that, but I scarcely see the difference between this and him actually fucking me silly. I guess it comes down to technicalities, but does Mav actually think he has to take a lie detector test at some point? He would pass the "have you slept with her?" question, but would epically fail the "have you both jacked off in front of each other?" question.

"Riley," he says after a few moments. My name sounds both wonderful on his lips and foreign, like it means something else now.

"Yeah?"

Silence. A beat passes. I can almost hear him grappling with what to say. I don't know what to say either.

Then, "Good night."

"Good night, Mav."

* * *

WHEN I WAKE up the next morning, the cabin is still dark. But it takes me a moment to realize it's because there are no windows. Inside, it's timeless.

I roll over, switch on the lamp, and look to see Mav's sleeping bag all rolled up. His pack is gone. I hoist myself up on my elbows and look around the rest of the cabin. It's empty again.

I get out of bed and check my phone, but the battery is dead. It always drains faster at higher elevations.

I get to my feet, slip on my ski boots and jacket, and open the door.

The world is white and bright and I have to shield my

eyes for a moment until I locate my sunglasses in my jacket pocket.

The cabin is located within the treeline, and though the trail we came up on seems pretty obvious thanks to orange trail markers stuck on the pines, it also looks like we're in no man's land. But that's the funny thing about the mountains, sometimes you think the desolation is crushing until you see a family of backcountry snowboarders glide past, waving cheerily.

But in this instance, I don't see any of that. What I do see is Maverick's tracks leading from the cabin to his skis and then the ski tracks taking off in a northwestern direction.

The sun is just above the mountains, so I estimate the time to be about seven-thirty, maybe eight. It's not like Mav to just leave like this without waking me up, but then again, we've never spent the night together before. This might just be what he does. We didn't have sex last night, but it was the closest thing we could get to it. Maybe I just freaked him out so much he had to bail.

But that doesn't explain why he left the sleeping bag behind and besides, I know Mav. He might be a player but I know he cares enough about me, at least as a colleague, that he wouldn't do that.

So I wait around, packing everything up and then standing around on my skis outside the cabin. The silly thing is, with my phone dead, I have no way of contacting Mav. We do have our beacons on, as that's generally the protocol when you're out with another person on the team, but I don't know if I should try and locate it yet and I'm pretty sure Mav has the locator in his pack.

I wait a few hours, until the sun is definitely closer to noon now and I'm starting to worry. I drink some water, eat some beef jerky, and think about all the different ways I want to kill him. I totally realize that he could be dead right now or dying, but I don't want to think about that (nor the fact that he just left me up a fucking mountain), so I channel it all into anger and annoyance because it's easier to deal with.

And then, over the snowy ridge, I see the top of his toque, followed by his determined gaze, charming smile, and a golden lab in his arms, cradling the large dog like a child. Mav skis toward me, and in that moment I forget ever being mad and I'm melting like butter in Sherpa tea.

"Found him," Mav says, his cheeks red, his brow covered with a thin sheen of sweat that sparkles in the sunlight. I don't think I've ever been so attracted to someone in all my life.

"You did," I say, unable to keep the grin from splitting my face. "Hey Charles," I say softly to the lab as Mav skis right up to me.

The dog licks my hand and then settles back into Mav like he's always belonged there. "What happened?" I ask.

"He had fallen off a ridge, pretty sure his leg is broken," he says. "But I can't splint it right now and he seems comfortable. So I'll ski down with him this way."

"I was worried," I say softly, stroking Charles's nose.

"I'm sorry," he says. "I went out for a piss just before dawn and thought I heard whimpering far off over the ridge. I grabbed my stuff and went. No wonder he wouldn't come after the treats, he couldn't even move. I had to do some solo rope maneuvers to get myself down there and then haul him up."

"You should have come to get me."

"I know," he says, looking sheepish. "You would have been a great help. But I looked at you sleeping this morning and…"

"And what?"

He meets my eyes, a flash of intensity coming over them. "You looked beautiful. I'd never seen you sleep before."

I try not to smile, feeling strangely embarrassed. "That's not for lack of trying on my behalf."

"I know. I just didn't want to disturb you. I'm sorry."

"You're forgiven," I tell him. "Let's get Charles back to his owner then."

I get my pack on, along with both sleeping bags, and we start skiing down the mountain, an easy and slow descent since Mav is skiing with a giant dog in his arms.

Hours later, Charles is taken to the vet in Castlegar and reunited with his owner, and Mav drives us both back to North Ridge.

As he stops outside my house, I can't help but linger at the passenger door as I get out, trying to think of what to say. Are both of us just going to forget what happened last night? I mean it wasn't sex, but it was something. In some ways, it was far more intimate than sex. That's what happens when your imagination takes over, and he gave my imagination permission to run wild.

"Okay," I tell him, hanging onto the open door. "That was fun."

"You're fucking right it was."

"Next time you're doing a dog rescue, know I'm your gal. Just remember to wake me up."

He gives me a lazy smile. "No promises, little minx."

God. Little minx. The name is conjuring up every lewd word from last night. Good lord, I still can't believe we did that.

I straighten my shoulders, trying to compose myself. "See you later."

"See you later," he says. Then drives off.

I exhale like I was holding my breath from the moment we first left North Ridge.

10

CHAPTER TEN

RILEY

THE BALD EAGLE BISTRO IS PROBABLY ONE OF NORTH RIDGE'S more trendy dining establishments. I wouldn't know, because for the weeks I've been here, I've been either making mac and cheese in my kitchenette or grabbing greasy diner food at Smitty's.

But today is Delilah's night off, and so her and Rachel asked if I'd go out with them for dinner and drinks.

I said yes, of course. Yes, because I want to get to know the girls better and yes because I need someone to talk to about what's been going on between me and Maverick. I don't even know if they'll want to hear about it because they probably see Mav as a brother (plus Delilah already told me to watch out for him), but if the opportunity presents itself, I'm taking it.

And I do.

I've only been at the high-top table with them long enough to order drinks and take a quick glance at the menu before Delilah says, "So, what's the deal with you and Mav?"

I take a careful sip of my drink before I answer, wondering what and if I should leave anything out. Like what happened on top of that mountain. Probably the hottest thing I've ever experienced without someone actually touching me.

"What do you mean?" I ask, extra innocent.

Rachel smirks at me and nudges Delilah with her elbow. "Look at her. She's blushing."

"I don't blush," I tell them. "If anything, it's the drink." I point at the dirty martini.

"You may not blush, but you still have a tell-all. You look guilty as fuck," Delilah says. "So, what's the deal with you and Mav? Still just co-workers?"

"Still just co-workers."

They both stare at me in dry disbelief.

I crack. If I'm a cookie, I'm crumbling. I sigh. "Okay, what do you want to know?"

"I don't know, anything," Del says. "Give me the gossip. I'm the only single one here."

"I'm single," I tell her imploringly, putting my hand on the table. "Believe me."

"So you're not sleeping together?" Rachel asks.

I shake my head. "No. We're not." They don't look like they believe me. "It's true. I mean, I want to. And he knows it. But we haven't."

"He knows it?" Del asks.

I laugh. "Look, I'm not a wallflower when it comes to men or sex. I go after what I want. And I've made it perfectly clear to Mav that I want him."

"And you still haven't slept together?" Rachel asks, eyes wide. "What the fuck? It's Mav! He's a fucking man-whore. He's slept with half this town."

Okay. Ouch. I didn't think that would bother me because I kind of knew that, but even so, it hurts. Jealousy flares inside me.

"Rachel," Del admonishes her.

"Sorry," Rachel says. "Really, I didn't mean to sound so crass. It's just…I mean, Maverick is Maverick. And you are you. He should be completely obsessed with you."

"That's true," Del says, nodding. "What's his deal?"

"His deal is that he wants his job more than me, and you know what? I respect that. I feel the same way. I didn't work my ass off all these years just to throw it all away for a night of mind-blowing sex." I pause. "That said, I know how to keep a secret. But he's just too stubborn to try."

"I still can't believe it," Rachel mutters, stabbing a plastic sword in her drink. The server comes by and we put in an order for nachos, spinach and artichoke dip, and popcorn shrimp.

"I'm not saying we haven't done…stuff," I eventually say after the server leaves.

They both snap to attention. "What stuff?"

I wiggle my lips, thinking it over. "Well…I made him tell me in explicit detail exactly what he would do to me if there were no rules. And…it was good." I briefly tell them about the cabin, not going into too much detail.

"I just can't believe that's all you've done," Rachel says. "Knowing the Mav I know, he should have fucked you senseless right there."

"Well he didn't," I remind her, feeling slightly annoyed. "Maybe the Mav you know and the Mav I know are different people."

"That could be," Del points out. "You work with Mav. You're not just some hoochie we went to high school with or some girl passing through town. He respects you. That much I can see. And he likes you too. A lot. So maybe that Maverick is new to everyone."

I shake my head, not wanting to get my hopes up. "Who knows."

"I just think it's crazy," Rachel says. "I mean look at you."

"What about me?"

"Well, you're flawless for one," Del points out. "I mean, you're super model perfect. Tall, thin, with great boobs and butt, and your face…god, if you can't get the guy you want, what hope in hell do I have?"

"You're gorgeous," I tell her. "You can have anyone you want."

"No," she says, her jaw going firm. "I can't."

"Well neither can I," I say. "Welcome to the club."

"I just think if I had your looks…I guess I'm just too tall. And too athletic. And my teeth are too big."

"Oh they are not," Rachel says to her. "What about me? I'm flat compared to you. You have awesome boobs. And smile. Mine is crooked."

"Am I supposed to share my flaws here too?" I ask, my eyes volleying between the two of them. "Because believe me, I have them. Everyone has them. But that's not what tonight is about, is it?"

They both look at me with blank expressions.

"I'm not going to join the pity party and throw myself under the bus so you guys can feel good about yourselves for a second," I continue. "Because, guess what, it won't actually make you feel any better. So fuck this sharing of the flaws. Why do women always do this? We should be celebrating our strengths. Let's stop talking about our cellulite, let's start talking about how amazing we are." I pick up my martini glass and raise it in the air. "Here's to Delilah and her gorgeous smile and Rachel and her stunning eyes and me and my tight, round ass."

At that, both of them burst out laughing, barely able to hold up their glasses. But we still manage to cheers.

* * *

I SHOULD PROBABLY GO HOME, but after the bistro closes Del takes a cab back to her place and Rachel is picked up by Shane. My house is in town so it's not far to walk from any place really.

But while I'm heading home, I decide I'm not ready to hibernate in my dark little basement suite. So I keep walking. The weather is doing this weird thing where it finally feels like winter is over again, though Mav and everyone else warns me that there will be one last brutal storm just as we hit April. Still, it's warm and the snow is almost all melted now. Not in the mountains or even at Ravenswood Ranch, but here in town it's all slushy and gross, but at least it's not ice.

With the balmy night air on my face, I decide to walk to the office. I don't think anyone will be there, which is good. It will give me time to go over maps and read up on past cases. Just something to make me feel like I'm still learning, that I'm catching up, that I'm not complacent. It's a tough business to advance in because every single case is different so you're always using different skills. Every now and then something will catch you off guard, but it isn't because you're ill-prepared.

Anyway, it doesn't hurt for me to do some extra prep and I figure, in my tipsy state of mind, that it's better to do it at night since I won't have weirdos like Neil and Jace watching over me. If it was Tony and Tim that would be great, since I really like them and they genuinely seem to want to teach me the ropes.

But when I get to the office, I see a light on inside. I haven't been here at eleven p.m. before, so I'm not sure if the office always has a light on, just in case, like a fucking light-house or something like that. Then again, it's the government and they'd shut down that shit so fast.

Then I see Maverick's truck outside and I know he's inside.

And I stop. Right there on the street. Because I know, *I know*, if I go inside that building right now, that small beige square building with vinyl siding, on the corner of Main and Seventh, that I won't come out of there the same person.

Something will happen.

And after everything that's lead up to this moment, I have to ask myself if that's what I want.

But of course it's what I fucking want. It's what I've wanted from the start.

I keep walking. I was prepared to use my key, but the door opens when I try the knob.

It's empty inside with only a small desk lamp on over Mav's work station.

There's a shuffle from the back, from the room with all our gear.

I quietly shut the front door behind me and head down the aisle toward it.

I poke my head around the corner and look in the room, all the backpacks, rope, and gear hanging from hooks on the walls.

Mav's broad back is to me. He's wearing a grey thermal shirt that stretches over his muscles, showing off every hard line. He's trying to untangle a mess of climbing rope that looks like it would take days. Last time I had that task, I gave up after five minutes, whining in frustration and passing it onto Tim who took the job without a second thought. Patience is not my virtue. In fact, I don't think I have any virtues at all.

Except for sexual ones. But in the grand scheme of things, I don't think they count.

I debate clearing my throat, giving some kind of sign that

I'm standing behind him. It's weird that I'm overthinking this at all. Who cares?

But right now, every single thing I do is taking on extra weight. Like it will all have consequences, all mean something.

So I stand there, and I'm pretty sure Mav knew I was here because he turns around so slowly, and when he sees me he doesn't seem all that surprised.

"Hey," he says.

"Hey," I tell him back, leaning casually against the door-frame, even though right now I feel anything but casual. "What are you doing here?"

"Well I work here," he says, lifting up the pile of rope. "And apparently no one else does."

I take a few steps into the room, trying to saunter casually, acting like my feet aren't filled with lead. "I hope that's not my fault. I passed my work off to Tim."

"You mean to tell me you didn't want to spend hours unraveling these, washing them, and drying them?"

"We have to wash and dry them too?" I ask, joking.

He shakes his head, runs a dirty hand over his jaw. "So what are you doing here?"

"I don't know. I didn't want to go home. Thought I would study terrain."

"Are you drunk?"

I shrug. "Not really. I went out for drinks with Rachel and Del."

"Ah," he says with a nod. "And how did that go?"

"It was good," I tell him. "I like them. But don't worry, we split up before things got crazy."

A smile tugs at his lips. "I can only imagine what crazy would be like with you."

I can show you, I think. I take another step toward him,

then another, until I'm right beside him. I take the rope from his large hands. "Need help?"

"Sure," he says, but it comes out throaty and he's right there, so close, and I can feel his eyes as they bore down on the top of my head. I feel it, the change in the room, like the ropes themselves are wrapping around my ankles and his, going higher and higher, keeping us tighter, more confined.

"So..." he says gruffly. "You want to learn the ropes."

I try to laugh, I do, because it's funny and he's making a joke, and if I laugh it will dispel the weird tension in the room that grows thicker the closer I move to him.

But I don't laugh because it's stuck in my lungs.

Because my breath is stolen away.

Because Maverick's hands are at my face, both large palms cupping my cheeks, and I'm staring up at him with big eyes, unable to catch up with what's happening. What's happening? How is this happening? How is he holding my face and staring down at me like I'm the final prize?

But he is. His glacier eyes burn into me with such intensity that the air catches in my chest and then the world around us seems to shrink, seems to whittle down, until it's just his skin against my skin and our eyes smoldering in an endless gaze and then he's leaning down, pressing his full lips against mine.

I open my mouth, his tongue slides in, hot and sweet and instantly I'm dissolving. His lips are soft yet firm, moving slowly at first, almost tentative, until it starts to build and build, growing more frantic by the second.

He's kissing me. He's actually fucking kissing me.

And fuck, he's good. He's so good. This is a kiss that I feel all the way in my toes, that snakes its way to my core, that makes me clench like crazy and I know I'm instantly wet. All from a kiss, his kiss.

Because it's not just a kiss. I would have thought after the other night, hearing his dirty words as I got off to them, that kissing would be an afterthought. But it's not. It's everything. Somehow he already knows how to kiss me perfectly. Our mouths move together so fluidly, it's like dancing. I could do this forever.

I think we might devour each other.

His grip on my face tightens, his fingers pressing into my skin and I can feel his urgency, the same urgency that's running through me now, causing my hands to disappear into his hair. It's short but thick, and there's enough for me to grab and tug.

"Fuck," he groans into my mouth and makes my nerves dance like I've tripped over a livewire. "Fuck, fuck, fuck. Oh God, Riley."

I whimper in response, unable to get any of the thoughts out of my head and out my mouth. I don't even think I have many thoughts, other than the disbelief that this is finally happening.

"Do you see now?" he says, pulling his lips away just enough so they still brush my mouth as he speaks. With one hand moving to the back of my neck and holding me in place, he takes his other and wraps it over my wrist, strong. He brings my palm over to his crotch and presses my hand there so I can feel the stiff, inflexible length of him outlined in denim. "Do you feel how much I want you?"

A wave of heat flashes under my skin as I hold him, so thick, so hard. I'm throbbing, wanting this so fucking bad. I'm starving for it, this fucking beast in his pants fighting to come out.

"Condom?" I ask, breathless.

I squeeze him as he chokes out the words, "Yes. I have one."

That's all I needed to know. I let go of him and step back and start stripping.

He stands there, surrounded by rope, his eyes traveling over me as I remove articles of clothes. First boots and socks, then my jeans, then my underwear, moving my way up.

His eyes fix on how bare I am and silently I'm thankful my hair is baby fine and the wax I had a few weeks ago is still holding on.

"Look at you," he whispers roughly, his gaze coming up from between my legs, to meet my eyes. Sky blue. Glacier. The deepness of ice. Such cold-colored eyes are lighting me on fire.

I remove my sweater, my tank top, my thin bralette, and then I'm completely naked in front of him. He doesn't even know where to look now. My tits, the tattoos on my arms and ribs, my stomach. He's taking me all in, the look on his face growing more intense, more carnal, by the minute.

"You're fucking perfect," he growls.

I grin and grab my breasts, teasing my nipples until they're hardened peaks. "I'm perfect for you."

"You are unreal," He shakes his head in disbelief, and then looks over my shoulder at the metal table we sort our gear on. "Get on the table."

I raise my brow. "Okay." I'm game. I turn around and climb on quickly with ease (thank God, because this is not the sort of thing that looks good when you're naked).

"On my knees?" I ask him as I'm on my knees, ass in his direction. I give him a sly look over my shoulder, playing the coquette, and wiggle my butt.

He opens his mouth to speak, licks his lips instead. Then, "On your back."

I lie down on my back, stare up at the ceiling. The metal is cold, biting into my skin, such a contrast to all the heat I have inside, the hot blood running through my veins.

I hear the slide of rope and raise my head to see him approaching the table, the climbing rope in his hands.

A thrill shoots through me and I swear I'm wet to my thighs already.

He stands at the end of the table, his expression so serious, like he's putting a lot of thought into this.

"You're still clothed," I point out. "This isn't really fair."

"It's fair," he says and reaches out, wrapping his big, wide hands around my waist and pulling me down along the table until my ass is almost hanging off. I immediately slam my palms down on the surface to keep me from sliding off, my abs working overtime.

He stares down at my pussy and slowly, carefully, parts my legs further.

"So fucking unreal," he says again. "Perfectly pink, tight, wet. You're so gorgeous."

More compliments. I'm not even sure how to handle them now. "My body is ready," I joke.

He grins and then quickly ties one of my calves to the leg of the table before doing the other. He's so comfortable with this, handling the ropes like it's an extension of himself. I know he'll handle my body the same way.

After my legs are tied apart, spread eagle, he comes around the head of the table and says, "Arms above your head."

I put them back and he wraps my wrists together before tying the rope to the table.

"I'm surprised you're letting me do this," he whispers as he works.

"You know I'll let you do anything," I tell him.

"Good," he says. "It's about time I'm in control."

I want to point out that he's been in control since the day I met him, constantly thwarting my advances, but I don't want to ruin his buzz.

As if to make a point, he tightens the rope, pulling my

arms an inch further, my back arching, nipples growing even harder as they point to the ceiling.

I moan as the discomfort morphs into bliss.

This is so fucking insane!

And yet feels so damn right.

He looks over me like I'm a feast and he can't figure out where to have his first bite. I don't think I've ever felt so desired before in all my life.

Then something dark comes across his face, his features tightening as he starts to run his fingers down my collarbone, between my breasts, over the flat plane of my stomach, before settling between my legs.

"Bet you didn't do this with Neil," he says, trailing his finger over my clit.

I blink at him in surprise while shivering from his touch. "Why, what?"

He shrugs. "I'm going to fuck that guy out of you. Like it never happened."

Oh boy. "Mav, it pretty much never did happen. I'm not going to go into details about it, right here and now when I'm naked and tied to a table, but believe me, you have *nothing* to worry about."

He shakes his head, jaw tense, eyes burning. "You're mine. You've been mine from the start."

I don't mind his alpha caveman talk. It turns me on. I'm his, he's mine. But still I say, "You sure have a funny way of showing it."

He frowns. "Don't make me gag you."

Oh, I am definitely down for that.

I grin.

He pushes one finger inside me. My grin disappears as my eyes close, my mouth falls open. I moan. With my legs forced apart, my pussy bared wide, his finger feels extra large and intrusive. Extra dirty.

"Do you like that?" he asks hoarsely. He pushes in two fingers. "How about that?"

I exhale, my breath shaking. "Yes."

"This?" Another finger is pushed inside. Three of them now, going deeper, deeper. I spread around him, squeezing as he goes. "I can't wait until that's my cock."

I open my eyes to look at him. "Then hurry the fuck up."

Though his eyes are blazing, he bites back a smile. "That's it. I warned you."

He leaves my view and when he comes back he's holding my lacy black bralette in his hands. He rubs the thin material between his fingers. "I don't even know how this is able to hold those up." He gestures to my full breasts.

"Underwire is the devil," I tell him before he shoves the silky material into my mouth.

Well, this is new.

Satisfied that I can't speak, even though I could spit the bra out if I wanted to—and I don't—he runs his rough hands down my thighs, squeezing and kneading them before he settles between my legs and drops down. I lift my head, staring at the sight of him there and he stares up at me from beneath his dark brows.

I watch, and he doesn't break eye contact as his flat, wide tongue starts licking me up and down, like I'm a melting ice cream cone.

I can't keep my head up for long.

It goes back against the table as his tongue sends wave after wave of fire through my body, the heat spinning in the middle and radiating outward. "Mav," I cry out softly, muffled, wishing I could grip the table, wishing my legs could crush his face. But I'm splayed open, so bare and vulnerable, at the mercy of his every move.

"So wet, such a good girl," he murmurs against me and

I'm raising my hips, bucking into his face, trying to get purchase. "Greedy too, but that doesn't surprise me."

"I'm going to come," I try to say through the bra, breathless, on the verge. My words come out muffled.

"What was that?"

I moan, my head lolling back and forth, trying to sort through the sensations running through me.

"You want to come?" He pushes his finger inside me again, razing against my G-spot.

"Oh God!" I cry out, nearly spitting out the bralette.

"You're ready to go, wound so fucking tight. I wish you could see this, how wet you are for me, how beautiful you look."

But while he goes on about how beautiful I look, I'm straining against the ropes, trying to get my hips up, trying to drive his finger in deeper. I want it, need it, more than I've ever needed anything. The drive to come is overwhelming. I might be going crazy.

"Please," I try to say.

"What?"

I spit out the bralette, gasp for air. "Please," I say loudly.

"What do you want?" he asks. His words are husky and I feel them in my skin. I want his words all over me, his mouth, his tongue.

"Your tongue. Tongue fuck me like you said you wanted to."

"I really like hearing you beg."

"I think I've been doing nothing but begging."

He doesn't say anything to that. I just feel the hot lick of his tongue, the perfect amount of pressure swirling around my clit and then I'm coming, a trail of sparks that quickly travels outward until I'm exploding like dynamite.

"Oh God, Mav," I yell, lost to the shockwaves, unable to

control my voice as it bounces around the room. "Mav, oh, fuck."

"God my name sounds so good coming from your lips."

I know he's watching me come and I hope he's getting a good show because I have no idea what's going on. The world spins out like a pinwheel and then I hear clothes being thrown to the ground and I raise my head in time to see Maverick taking off his clothes.

Dear. Fucking. God.

I don't think it's just the lingering orgasm clouding my judgment, but his body is even more unreal than I thought possible. The man is built like a god, like some powerful, inhuman, immortal from the past, one who rules seven king-doms and rides a chariot into the clouds. That kind of god.

Every single inch of his body is ripped. Taut. Hard. Perfect.

Tattoos of all sorts, geometric designs and words and animals decorate his torso, his chest, his arms, his shoulders. It's crazy to think that I've been around him so much, working with him constantly, and yet I've never had a glimpse of these. Fucking winter weather, all these sweaters and jackets kept on hiding the goods.

And what goods they are. He's pure, beastly, godly, sculpted perfection from head to toe.

He knows it too.

How can he not?

Especially when he has his python of a cock in his hands, thick and dark with need and ready to do some serious damage. I mean, just look at that cocky smile on his face. He knows.

He expertly rolls on a condom and then saunters over, his giant dick swinging as he comes, looking so big even against the vastness of his thighs.

He stops at the end of the table, between my legs, where

I'm still pulsing, and grips the base of his cock, rubbing the fat tip up and down over me. I'm sensitive, too sensitive, and I cry out, cringing, but he's persistent, knowing what I want and need even if I don't, and then it fades into want. I find myself aching for him all over again, the need inside me winding and winding and winding.

For someone who was quite talkative earlier, Mav has certainly gone quiet. I stare at his face, taken by the pure lust burning out of his eyes as he looks at me. My skin grows hot and tight, impatient under his gaze.

He puts one hand at my waist, gripping me so hard I can barely breath, as he positions himself against me. I'm tightly tied up, I'm not going anywhere, but even so his grip doesn't loosen.

There's little time to think about it.

With one swift movement he pushes himself in and all the air leaves my lungs, my mouth is open and gasping and the sensation is too much, he's too much, that I don't know how to handle this.

"Oh, fuck me," he groans, still sliding in. "You're so damn tight, like a fist. How'd you get so tight, little minx?"

He exhales, his breath shuddering, his back arched and head back, displaying his Adam's apple. He then looks down at me through long lashes and heavy lids. "Are you okay?"

I nod, but I'm not sure if I am, I'm so tense and he's so big and I'm so tied up and...

He pulls out, slowly, inch by inch, then pushes back in, over and over until...

Oh, fuck, this is good.

So crazy good.

I'm no longer tense, not in that way. I stretch around him, feeling impossibly full, like I can barely contain him. The feel of his cock inside me, so stiff and hot and wide, he eventually becomes the perfect fit, moving inside me like it's second nature, like our bodies know each other, like we do this particular dance every night.

With each push, I feel like we're fusing, going deeper in time and space, not just into each other. Somehow he knows exactly how to work my body, to give me what I need.

My neck is starting to hurt but I want to keep watching him because he's watching me, staring in lewd fascination at his cock as it disappears deep inside me. His brow contorts, full lips fall open on a moan and he picks up the pace, thrusting harder, faster.

His grip is still rough and he's fucking me hard, wild, his hips slamming against the edge of the table. It's starting to move across the floor, an inch here and there, and I'm getting fucking pounded, over and over again. I'll have bruises around my wrists and ankles tomorrow, probably my waist and thighs too.

So. Good.

"Sweet Jesus," Mav croaks hoarsely. Sweat is starting to trickle down his face, dripping onto my stomach. The whole room vibrates with the sound of sex, our sex, his quick, heavy breaths, the slap of skin, the scrape of the table legs, my heart fluttering in my ears. Faster, harder, deeper, Mav doesn't give in, doesn't give up. He fucks me like it's his job, like he's trying to save me.

This man is a goddamn national treasure.

"You're coming again," he tells me and slips his hand over my clit.

I immediately cry out, so hair-trigger sensitive.

"Your noises will be the end of me, you know that," he goes on, and then starts grunting rhythmically with each rut. "Your wet, dirty little moans. Fuck, Riley. I don't have long." His voice breaks off as he groans again.

I feel like the universe is expanding inside me. There isn't even enough time to warn him that I'm coming but it doesn't matter because the second I start to let go, my back arching, my hips fucking into his, he lets out a low guttural groan that vibrates through me and then his head goes back, his pumps slow and he shudders endlessly, coming and coming.

Once again, I'm flung out into stardust, my heart bursting like a firework, my world all colors and shapes that feel like surrender. Eventually his grip on my waist loosens and my skin tingles. He probably left a palm print behind.

So fucking...*good*.

I can't even...

Seconds tick past. Maybe minutes. I can only stare up at the ceiling, waiting for my breath to return, for my heart to slow, for my brain to stop spinning. I feel fucking drugged, like I don't even know where I am. But I know where I am. Tied to a metal table in the storage room and Maverick is *still* inside me. I'm still pulsing around him but even that eventually slows.

He exhales loudly and pulls out and suddenly I'm hollow, bereft. The feeling is so unwelcome that it snaps me back to reality. I hear him roll off the condom and toss it in the trash and then he starts to undo the ropes.

"You okay?" he asks me, as he does the ones around my wrists, peering at me with such tenderness and concern that I feel like I'm thrown for a loop once again.

I swallow, nod, say "yes" but it's just my lips moving.

He gives me a soft smile and then slides his arm under my back, slowly helping me up to a sitting position.

The room spins some more as the orgasm still holds on, sticky-sweet. If this was my bedroom, I'd insist he stay over. But it's not. It's our work. It's a room lined with tents and sleeping bags and numerous skiing packs and hiking backpacks and boots and helmets and ropes and emergency kits and skis and snowboards and snowshoes and it's everything

I've worked so hard for. To be at a place like this that has stuff like this.

And then it hits me, the fact that we just had sex at the office, where anyone could have walked in and seen us. We've been fighting against the rules for so long and when we finally throw the rulebook out the window, we lose all common sense.

"What's wrong?" he asks me as he frees my legs. "Did that hurt?"

I shake my head. "We could have been caught."

"It's after midnight now," he says but I see the worry on his brow.

"It doesn't matter. Someone could have come in here and seen us. And then we'd be out of a job."

He rubs his lips together, thinking. "Okay. I guess we got carried away."

"Yeah," I say. *It shouldn't happen again.* I can't believe those words are even in my head but they're there. And they are right. It *shouldn't* happen again. But I'm going to bet it probably will. "We just need to be more careful next time."

Mav tilts his head, looking me over. "Next time?"

"I don't think you're done with me yet," I say, getting off the table, and feeling vulnerable naked for the first time. I start gathering up my stuff so I don't see the expression on his face. I don't want him to think it's over, to want that.

"You're right," he says, pulling on his jeans. Relief runs through me. "I'm only getting started with you."

I nod at the trash can. "Then you probably shouldn't put that there. Who knows what people will think if someone finds it."

"Right," he says, running his hand over his face as he looks at me, his eyes growing wild.

"What?"

"Nothing," he says, going over to the trash can and fishing the condom back out.

"*What?*" I repeat, folding my arms across my chest.

He comes over to me and, with his free hand, grabs the back of my neck and pulls me to him, kissing me hard.

"You," he says as he pulls his lips away. "Just…you."

He holds me in place, his earnest eyes searching mine, a million words tumbling behind them, things he's not saying.

Then he lets go. "Need a ride home?"

I nod.

Ten minutes later I'm dropped off at my place, crawling into bed and trying to figure out what the hell just happened.

I fall asleep and I'm still not sure. All I know is that I've never felt more alive and Maverick bleeds into my dreams.

CHAPTER ELEVEN

MAVERICK

"John!"

I blink and look over at Fox. It's rare that he calls me by my real name.

"What?" I ask. I'm standing out on the deck that takes up the whole front of the house. Because of where the chalet is built at the base of the mountain, we have a pretty sweet view over the town, the river, and the valley stretching beyond. You can even make out a few of the barns at Ravenswood. Or, at least you could, if the cloud cover wasn't so low it obscured half the town.

"I've been calling you for the last few minutes," he says gruffly, brows knit together. He's in a mood, I can already tell. "Couldn't you hear me?"

"I was looking at the view," I say as he comes over.

He looks over the foggy landscape and cocks a brow. "Right. What's with you?"

"Nothing?"

"You've been locked in your head for the last few days. That's not like you. What's up?"

"Nothing," I repeat. Nothing I want to get into anyway.

The fact is, I've been thinking about Riley non-stop. I can't get her out of my damn head, not even for a second. I haven't seen her since that night in the gear room. In fact, because I haven't seen her—our schedules aren't crossing—I'm starting to wonder if that night ever happened.

Because, fuck, that was the best sex I've ever had. I mean…Jesus. The first time I'm inside her and she lets me act out the dirty fantasies I've had about her since the day we met. I don't know what guy at North Ridge SAR hasn't thought about tying someone up in climbing rope and fucking them senseless.

It's almost too good to be true. No, Riley is too good to be true. That little minx is like God dropped off the world's most perfect woman right on my doorstep. Only when I look at the package closer, it says "do not touch."

I certainly didn't listen. I touched her everywhere I could. As much fun as it was to have her tied up like that, wanting and waiting and vulnerable, it was hard as hell trying to keep myself together. I'm surprised I lasted as long as I did. I'm surprised at a lot of things.

But I'm not surprised about my feelings for her. That little taste was everything and yet wasn't enough. I'm hungry. I'm like a fucking junkie. Her skin, her taste, her breathless little sounds—it's all that can satisfy me right now.

Of course, I don't want to discuss any of that with Fox, though I can tell he wants to ask. I always kiss and tell, but not this time.

"Okay," he says. "Well, I'm heading up the hill for a ski? Want to come?"

"Nah," I tell him. "I should take Chewie to the dog park."

He watches me intently and then seems satisfied with that answer. "Does that poodle still have a crush on her?"

"It's hump city. Population: Chewie."

But that's all a lie. Not the poodle thing, there is a poodle at the dog park called Rubble that likes to hump Chewie all day long. It's just that I'm not going there today. It's Sunday and I'm not the only one with the day off.

As soon as Fox leaves, I text Riley.

Hey little minx. Want to come for a trail run?

The thing about working for search and rescue is that in our downtime, we have to stay active, keep learning. So that means running through the snow and up mountains, it means doing climbs, it means breaking into ice ponds and rescuing each other for practice. So, really, what I'm suggesting is good for the both of us.

She responds back right away. **I'm in. Where?**

Come meet me at my house. Do you know where I live?

Three dots flash and disappear. Then flash and disappear. Finally, the text comes through: **I wouldn't be a very good stalker if I didn't.**

I laugh. **Good girl. See you soon.**

I stand there on the deck waiting about thirty minutes, and I see Riley running up along the sidewalk toward the house.

There's a smile on my face the whole time I'm watching her. I'm not sure if she's as klutzy as she proclaims she is but there's obviously some mind over matter shit going on as she tries to navigate the sidewalks that are slick and half covered with melting grey patches of snow.

My inner thirteen-year old has a moment.

Just as she's coming up the driveway, I scoop up a handful of wet snow from the railing, press it into a snowball and pelt it at her head.

Plomp.

It lands right on her beanie and she cries out, "The fuck?" and the moment she looks up at me to see where it came from, her feet start sliding on the driveway in every direction.

Oh shit.

She goes forward for a moment, then backward, then she just kind of throws herself into the snowbank on the side as a last-ditch effort to save herself.

I burst out laughing. I shouldn't and I should also feel bad that it was my snowball that brought her down, but that was probably the funniest thing I've seen in a long time.

Of course, I'm not a complete jerk. I quickly run down the stairs and in seconds I'm at her side, grabbing her by the elbows and hauling her out of the snow.

"Sorry," I tell her, "so sorry."

"You fuck," she seethes as I pull her to her feet. "What are you, twelve?"

"I believe I was having a thirteen-year-old moment."

"I bet you were," she says. Then she scoops up a bunch of snow in her glove and before I know what's happening, she yanks at the collar of my sweater and drops the snow inside my shirt, pressing it in.

The cold makes me yelp. Fuck!

"You dick," I tell her, waving the sweater, trying to get the snow out and off my skin.

She sticks out her tongue. "Tit for tat."

"I'll believe it when I see a tit," I tell her, still feeling the cold.

"So is your dog coming with us?" she asks.

"Huh?"

"On our trail run?"

"Oh," I say slowly. "You actually thought we were going for a trail run?"

She glares at me. "This is a booty call?"

I honestly didn't think she of all people would have a problem with a booty call, especially after we screwed the other night, but now I'm second guessing everything. Shit. What if that was it? Like, she got her fill of me and now wants things to stop.

"Uh," I fumble for words.

She rolls her eyes. "I'm down for a booty call, Mav. I just think we should actually go trail running as well. You said yourself that even when it looks like winter is on the way out, we're usually hit with one last wallop."

Man, she is way more on the ball than I am. And she has the right idea. If we're going to screw around in secret, then we might as well keep working hard as well. Otherwise it just feeds into the reason why there are rules to begin with: you get distracted and sloppy and when that happens, people die.

"Okay," I tell her. "Give me a few to get dressed. Want to come inside?"

"How about later?" she says, her stance firm, because she probably knows the second she steps inside my house I'll be tearing off her clothes.

I head inside and slip on better pants and shoes and then come back out, Chewie whining pitifully the whole time.

"The dog isn't coming?" she asks me while I join her side.

"Chewie? She's got short hair, so she has to wear a sweater, and that sweater is wet right now and also, she's chubby and slow. So no. She's not a running into the snow trail dog. She's a pass out in front of the fire dog." I pause. "Which was my original plan."

"Later," she says, swinging her ponytail over her shoulder. "Let's go."

The easiest and quickest trail from my house is up a few blocks on Yates street until you come to the trail heading to Bridal Falls. In the summer, it's packed with tourists, but in the winter, when the falls are frozen over and the trail is full of snow, there's no one up there.

We take off running, our trail runners going over the

snow with ease. Because of the recent melt, there's only a few inches of snow and the higher up we go, the more stable the trail gets.

After a half an hour of running we finally reach the waterfall, the low cloud cover having parted for this moment.

"Wow," Riley says breathlessly as she leans against the railing. "I can imagine how powerful it is in the summer."

"I think I prefer it like this," I tell her. The water is trickling now underneath the layer of ice. It's perfect, like someone decided to make a waterfall ice sculpture. "It's calming. The opposite of chaos."

She seems to think as she looks me over. Her face is lightly sweaty, her cheeks and nose bright red. She's breathless and yet she's taking my breath away. "But you love the chaos."

"I do. But, I think sometimes it gets old. Or tiring. I love getting that call, knowing that when I head out there, I'm doing something brave and important. It's exciting. It's addicting. It's like nothing else." I pause and take a deep breath. "But the older I get, the more I see other side. The peace. The quiet. I'm not sure what that means."

She comes over to me and puts her hand on my cheek. "It means you're getting older and the world is getting wilder and sometimes our hearts need a little peace. That's all."

"You're so wise," I whisper, half joking, half serious. Our faces are so close, intimate, her lips begging for a kiss.

"I'm many things," Riley says, her hand coming off my face and trailing all the way down to my crotch "But wise isn't one of them."

I clear my throat, my limbs tense, my dick already throbbing at the mere suggestion of what might happen. I'm wearing rather tight jogging pants too, so there's no hiding it.

"Riley," I say quietly but I'm not sure what else to say because there's no way in hell I'm going to stop *this*.

She bites her lip, looking extra coy and drops to her knees in the snow, yanking down my pants and briefs.

My skin is immediately shocked from the cold and I gasp. She looks up at me with big sex-kitten eyes and takes off her gloves, dropping them in the snow, before taking the length of me in her bare, warm fist.

"Any objections?" she asks sweetly.

My God. I could never object to a single thing she does.

I shake my head and watch as she draws a long, thin line with her tongue from the base of my cock to the tip. I'm tempted to reach down because I know what I want but she reads my mind and rubs the tip across her lips like my precum is lip balm.

"Fuck," I groan, reaching down and grabbing hold of her hair, half-pulling it out of her ponytail. "God, you're so fucking good."

"Mmmm," she murmurs, running her mouth up and down over the hardened ridge and I'm helpless at the vibrations. "I can tell you've wanted this."

I groan, my fist tightening. I know I can be rough with her but we both seem to like it. "I've been wanting to fuck those lips of yours since the moment I first saw you."

"And I've wanted nothing more than to drop to my knees and suck this perfect dick," she whispers hoarsely. "Match made in heaven."

This is heaven. Standing here beside a frozen waterfall, Riley on her knees in the snow, slowly slipping my cock into her mouth. "I want you to swallow when I come. I want to feel your throat move."

She pulls me out of her mouth in one long draw, her lips making an audible popping sound. "What makes you think I wouldn't swallow?"

"I don't know. There has to be a catch somewhere."

"As long as you take me as I am," she says, pausing to tease the rim with her tongue, "there are no catches. No surprises."

"Oh but that's where you're wrong, little minx. Every day I'm surprised at how more perfect you become."

Every day you become more ingrained my head, in my heart, I'm starting to think I'll never be rid of you.

You're under my skin.

You're there to stay.

But I don't say any of that because even the feelings are too raw for me to process. I've honestly never felt this way before and the more time I spend with her, the further I'm pulled under. New territory. It's frightening.

And oh so real.

"You sound so hungry," I say gruffly, my grip rougher, pushing harder into her mouth, as much as she'll take me. The sounds coming out of her are messy, greedy, like she can't get enough. I don't even think she's moaning for my sake, she seems to be insatiable for my dick.

And I'll give her as much of me as possible.

"You're beautiful,

you sweet thing,

these perfect lips.

You feel so good."

I'm saying words but not really hearing them. The urge to come is building inside me, rising hot and fiery, and I'm desperate for release. I fuck her mouth harder, my fist anchoring her head in place, deeper and deeper and then I'm coming.

It's hot as it shoots down her throat and then I'm watching as I'm still emptying and she's trying to swallow. It's messy, spilling over her lips. It's the hottest thing I've ever seen. Her tongue swipes out, bringing more of me into her mouth, still gripping my dick.

I'm surprised I didn't fall over during that. I'm fucking spent. I could curl up in a ball in the snow and sleep forever.

"Thank you," I whisper, my face to the sky, eventually letting go of her hair. I then pull up my pants, every part of me extra sensitive, running both hot and cold.

"Thank *you*," she says, getting to her feet. "I like seeing you like that."

I look at her through heavy lids. "Like what?"

"Powerless," she says.

She's right. I'm completely powerless and at her mercy.

"Okay," she says, dusting off her knees. "The waterfall was great and that was even better. But now I'm cold."

"I have a hot tub," I tell her.

"Sold."

It's not long before we're back down the trail and at my house.

"Are you ready to meet Chewie?" I ask her as we stand outside the front door.

Riley nods eagerly.

I open the door, and as expected, Chewie comes tearing out of the house. She runs right past us and down the driveway and then right back up in a tight circle, running around the two of us over and over again, ears back, smiling, tongue hanging out of her mouth. I probably looked like that earlier.

"She's got the zoomies," I tell Riley, putting my hand at the small of her back and ushering her inside.

"What are the zoomies?"

"When she zooms around like that." I clap my hands at Chewie. "Hey, Wookie Butt, get over here."

Riley snickers. "Wookie Butt."

"Believe me, you don't want to hear all her nicknames, though I'm sure by the end of the day, you will."

Chewie comes barreling inside and up the stairs. She gets

these energy bursts every now and then, which is always amusing, but it also means she's going to crash soon. Which is perfect. I can't say the number of times this dog has cock-blocked me at one point or another.

I almost bring that up to Riley as we're climbing the stairs to the main floor, but I manage to keep my mouth shut. Most women don't care who I fuck around with because most women don't stick around long enough to care. But with Riley, even though she has this *don't give a fuck* attitude, I don't think she'll take too kindly to me talking about past conquests.

I certainly don't want to hear about hers, especially when it comes to Neil. I really hope I erased that prick from her system.

"This is like a ski chalet," Riley says, looking around. Chewie continues to zoom around the living room, going in circles around the coffee table, though she's already tiring.

"That's what we were going for," I tell her. "Fox and I bought it together four years ago. He sleeps in the loft upstairs," I point to the top of the cathedral ceiling. "That was all open before but we had it closed in. I'm down the hall."

She walks to the large cathedral windows that look over the balcony and then the town, then past the fireplace and the fuzzy bearskin rug in front of it. "Hope you didn't kill that." She points at it with pouting lips.

I shake my head. "My grandpa. It was a dangerous grizzly too, kept eating our sheep. Believe me, I'm not a hunter."

"A mountain man and not a hunter."

I shrug. "I have too much appreciation for nature. But I also respect those who do hunt. Fox does for deer and elk. So does my dad. They use all the meat. No one in this town touches the predators. The wolves, the bears, North Ridge pretty much leaves them alone unless they're a bother."

She seems to appreciate that. She points at the fireplace

157

with her boot. "Are you going to light this baby up? For after the hot tub?"

After the hot tub? Jesus. For some reason I thought she would bail after, but she doesn't seem to be going anywhere. And why not? We have all day. Kind of.

"My brother might be home when it gets dark. He's on the slopes right now."

"Then you'll have to fuck me quick. You can do that, can't you?"

"I can," I tell her, walking over to her and taking her hand. "But maybe I want to take it slow. There's no rush."

"There's a rush if you're screwing me on the rug when your brother comes home," she points out.

"You're so crass," I can't help but comment.

She smiles playfully. "You love it."

And I do. But honestly, and this is going to sound kind of lame, I wouldn't mind some tenderness from her. I've only seen it a few times, like when she was coming, wrapped in rope. Those moments after sex, she's soft and fragile and open. She's someone I feel I can protect, who *wants* to be protected. Most of the time, Riley acts like it's the last thing she needs.

But *I* want that.

I want her to need me.

While all of this is warring inside my brain, Riley reaches up and runs the tip of her finger down the bridge of my nose and over my lips and chin. "Come on, mountain man. Let's get wet."

I grab some towels from the linen closet and then take her hand and lead her through the kitchen to the back deck where we have the hot tub. It's a small one but it backs out onto the mountain and there are huge Douglas firs between our house and the next so there's complete privacy.

Snow surrounds the hot tub, biting into my bare feet after

I've stripped naked. I pull back the cover, steam rising, and quickly get in.

"Fuck it's hot!" Riley cries out, laughing and shivering as she gets in. "And so cold!"

"Man, you're hard to please."

I can't take my eyes away from her body. Her breasts, full and perky, her hard rosy nipples, the sleek curve of her waist, the meat on her thighs. By the time she eases herself in, I don't even feel the heat anymore. I'm hard as a rock and ready to go again. This woman will never tire me out.

"Come here," I tell her, grabbing her by the back of her neck, relishing how delicate she feels in my grasp. I pull her toward me and crush my mouth against hers, my tongue sliding in, ravenous, hungry. She tastes sweet.

Her hands sink into the water, grabbing hold of my dick, just as she had earlier on her knees, with purpose, with lust. I love how much she loves this, like she couldn't keep away if she tried.

I grab her by the waist and lift her up and she grabs hold of the tub edge behind me for leverage. She lowers herself onto me, not making a noise, not even breathing. Her eyes meet mine and for a moment she looks startled. Our faces have never been this close before while I'm inside her. It's beyond intimate.

It's probably why she looks away.

Hot tubs are notorious for sounding sexy but actually not being so when it comes to practice, but Riley is superhuman and she's slick and wet and luscious inside. She's so fucking good, so small, and warm. Almost as warm as the water we're in. She moves her body up and down my shaft with confidence, knowing what she wants, what I want.

"Look at me," I whisper to her and my words come out hoarse.

She reluctantly brings her eyes back and I lock them in

with mine. I want her to see how I feel about her, not just what she's doing to me physically, because that's impossible to miss, but I want her to see *in* me.

"There you are," I say.

She gives me a soft smile in return before her eyes close with pleasure. She leans forward and takes my bottom lip between her teeth and tugs. Then she kisses my chin, my jaw, my neck. I take over the rhythm, moving her up and down over my shaft in long controlled movements. I wasn't kidding about earlier when I said I wanted to take things slowly but the reality is, the slower I go, the faster I want us both to come. My mind and body are at war with each other.

"Does that feel good?" I ask, wondering why she's not saying anything. Usually she's quite talkative.

She moans her response, digging her fingernails into my shoulder. But still, it's like there's something holding her back. I don't want her to hold back, I want her to let loose, be loud, tell me how much she wants me, how badly she needs this. I want to know she wants this as much as I do.

My mouth drops to her breasts, sucking her nipple in, swirling my tongue around and around until I feel it stiffening in my mouth.

Her moans get louder and I'm rutting up into her deeper. I'm packed in so tight and she's squeezing around me, the entire length of my cock in a warm, hot grip. I try and keep it slow and controlled but the truth is, I'm getting ravenous. I could fuck a lot harder than this.

"Tell me what you want?" I ask her, my way of checking in. "Tell me if…" My words fail as she starts to ride me harder, matching the speed of my thrusts, her pattern to mine. "Fuck."

"Just this," she says thickly, licking and biting my neck until I'm near the point of no return. "Keep going. Keep going."

I take in a deep breath and try and keep the pace. The steam rises up around us and I take a hungry kiss from her lips, tasting like chlorine and sweat.

I've never had such ease with a woman before, this grinding and rocking of our bodies together, like they move as a singular unit.

And soon we're moving fast, fucking hard, the water is splashing over the sides of the hot tub. She's all around me, so wet and wild and ….

She's *so* good.

Unreal.

I want her to come so hard she sees stars.

Impulsively I grab her ponytail, wrapping it around my hand, and then yank her head back so the delicate arch of her neck is exposed as I slam her up and down on me.

"Fuck!" she cries out. "Oh God. Mav."

It's not from pain, and if it is it's from a pain she likes. A lot. I can feel her coming before she even says another word.

Her mouth drops open. Nipples harden. She rolls her hips, her chest shiny with sweat and water and she starts shuddering around me, squeezing my cock, tight, tight, tight.

"Mav!" she yells and moans and moans, her noises echoing through the forest, bucking against me wildly.

That does me in.

I let myself go. No holding back anymore.

I pump harder up into her as I come and I don't know if she saw stars but I'm seeing them.

Holy shit.

A garbled mess of words spill out of my mouth as I spill into her, thrusting and thrusting until I'm emptied.

And that's when I realize I didn't use a condom.

I was going to wait until we've both calmed down until I bring it up but she beats me to it.

"We didn't use anything," she says softly as she raises her

hips and climbs off of me.

"I always use something," I tell her earnestly. "Always have. Just in case. But I'm clean. You can believe me on that."

She nods. "So am I. You'll have to take my word on that too."

And of course I do. I'll take her word on anything.

I lean over and kiss her gently. "It felt so good being bare inside you." I rub the tip of my nose against her and she stares at me with big eyes. But if the intimacy scared her earlier, it's not scaring her now.

She smiles and kisses me back. "Yes, it did."

"So you took the dog to the park, eh?"

Both Riley and I spin around to see Fox standing by the sliding door. He's not amused.

Riley doesn't even move to cover up her breasts so I place my body in front of hers. "You're back early," I tell him.

"Yeah, I am," he says. "And by the way, your dog ate one of my boots while you guys were…whatever."

He turns around and heads back in, and through the glass door I can see Chewie staring at us with a proud look on her face.

"That dog," I mutter to myself. "Good thing she's cute."

I look back at Riley.

"Does he care?" she asks.

"Who, Fox? Yeah but he'll get over it. He has a lot of boots."

"No, I mean about us."

"Oh. Nah. He'll probably high-five me later."

"You guys are really playing up this whole bachelor pad thing, huh? You're like Joey and Chandler."

"Which one am I?"

She thinks for a moment. "Joey."

"Aw man. But he's dumb."

"But he gets laid."

"But Chandler gets laid too."

"Yeah, with Janice and the woman with the missing leg."

"He ends up with Monica."

"Monica is batshit crazy."

"Okay, so then Fox is Chandler."

"No Fox is Ross. I barely know him, but I can tell you he's one hundred per cent Ross Gellar."

"But Joey never lived with Ross."

"Yeah he did. Don't you remember?"

"That was Rachel."

"Oh yeah."

Our conversation continues like this for a while until we both remember that Ross did in fact live with both Joey and Chandler for about three episodes, then when we start getting wrinkled from the water, we get out. I wrap her up in a big fuzzy towel, making sure Fox wasn't looking, and we go inside. I throw a few logs on the fire, settle us both down on the bearskin rug, and have a beer.

Obviously, nothing else happens between us and we're just sitting there chilling. Mainly because Fox is a weirdo and sits down on the living room couch with Chewie, staring at us and trying to make sure it's all as awkward as possible. He succeeds. When it starts to get dark out later, I drive her home.

"Thanks for coming trail running with me," I tell her as she steps out onto her sidewalk. "And, you know, the blow job and the hot tub sex."

"Thanks for inviting me," she says. "Tell Fox that next time he's welcome to join us in the hot tub."

"You don't fucking mean that." I am *horrified*.

She laughs, loud and contagious, and slams the door, giving me a quick wave before she hurries through the cold and into her house.

That little minx.

1 2

CHAPTER TWELVE

RILEY

THE TEXT COMES AT ELEVEN AT NIGHT.

I worked all day at the lodge with Tony, giving a talk to young kids about mountain safety, followed by a few runs (Fox gave us lift passes), so I went to bed around nine, totally exhausted.

But despite being tired, my mind won't shut off. It keeps thinking. I'm not even in control of my thoughts, they're just going every which way. They're thinking about Levi. They're thinking about my parents. They're thinking about the future. They're thinking about the people I've rescued. They're thinking about this town. And most of all, my thoughts seem to center on Maverick. Every part of him.

So the text doesn't wake me up, though when I hear it I groan loudly because I'm so cozy and warm in bed and the last thing I want is to get out, get dressed in my gear and head into the cold night. For once, I just want to be a normal person who has a nine to five and can expect to get some sleep at night.

But when I look at the message, it's not about search and rescue.

164

It's from Maverick and it says, **Spend the night with me.**

My heart jumps and skips and swells.

Fuck. I'm losing my head here. Even just a two-line text for sex is making me giddy, filling my chest with champagne bubbles.

Are you going to pick me up? I text back. I can definitely walk to his place if needed but...

He texts back:

I'm outside right now. I'll wait.

A grin splits my face. I'll get out of this warm bed if I can go right into his.

Not that he hasn't been here before. It's been a week of us sleeping together whenever we can, which meant an afternoon sex session in my room, then the next day we fucked in the backseat of his truck, parked down a deserted road.

But I've never stayed overnight at his house, so this is a big step.

Stop thinking in steps, I tell myself. *There are no steps when you're just fucking.*

I've become pretty good at ignoring that voice though. Because right now, there are steps. Steps that are bringing Mav and me closer, beyond being boss and employee, colleagues, beyond having casual sex. Each moment we're together, I feel that rope wrapping us tighter.

I'm not sure what to do with the feeling. I know I should push it away to feel safer, to protect myself. Because what are we really doing here? We both know that what this is can't morph into anything more or we'll lose our jobs. I can keep sex a secret but anything more than that is going to get harder and harder. There will be a straw that breaks the camel's back.

At the same time...god, it feels so damn good to be with him. The way he looks at me, the way he touches me. The things he says, both so possessive and sweet, soft and rough.

He makes me laugh too, so much. He gets me, brings out my silly side while I bring out his. I just...I can't get enough.

I can't get enough of him.

I shove my birth control pills into my backpack, along with clothes for tomorrow, toothbrush and face wash, and then I'm slipping on thick leggings, an oversized sweater and heading out the door.

His truck is running at the side of the road, the exhaust billowing up into the sky. The sight brings me peace, warms me like a hot bath. Amongst the unending darkness here, the cold air, the desolate peaks rising into the stars, he's shelter. My shelter.

I run toward him and quickly get in the passenger seat.

He leans over and kisses me, soft, long and sweet. "Hi," he says, looking deeply into my eyes. Yowza.

"Hi," I say back as I pull away, rubbing my hands over my legs. "Damn it's cold tonight."

"I know. I figured I'd use you as a heater."

"How romantic."

"I think we might get hit with another storm," he says to me as we drive off. "Forecast isn't calling for it, but I feel it in my bones. Normally we would see some geese flying in for the spring but I haven't seen any yet."

"That's when you know you're in the backcountry," I joke. "Using geese to predict the weather."

"They're better than the weather app," he points out.

Soon we're pulling up his driveway and I stare up at the house. All the lights are off. "Is Fox home?"

He nods. "Yeah. But don't worry, we'll be in my room."

"Will he be in the room too?" I ask, knowing how Fox was trying to cockblock Maverick last time. It was funny and I love seeing him rile Mav up as good brothers do, but if we're getting down to business, I definitely don't want his brother there, no matter how good looking he is.

"What do you think?" he says. "If he shows his face, I'll show him his ass."

We go inside and he grabs my hand, leading me past the living room where Chewie is snoring, all the way to his bedroom.

It's a nice room. Sparsely decorated but that seems to suit Maverick. Just a bunch of maps nailed to the wall along with some framed concert posters. In the corner is an overflowing laundry hamper beside an acoustic guitar. On his desk pushed up against the wall are a bunch of coffee cups. I have a feeling they were all over his room earlier and he did his best trying to tidy for me.

"It's nice –" I try to say but he cuts me off, his mouth pressing down on mine, his hands going for my waist, my breasts.

I'm pushed backward, walking fast until the backs of my legs hit his bed and then I'm pushed down and he's standing above me, ripping off his shirt.

This sight never gets old.

He's already breathing hard, his hard chest rising and falling. His eyes rake all over my body, making every inch of my skin hum and buzz with anticipation. This man doesn't even have to lay a finger on me and my body is already primed to let go.

"I've missed you," he says roughly.

I swallow, his words hitting my gut and making it warm and fuzzy, making it matter more than he can know.

"Good," I whisper. *I've missed you, too.*

He grins, giving his head a quick shake. "I've said it a million times already but you, my little minx, you are absolutely unreal. How the fuck did I ever get so lucky?"

"There's no such thing as luck," I tell him. "Just timing."

"There you go, being all wise again."

167

"Are you just going to stand there and look at me or are you actually going to do something?"

He laughs, bites his lip. Takes off his pants.

His gaze turns predatory as he stands above me. All muscle. All beast. His hard, thick cock in his hand.

"Beg for it." The words come out as a growl.

I lift my top over my head. I'm not wearing a bra.

I run my hands slowly over my breasts, stomach, down below the waistband of my tights.

"This is me begging," I murmur.

I pull off my tights and kick them to the floor.

I'm not wearing underwear either.

His eyes spark and then he practically leaps onto the bed, covering me with his body, making me feel as small as a mouse under him.

At first I think I'm going to be crushed, then instantly devoured, but he pulls back and moves slowly, deliberately. He positions himself so he's lying on top of me, his warm chest pressed against mine, his elbows planted on either side of my head. He peers down at me in such a way it starts unraveling some part of me I keep tight and hidden, a spool of thread in the dark.

"What is it?" I say softly.

He doesn't say anything, only gazes at me with deep longing.

Then I feel it.

The fear.

In his heart.

In my heart.

Tenderness is the unknown.

He keeps his eyes on mine, burning with lust that I can't help but feel the flames and I'm so turned on already that I'm ready for him.

This man can do anything to me.

And yet…a part of me is scared for more.

For more of him.

For his heart.

"Riley," he groans as his fingers find my clit, teasing it, his eyes never breaking from mine. "You're drenched, sweetheart."

I give him an anxious smile. All this eye contact and unsaid words has left me rather nervous. I'm never nervous and yet here I am. "I've been waiting for you."

"Just the way I like it," he says gruffly as he grabs my hips and pulls me closer. "Waiting and ready." I bring my leg up, hooking it around his waist, keeping him against my hips. I'm starting to get impatient, the ache inside me increasing with each slick stroke of his finger.

"Slow," he whispers to me as he reaches for his cock and runs the crown of it up and down my clit, pausing to dip it briefly inside before bringing it back up. The sound is so loud in this room, so wet, it's graphic. "Slow."

And he wants it slow. He keeps repeating the word, over and over as he kisses me everywhere, hot little bites. "Slow as we can go."

My eyes close, surrendering myself to this torturous tease. He's not pushing in, it's just a lazy slide, back and forth, but I feel myself opening for him anyway, my body starving for more.

"You want more, little minx?" he murmurs, his voice so thick with need that I can't even answer him. I nod, relaxing back into the bed. I'm both relaxed and tense at once, surrendering and spurring him on as he rubs against me, over and over again.

This is so fucking *decadent*.

As if he's teasing me, he grips my hip as he pushes himself inside me from the side. He's bare and thick and long and I love the fact that we're not using a condom, that we both trust each other enough.

And just as he said, he does it slowly.

So slowly that I'm starting to buck with impatience.

"Easy," he murmurs, his voice throaty with need. "We have all the time in the world right now."

He's right. I take in a deep breath, trying to calm myself, to stop that need to climax, that quick chase of release. I try to focus on every single thing that's happening, from head to toe, just letting it all sink in. It feels good, then it feels too much, then I don't even know what I feel because all I feel is Maverick. He's taken over my whole world.

"Want me to go faster?' he asks through a groan. "Harder?"

I shake my head but can't speak.

It's better than good but other words are escaping me right now.

"Fuck Riley," he moans. "Oh, fuck."

His grip tightening on my hips, sliding up to my waist, to my breasts where he pinches my nipples, hard.

I buck up to him, unable to hold back the pleasure and the pain from ripping through my system.

"Unreal." He groans, his eyes blazing in intensity. "You're not real."

I might feel perfect right now while his cock is sliding deep within me but I don't feel unreal. I'm one hundred per cent real.

This is me.

This is him.

"I'm real," I whisper to him.

"Do you promise?" He's watching me, watching himself, watching *us*, where his cock sinks into me, his shaft wet. "Because," he trails off, breath hitching, "this feels like a dream."

It's like the world's best dream.

Slow.

So slow.

So real.

So much.

Too much.

He rocks against me and it starts to spark fires, flint against rock, and these fires are building and building through my core. All the ice around us melts.

I don't want this to ever stop.

Then the orgasm comes for me.

Just a tease.

Just a whisper.

"Are you going to come?" he whispers. "Come for me."

"Almost," I whisper, my voice choked with my sudden hunger for him. "God, I'm almost…"

With a roar that tears from his throat, he starts rutting faster, one hand at my back to hold me in place, the other in my hair, making a fist. Because we're fucking on our sides, he's able to slide in deeper than ever, hitting me where my body is begging for the sweet release.

I want this man forever.

My thoughts don't even shock me right now, even though I've never thought them during sex before. But this is more than just sex. I can't deny it anymore.

He lets go until we're shuddering with the power of a thousand snowstorms and I can't hold on forever.

I also can't keep my eyes off of him, the muscles in his neck are corded and strained as the sweat rolls off of him, his eyes are lost in a fiery haze. His tattoos seem to dance against his skin. The sounds that come out of his mouth with each thrust are primal and raw. He's an animal.

The bed slams back against the wall, the sheets are pulled loose, my breasts are jostling and I hope we're not waking his brother but fuck it, I don't care. Not now. Not when I'm *this* close.

"I'm coming," I cry out, my voice ragged, trying to hold his gaze. He holds mine back, his eyes burning, goal reached.

Then I'm twisted and crushed as the orgasm washes over me like an avalanche. But there is no cold, it's just heat and ecstasy and being buried never felt so good.

"Fuck," Maverick yells, the bed shaking, his sweat dripping on me.

Then he lets out a long, rough moan, shoulders vibrating as he comes.

I'll never get tired of seeing this, hearing this, feeling this.

This beast of a man brought to his knees.

The thrusting slows.

Slows.

His fingers let go.

He collapses beside me, breathing hard, eyes heavy-lidded.

Sated.

"We should have sleepovers more often," he says, giving me a wry smile.

No kidding.

"So," I say to him as he pulls out and gets off the bed. "Are you a cuddler? A kicker? A snorer?"

He laughs. "Don't you want to find out for yourself? Where's the mystery?"

"Sometimes I talk in my sleep," I warn him. "But I don't cuddle."

He looks crestfallen. "You might change your mind with me. I can cuddle all night. You're my heater, remember?"

But after we've both washed up and gotten ready for bed, I find myself gravitating toward his arms. They're so big and strong and as they wrap around me, I realize that cuddling might not be so bad after all. At least not with this guy.

"Good night," he says to me, kissing the top of my head.

And there I go, melting inside like sugar.

"Good night," I whisper back and his heartbeat lulls me to sleep.

* * *

WIND CUTS into me like a knife.

I'm standing precariously along a ridge a few feet wide. On both sides the mountain falls away, loose shales at first that turn to sheets of fresh snow that plunge into the void.

I don't know how I got here, which must mean this is a dream. Dreams never have a beginning, they always drop you somewhere in the middle. And in this case, I'm dropped on a mountain's spine.

In front of me the spine curves up, leading to a peak but there's snow blowing around, obscuring my vision.

Behind me there's another peak, a place I've just come from. I can feel it but I can't turn around to see it.

I don't want to see it.

I don't know where to go or what to do. My feet feel like lead, which is what this would probably feel like in real life.

"Riley," Mav's voice floats into my head and up ahead the storm pauses enough for me to see the outline of the mountain and the strong silhouette of Maverick. I'd recognize his shape anywhere. It instills a sense of power and wonder in you. It represents all that's safe and unsafe at once.

He's holding out his hand for me.

I start walking toward him like I'm on a tightrope, my body off-balance, teetering dangerously close to the drop-off on either side.

Then something grabs me from behind, holding me by the collar, spinning me around.

I gasp, finding myself face to face with Levi. But it's not

the Levi that I remember, not the way he was when he was alive, so bold and full of life.

Just like Maverick.

No, this Levi is blue, dead, with white eyes of snow. They stare at me and though they look blind, I know he's not.

"How could you," he says to me, icicles for teeth. "How could you love someone else? Didn't you learn anything?"

I open my mouth to speak but there isn't anything to say.

Levi lets go of me, then shoves me backward.

My feet go for the ridge and then it's gone.

I'm falling, sliding down the icy slope, my fingernails digging into the ice, trying to stop, leaving bloody trails, red stripes on white.

I fall and fall and fall.

Then wake up.

Gasping for air.

I can't breathe.

I'm in the dark and there's ice in my lungs and –

"Riley," Maverick says. "It's okay, it's okay." His hand is at my back, I'm sitting upright, panting, my hands gripping his duvet.

"It's okay," he says again, voice soothing. "You had a bad dream. It was just a nightmare. Just breathe, baby."

Baby. That word brings me around. He hasn't called me baby in any of my dreams.

I nod. "I'm fine," I whisper. "I'm fine, it's just…" I breathe in, out. *Riley, keep it together!* "Yeah. A dream. Just a dream."

He keeps one hand rubbing up and down my naked back, the other grabs my hand and squeezes it. "Want to talk about it?" he says softly and as my eyes adjust in the dark, I can see the concern on his brow, his gaze searching my face, his brows as they knit together.

"It's okay."

"Are you sure?"

I nod.

He leans back into the bed, gently pulling me down with him. "Come here," he says, his arm going around me, holding me to his chest. I hear his heartbeat, let the heat of his skin sink into me until slowly I'm warmed again.

His fingers play with my hair, gentle, so gentle, his other hand holds onto mine, clasped over his chest. He swallows, a noise that sounds large in the dark. "I'm glad you stayed over," he says, voice barely audible.

I smile against his chest. "Even though I wake up gasping from nightmares?"

"Even that. Especially that," he says. "I want to see all parts of you Riley, not just the ones you choose to show me. I want to see the real you, the one you hide away."

"Who says I hide anything?" I say.

But fuck, I do. And he knows it. He knows it.

"We all hide something," he says.

"What do you hide?"

He sighs softly. "Everything."

I think about that for a moment. "Why?"

He lets out a chuckle. "Damn it, Riley. I don't know. It's too late for this talk."

"You brought it up, Mav."

He sighs and I can hear him chewing on his lip in thought. I have patience. I wait. I don't push. I want so bad for something raw from him.

Eventually he speaks. "Because...that's the role I play. I mean, my name is fucking Maverick. It's not even real. So who am I? Maverick, the happy-go-lucky playboy mountain man, always up for a good time, for a good fuck, for a good laugh? Or am I John?"

"And who is John?"

"John is...John is someone who wants to be taken seriously. John is someone who hasn't quite...he hasn't...I

175

haven't really moved on. From things of the past. I've just kind of pushed everything aside and I don't know. It scares me, to have to deal with that one day."

"Why can't you be both John and Maverick?"

"I don't know," he says after a few beats. "I don't think anyone wants both."

"I do," I tell him, raising my head and resting my chin on his chest, staring at him in the dim light. "I want both of you. I want Mav, that fun, fearless man, the one with the tattoos, who fucks me like a champ. And I want John, the one who is afraid and doesn't let anyone know it. The one who wants respect more than anything else. The one who would risk life and limb for people he doesn't even know. Why can't I have both?"

His eyes meet mine, so stark in his gaze. "You have me," he says. "All of me." He pauses. "Do I have all of you?"

My heart clenches in my chest. The truth feels foreign to me.

"I want you to," I say slowly. "But…what are we doing?"

"We're spending time together. Because we like each other. Because we're so damn good together."

"But then what?"

He frowns, tucking a piece of hair behind my ear. "You don't strike me as a *then what* kind of person."

"But our jobs, Mav. Are we just going to sneak around forever?"

He sighs, closing his eyes for a moment. "Would it be so bad?"

I start running my finger over the designs on his chest. He has the province of British Columbia outlined, a star where North Ridge is. "It's better than the alternative," I tell him. Which would be to not have him at all. I couldn't deal with that, couldn't imagine waking up each day and not having this to look forward to.

"So then," he says, "we just keep doing this. We keep getting to know each other. We keep having fun."

Fun.

God, that word *hurts*.

For someone who has prided herself on being a barrel of monkeys, a woman of no fucks given, someone who lives for fun…

That's not what I want. Not anymore.

I want…everything.

His heart.

His big, blooming heart.

There you have it, I tell myself. *Ease up on your feelings, you're just having fun.*

I give Mav a quick smile, trying to pretend this isn't bothering me at all. "I can have fun."

Sex is my default mode, my deflection. It's a role I play so well. My hand slides down lower over his rigid abs and flat stomach, heading down, down, down.

"I know you can," he says softly, grabbing my hand and pulling it up and back to his chest. "And I love it when you do, baby. But tonight, we sleep."

A protest is on my lips but honestly, I'm exhausted. I nod and close my eyes, feeling myself drift away in his arms, my head on his chest. There's so much safety and comfort in his bed as I drift away.

I want him to be my shelter through any storm.

A shelter for my heart.

But I'm in love with this man.

And who is going to save me from that?

CHAPTER THIRTEEN

MAVERICK

A KNOCK AT MY BEDROOM DOOR WAKES ME UP.

I open my eyes, the room a purple grey. It's early.

Riley is sleeping in my bed next to me, her back to me, her chest rising and falling. I take a moment to watch her, still in disbelief that this gorgeous creature is in my bed, looking so small and vulnerable. Something in my heart aches for this scene, makes me want to lock it in my head forever. What if this is all I get of her? What if this is it?

The knock repeats itself and I carefully get out of bed, trying not to wake her, and open the door a crack.

Fox is on the other side, frowning at me.

"Are you alone? Why aren't you opening the door?" He's trying to see into the room.

"I'm naked, dude," I whisper. "You want to see the family jewels and compare them to your own?"

"Why are you whispering?" he asks. Not whispering.

I look over my shoulder at Riley. She's still sleeping. I eye Fox through the door. "I may have someone in here. She's sleeping."

"Riley?" He looks impressed.

"Yes," I hiss. "Now what do you want? It's cold and that doesn't do my dick any favors."

"Again with your dick."

"*Fox.*"

"Just wondering why your truck is still here. Aren't you working today?"

I groan. "Shit. Yes. Fuck it, I'm calling in sick."

"Really? You're already doing this? What happened to not breaking the rules?"

"Yeah, well obviously I've broken them in a million different positions already."

Fox rolls his eyes. "I guess you're the boss."

"Yeah, I am. Thanks for getting that. Have fun on the slopes."

He studies me for a moment, not smiling. "Just watch yourself, that's all."

"Why? For what?"

"If you don't know, I can't help you."

"But I don't know."

"Then I can't help you." He turns and heads down the hall. "Just play it safe, okay brother? And don't forget about your damn dog while you're having all the sex. If I come home and she's pissed everywhere, I'm going to be very upset."

"Heaven forbid you get upset," I mutter to myself, gently closing the door.

But when I turn around, Riley has rolled over and is looking at me through sleepy eyes under the mess of her blonde hair.

"Sorry," I tell her, quickly getting back into bed with her. "The drawback of living with your brother. It'll be better in the summer. He's away fighting those fires for weeks at a time, living in camps. It's only in the winter that we really have to share."

She looks at me with big eyes and I wonder if what I've

said has surprised her, if she thinks that we won't be a thing come the summer months.

I find myself rambling. "Honestly, when we decided to buy the house it just made sense. The market was at a low and it's slowly picking up. We wanted to invest. It's so expensive in this province that eventually the small towns are going to get popular too. We've made an agreement where… well, anyway, doesn't fucking matter. We won't be roommates forever, it's just what makes sense for now."

She stifles a yawn. "You talk a lot in the morning, you know that?"

"Maybe you make me nervous."

A sly smile spreads across her lips. She likes the thought of that. "What time is it, anyway? Don't you have to go in today?"

I shake my head. "I'm giving myself the day off."

"Then I should probably go in," she says, suddenly determined, making a move to get out of bed.

I quickly grab her arm and pull her back down. "Please, don't go."

"But –"

"No buts," I tell her. "The weather has been great so far, it hasn't changed yet. We'll go in if there's an emergency but…I just want to be with you. Here. All day. Please, stay with me. Spend the day with me."

She's thinking about it, her eyes looking elsewhere in the room, then the window, trying to judge the weather, or maybe something else.

"Riley," I say, hoping she can hear the pleading in my voice. "*Please*. Just…stay with me."

She exhales and tucks a strand of hair behind her ear, peering at me. "Okay."

I can't describe the way my heart feels, like I'm being flooded with relief. Something so fucking simple, just her agreeing to stay here for the day, and I'm happier than I've been in a long time.

"You're such a good girl," I say to her, grabbing her face in my hands and kissing her, soft and hard all at once. "I'm making you Maverick's Famous Pancakes."

"Oh my God," she laughs against my mouth, a sound that shoots straight to my chest. "Please don't tell me there's hot sauce on these ones too."

"You'll see."

We get out of bed but we take it slow. I make coffee and she drinks it in the kitchen just wearing one of my flannel robes that's oversized on her, plus a pair of too-big shearling slippers. She cups the mug with both her hands, wild pieces of blonde hair in her face, and watches me intently as I start making breakfast.

She is ridiculously adorable.

I'm trying hard to impress her. Maverick's famous pancakes are actually normal pancakes but I add bananas, walnuts, slices of bacon, and top it with brown sugar instead of maple syrup. I know, how anti-Canadian of me to forgo the syrup that's supposed to run through our veins.

We eat the pancakes at the kitchen table, Chewie hanging around at our feet, hoping for the occasional piece of bacon.

This feels right. I've never had a woman over who stayed for breakfast and I certainly never made anything for them. The few relationships I'd been in, I rarely had them over. What was the point when I was on call? Everything was always kept at a distance. And it wasn't always me breaking it off with them, sometimes they broke it off with me because they didn't want that distance and they didn't understand my job.

But with Riley, she understands my job – in a way, she is my job. And I want to close the gaps. I want there to be no distance between us.

There was a softness to her last night. When she woke up from the nightmare, I didn't have the heart to tell her that she was calling for Levi. I know that dreams can be personal and what happened with him is something she keeps dear to her heart. To bring it up would be to intrude, especially when she's so vulnerable.

I just want her to keep being vulnerable.

I want *tender.*

And that shocks me, because I've never been a tender kind of guy. Riley is slowly but surely rewriting me.

"That was amazing," she says to me after she's scarfed down the pancake. Must I mention that I *love* the fact that she eats. She makes no apologies for it, just like she makes no apologies for the way she is. That is so rare.

"You're amazing," I can't help but blurt out.

She gives me a coy smile. "Right back at ya."

"I mean it. You don't even know why."

"Okay, why?"

"Because you're so unapologetically you. You don't give a fuck."

She considers that. "My give-a-fuck meter is broken and it never even worked to begin with." She pauses, looks up at me through long lashes. "But I do give a fuck about you."

I laugh. "That might be the most romantic thing I ever heard."

She shrugs, pushes back her chair and gets up. Drops her robe so it falls to the ground. She's completely naked underneath.

"I'm cold," she says. "Put on a fire."

Fuck me. She's trouble.

"I'm hard," I tell her, getting up, pressing my palm against the erection in my pajama pants. "And I can set you on fire"

She giggles at that, shaking her head, and walks naked around the table and over to the fireplace. "I'm serious," she says, getting down on all fours on the bearskin rug. "Put on the fire and then warm me up."

Jesus. She doesn't stop.

I follow her, trying to ignite the logs while she stares up at me from the rug with sex-kitten eyes, wiggling her ass in the air.

"You fucking tease," I whisper hoarsely. "You're going to get it."

She cocks a brow.

The fire lights.

I strip quickly, feeling electricity running through my veins, a sense of urgency unlike any before, and then I'm coming around her from behind on the rug, prowling like she's the prey and I'm the hunter, or maybe it's the other way around because I'm in her pull, her power, and there isn't anything I can do about it.

She's on her hands and knees beneath me, her hair spilling around her like a blonde cloud, looking so flawless and pure and soft against the fur rug. My cock juts out between us, bobbing as I move above her body, and the need to drive myself so deep inside her is more dominant than ever.

It's the need to claim.

To make her mine.

That primal, animalistic instinct to take and hold and possess. As caveman as it sounds, it's real and raw and it's an ache in my chest, clawing its way out of me.

With her ass facing me, I place my tongue on her firm cheek, making long, wide licks up and then down, back and forth, while I'm squeezing her skin. Her ass is so tight and round and perky, a peach I could bite into all day.

She rises her hips into me, pressing her ass into my mouth.

She wants more.

Of course she does.

Even with my cock almost painfully rigid, everything swimming with this heady infatuation, I slide my finger down her ass, parting it.

"Do you like that?" I whisper. Everything is wild and tense. "Do you want this?"

She makes a sound, tight and breathless, that sounds like "yes."

I draw the finger back up, and she rotates her hips for purchase.

Greedy.

I lower my head and gently blow on her.

She stiffens again, then presses herself back.

More.

I slide my tongue in slowly, my heart intent on climbing out of my chest.

Riley sucks in her breath sharply; the exhale is a low groan I feel rumble all the through me, hotter than the flames dancing around us.

I slide my hand around, finding her clit and lightly petting it until she's moaning again, her hips circling for more.

Her legs spread wider on the rug, giving me greater access in all ways and I'm experiencing her in a whole new way. She's opening up to me, putting her pleasure in my hands, and offering herself. She's vulnerable, something so rare for her, and I want to drown in this tenderness.

And yet I want to be oh so rough.

I can feel her close to coming. She's panting, her body growing warmer, on the verge. Her nails are digging into the rug.

"Oh my God, Mav," she says hoarsely, and I nearly lose my fucking mind. "Keep going. Keep going."

I do. My tongue plunges in her ass, fucking her so tight,

and my fingers stroke and circle. She's panting, breathless, needy.

She's incredible like this, about to throw herself over the edge.

And then she goes. It happens quickly, and I feel her unravel under my tongue, my lips, my fingers. She tenses for a split second and the world seems to still, tipping on its axis, and then she's shattering, arching her back, crying out my name.

"Come inside me," she says, voice a broken whisper as she rides out the wave. "Right there."

Fuck yes.

I grab her hips and pull her back into me, my hands so large around her waist, my cock positioned. Good lord, I can't believe she's letting me do this but I'm fucking doing it.

I hold my breath and carefully, slowly, push inside.

Oh.

Fuck.

It's.

So.

Good.

She gasps but pushes back into me to let me know I should keep going. I take it as easy as I can, my movements slow and deliberate.

"Is this okay, am I hurting you?" I murmur, hoping she's at least getting some kind of thrill out of it and grateful that she got off moments before. Before she has a chance to answer, I let go of her hip and my hand slides between her legs. Her cunt is still pulsing from her earlier orgasm, so I know to take it even gentler.

She immediately relaxes into my fingers. The muscles along the length of her back smooth out, and her head hangs down limply as she gives herself to me. The fire makes her hair glow like a halo.

"You're so beautiful," I whisper to her gruffly. "You feel so good. You're so good."

She's silent and breathing heavily but her body responds to my touch like a finely tuned instrument. I push in and out, and her ass is so goddamn tight that I don't have much time. I can't seem to get air, my skin is running hotter and hotter, tighter and tighter, like I have a sunrise coming from within.

My fingers work faster as I pump harder, with as much control as I can muster. The rug slips back and forth and I know at some point we might slide right into the fireplace.

There is so much going on.

And yet my only real thought is her.

I groan, the relentless energy building inside me as I push in to the hilt, the pressure reverberating through me.

She's so tight.

So good.

So good.

My body gets warmer, tighter, and a heated coil builds inside, layer by layer, until I know I don't have long.

And now I'm teetering over that thin line, that edge, that drop.

I'm not alone in it.

She comes hard, shaking so violently that it makes me shake. My lower back tightens, and everything inside me cracks while an animal-like growl is ripped from my throat, echoing around the living room as I pour into her. It feels so good, I can't even feel my knees. I don't know my name.

Her noises are soft compared to mine this time around, and we're rocking together, joined, until everything inside me is gone.

I nearly collapse on her back which is now covered in my sweat and it takes all my strength to keep holding onto her waist, to keep myself up.

"Fuck me," I manage to say, unable to catch my breath, my

heart pounding so hard in my head that it's making the room shake. "Fuck, Riley…that was…you are…"

"No, you are," she says, looking at me over her shoulder. Her face is bright red, either from facing the fire or from her orgasm or from both, her hair sticking to her damp forehead. Her eyes are hooded.

She looks like I just fucked the life out of her.

She certainly fucked the life out of me.

I pull out, not caring for now that some of me drips on the rug, and lie down on my back beside her. I stare up at the high ceiling, the knots in the wood.

"Best day ever," I eventually say, my chest still rising and falling.

She peers down at me. "It's getting there."

I raise my brows. "What? What could be better? You just came twice."

"Do you have Netflix? And beer? And popcorn?"

"It's, like, ten a.m."

"So?"

"Well, yes then."

"Can we drink beer and eat popcorn and watch Wayne's World? And then Happy Gilmore? And maybe Ace Ventura after?"

I grin stupidly at her. I'm not sure I've ever been so happy. "Okay. Now it's the best day ever."

She leans over and kisses me on the lips. "And we've only just begun."

CHAPTER FOURTEEN

MAVERICK

WHEN I DROP RILEY OFF AT HER HOUSE LATER THAT EVENING, the both of us are spent, not just from the day of sex but just the day of letting each other in. I don't know about her but after today...*fuck*. There's no going back anymore. This woman is becoming everything to me. I can't think straight, can't see straight. My skin, blood, bones, still hum with the feel of her, like she's imprinted herself deep, down to my marrow.

It's enough to drive a man mad. Wild. And I've never had anything in my life throw me for such a loop before. It's that adrenaline I get when I get the call, the thrill when I'm rappelling down an ice-covered cliff, the wonder of seeing a pack of wolves running off in the distance, oblivious to someone as insignificant as me. She's every unexplored mountain, every wild river, every storm that catches you by surprise.

She's a force of nature.

Super, Natural, Riley Clarke.

But she's not mine. And sometimes I think I might not be able to tame her. Sometimes I think I shouldn't. Because she was right to ask last night, about what we are doing. She was right because I've thought it too. Where this can go? How can we ever become anything more than sex, because if we do, we lose our livelihood. Sex can be a secret; a relationship is harder to bury.

And, *fucking eh*. Am I even ready for that? In this line of work? Committing myself to someone, knowing I could lose them, that it could ruin us both in the end?

All I know is that I've never met anyone who is more addicting than search and rescue. Those thrills I seek, the validation, it's all inside *her*. We work in a team, but we're a team of our own, the two of us, a team with nowhere to go and no one to rescue but ourselves.

I'm sitting in my truck now, just outside the house. The lights are on and I can see Fox's shadow pass by the large windows but I don't want to go inside yet because he'll grill me. I think it's his favorite hobby, pestering me about the women I date just so he doesn't have to think about his own romantic shortcomings.

But eventually I have to go inside, so I get out of the truck and the door is almost immediately slammed back against me. A burst of wind has come out of nowhere, rising hard and fast from the direction of Ravenswood and Cherry Peak to the north.

It's a cold wind too, immediately chilling me to the bone. After the near balmy temperatures, I wonder if this is the storm I've been suspecting. The wind dies down almost immediately but that one burst has me on edge.

When I wake up the next morning, it's four a.m., a long time before my alarm goes off. I get up and look out the window. The wind is howling now but there's no snow, just the high, eerie whine as it whips through the trees.

I wonder if Riley is up, listening to the storm. I have a feeling she is.

I text her, **Hey, you awake?**

I then wait, wishing I hadn't done that. She'll probably assume it's a call to go out and I'll wake her up for nothing.

But she texts back, **Yes. Can't sleep.**

Want company? I text back and I know, I *know*, I'm pushing things here. But fuck, she was pushing it for so long, I figure it's time I return the favor.

Don't you have to be at work in the morning?

I text back. **Don't you?**

But I take that to mean she wants company because she didn't exactly say no, so I get ready and head out the door. It's funny, to feel so comfortable with someone but we're still in that stage where we're really not sure about what we are and how every text or word or look can be too much or too little.

Soon she's letting me in her suite and I'm kissing her and we're falling backward onto her bed and I'm taking off her tank top, sucking on her breasts, her neck. I push inside of her and I know I've found that peace I crave, that balance to all the chaos.

It doesn't just stop there.

Like the day before, we keep touching each other, sinking into easy, constant sex, our bodies constantly entangled. I swear we fuck for hours, this slow, drowsy, descent into this world we've created for just ourselves.

I've just pulled out of her, my back stinging from her nail marks, my muscles cramping from the night of effort, when my phone buzzes.

I glance at the glowing clock radio—seven a.m. now, I'm not supposed to be in for another hour—and fish my phone out of my jeans.

There are a shit ton of missed calls.

"Oh fuck," I mutter.

"What is it?" she asks.

I shake my head, looking them over. "How did I not hear these come in?"

"Because we were having all the sex."

I glance at her. "Why didn't your phone go off?"

She looks put out. "It died after you texted me. I figured any call would go to you. What is it?"

I sigh and sit down on the bed, scrolling through them. "It's nothing. Well, a climber fell at the Kokanee Glacier. Six-hundred-foot drop. His partner came back in the middle of the night. It's pretty much a body recovery now."

"Who went?"

"I don't know." I text back Tony and wait for his reply.

To his credit, he doesn't ask where I was. Or where Riley was. He says that Tim and Jace went out. I relay this to Riley.

"Don't they need us?" she asks, bringing her knees to her chest and tucking her covers over them. In the hazy morning light, she looks so young, fresh, innocent, her blonde bedhead spilling all around her.

I shake my head. "No. To recover a body...you can do it alone. Usually I'm doing it."

She swallows and looks down at the pattern on the bedspread. "I've only seen one dead body. I don't know how you do it."

"It's part of the job," I tell her, leaning against her knees. "And someone has to do it. We aren't always about the rescue. Sometimes the searching is more important. People deserve to be buried properly. Loved ones want to know what happened. So I go out there and I retrieve the bodies and maybe they aren't alive but they're safe. You know?"

She blinks, staring at nothing. "But...how do you *do it*? Face death? Doesn't that...affect you? I mean, you're so normal."

I laugh softly. "Am I? I believe I told you the other night that there are two people in me, John and Maverick."

"You know what I mean." Her eyes are grave. She's serious.

So I'm serious too. "Look. It's not easy but you do get used to it. But for me, I've maybe recovered fifteen bodies or so, it's a balance of being respectful while keeping your distance. There have been climbers who have fallen. Backcountry skiers buried in an avalanche. I've helped recover bodies in a plane crash, a Cessna where a father and daughter died together. Most of the time though, someone has taken their own life. Sometimes it's a shotgun in the mouth in the middle of the forest and I don't find them until after the wolves have. Other times, they jump over the waterfalls, like Bridal, or hurl themselves off of Cherry Lookout. It's…so stark and raw and intimate, you know, to be the one to pick these people up after they've decided to end their lives. You're seeing some part of their life that no one else ever will."

"But your mother…" she says and then clamps her mouth shut.

I know what she means. "Maybe that's why I do this," I tell her. "Because my mother drowned herself and had there been someone in SAR around at that time, maybe they could have gone into that river and saved her. Maybe they would have given her the help she needed. Maybe…she would still be here today and I would still have a mother."

It's hard to swallow and I'm getting choked up. I close my eyes and inhale deeply through my nose.

"Mav," Riley says softly, getting to her knees. She wraps her arms around me and holds me close, resting her cheek on my shoulder. "It's okay. I'm here."

Are you? I think but I don't think too much. My emotions are running high lately and I can't stop the few tears that fall from my eyes.

But this isn't how I want to start this day. I need to get it together. Riley is unraveling me with every second we're together, like when you're climbing and there's too much slack in the ropes and you know it. Eventually there will be nothing to hold you up. Eventually you'll fall.

I get up and shake it off. "Let's go in to work," I tell her.

* * *

THIRTY MINUTES LATER, the two of us are coming into the office together.

Tony is at his desk and looks up with a smile. At least this guy is always smiling.

"You're here."

"In the flesh," I tell him. "Where's Neil?"

"He went out for donuts," Tony says. "Need to keep that boy busy."

"Any word from Tim or Jace?" Riley asks as she takes off her coat and hangs it on the rack. I love how no-nonsense she can be sometimes, how easily she goes from sex kitten to vulnerable to a goof and back to one serious ass-kicking SAR.

"Tim has the body," Tony says. "Jace is relaying. Police are with the climber by the road. Should take them about three hours to get down though."

"Why so long?" I ask. From what I understood, the ice walls that the climbers were using were quite close to the trailhead, maybe an hour's hike.

"This wind," Tony says, gestures to the trees wavering outside the windows, "it's coming from the glacier and beyond. It's a fucking mess up there. I can barely get them on the radio."

A cold knot forms inside my stomach. "I think we should go for backup." I look at Riley. "You in?"

"Always," she says, grabbing her coat and putting it back on.

I look at Tony. "Stay here and be base. And don't let Neil eat all the donuts."

"I'll save you a maple glazed."

Riley and I get our gear in the truck and head out. It's about an hour drive to the glacier and she's lapsed into silence, staring out the window at the weather. The wind is still howling and now light flakes are starting to appear. As long as they stay light, it shouldn't be a problem, but if they get any heavier, then the avalanche risks rise. The glacier can be notorious for that, another reason why I think we need to be there.

But her silence is telling after a while.

And I have questions.

"You never talk about Levi," I say to her.

She stiffens slightly but keeps her eyes focused outside.

"There isn't much to say," she says after a few beats. Her words are careful.

"He was your friend, wasn't he?"

She nods. "Only friend."

"Just a friend?"

Now she looks at me. "What makes you say that?"

I give her a quick smile. "I don't know. I just feel it. The closer someone is to you when you lose them, the less you want to talk about it."

She watches me for a few beats, thinking, then sighs, leaning her head back against the seat. "Yeah. Well, I was in love with him. Ever since high school. He didn't know it though."

"I'm sure he did. There's no way you can love someone and not have them know it."

A line forms between her brows. "You've obviously never pined for someone before."

I think I might be pining right now.

"What I mean is, *you*, Riley. Your heart and soul just beam out of you, like a sunburst. You've got all this joy and life in you that you can't possibly contain. There is no way in hell that Levi didn't know how you felt. He knew, believe me, he knew."

She watches me for a few moments, confusion and fear washing over her features, until she says, "If that's true, he never addressed it."

"Sometimes it's difficult with friends. You don't want to ruin a good thing. Take Fox and Del for example."

"Yeah. What is their deal?"

"It's what I said. They're like sister and brother. Good friends to the end. But there's something else there that neither of them are facing, because if they do, it means that everything they are to each other is at risk."

"That's sweet that you care."

"Sweet? No. I'm not a matchmaker and I don't necessarily believe in their romance. But Fox is a short-tempered grump. Just like our father. But worse, because he's sexually frustrated over Del and doesn't even know it. Love would calm him down, bring him peace."

"Love is chaos."

I give her an odd look. But she's right. Love is chaos.

I think I might be falling in love with Riley and I've never felt more turbulent in all my life.

I clear my throat, trying to push those feelings away. "Anyway, the reason I'm asking about Levi is that –"

"You want to know if I'm capable of loving someone."

I blink at her in shock. "What? That is not what I was going to say."

She shrugs. "Sometimes I wonder myself."

What I was going to say had to do with the dead body. I know she found Levi's and I don't want her to be traumatized all over again if it turns out we have to help take the climber out. I'm not sure if Tim has a body bag packed with him or not.

But I let it go because, really, it's dumb of me to ask. Riley is more than tough and she can handle everything that gets thrown at her. Even if she's crumbling on the inside, she has enough bravado to do the job properly and I suppose that's all that matters in this line of work.

When we finally get to the trailhead, we have a quick meeting with the RCMP officer and the distraught climbing partner. The police always have to be called in when someone dies, especially to make sure foul play isn't suspected. It never turns out that way either, but there are also special precautions that we have to take when we're investigating the scene.

Then we head up. Our packs are extra heavy today because we're both carrying 600 feet of rope in case we need it, plus ice axes, helmets, and crampons. It's almost all vertical, so there's no skiing in and the snow is too wet for snowshoes, so we're hiking in our boots. Thankfully it's a popular trail for ice climbers or people wanting to see the glacier so the snow is hard packed and we're not sinking in too much.

The weather, however, is like one big fucking hand in our faces, trying to hold us back. We push through, but it's hard. I keep looking over my shoulder at Riley, just her eyes visible through the balaclava that covers her face, frost and ice building up on the fabric.

Finally, we break through the treeline and head up a couple of ridges before we come to the glacier. I'd been trying to radio with Jace on our way but things aren't coming in clearly. All I got is that they had to take a higher route along one of the saddles before cutting down the glacier at an angle.

We can see them now, halfway across, tiny dots on

endless white. Tim leads, holding the body bag on the litter, Jace keeps up the rear.

"This isn't good," Riley says.

I look over at Riley. She's pulled down her mask, staring at the ice field with trepidation. Her pallor is white as snow. She looks at me. "I don't like this."

I put my attention back on the team. They seem fine. Slow, but more than capable as they cross. "Why?"

"I don't know. The storm, the way the snow is sitting at the top there, those cornices are overloaded. All of this is fresh powder, it's been dumping here for hours, probably since yesterday, after those weeks of snow melt? No. I don't like it."

"Why don't you wait here," I tell her. Granted it's not the best spot where we've stopped. We've just come up the spine and while the slope into the glacier is easy and gentle, the slope behind us is four hundred feet of pure ice that eventually drops off into the abyss.

"Why don't we wait for them to come to us," she says. "No point putting extra weight out there."

"I wouldn't be much of a leader if I didn't go out there and help," I tell her. "I should have been the one to take the call this morning. I should be there."

A wash of shame comes over her eyes and she diverts them, looking to the glacier. I didn't mean for it to sound the way it did, that I was angry that I was having sex with her this morning instead of being where I needed to be.

"Okay but..." she trails off just as a *whumpf* sound echoes down the glacier. Instinctively we both look up at the top and see a massive cornice of snow break away and fall onto the slope below.

The trigger for an avalanche.

"Run!" I yell across the glacier but it's pointless because Tim and Jace have both heard it too and have stopped, staring up at the giant sheet of snow – two football fields worth – that's barreling toward them faster than anything they can outrun.

I've seen plenty of avalanches before. Despite how destructive and deadly they are, they're also awe-inspiring. It's probably why so many die in them. Not only are they hard to predict but when you see them, you can't look away. It's supernatural, ravishing and horrifically beautiful. A heard of ice horses stampeding toward you on white crested waves.

I'm powerless. I can't yell, I can't move, though moving won't help anyone right now. I can just watch as the snow comes down in a relentless blast, the powder clouds rising high into the sky. In seconds Tim, Jace and the climber have vanished, disappeared under the cover of snow and then the wall starts moving up the edges of the bowl, coming for us.

It should stop just below us, the momentum already slowing, but it's still rising, crawling up the ridge to where we are, reaching for us with icy fingers.

Instinctively I move in front of Riley to shield her, even though I know the worst we'll get hit with is a face full of powder.

But she screams.

I turn around in time for the powder cloud to hit my back and to see her stumble backward away from me, arms wheeling around trying to keep her balance on the thin line of the ridge.

"Riley!" I cry out, lunging for her.

But it's too late.

She falls backward, ten feet down onto the slope of ice and starts sliding down, fast, first on her back and then flipping over, trying wildly to grab hold of the ice as she slides.

I don't think.

I just move.

I leap off the ridge and land on my stomach, arms out, sliding down right after her, head first.

The slope is pure ice, fifty degrees slant, and I'm hurtling down faster than a car, my hands stretched out in front of me, trying to be as aerodynamic as possible to catch up. I have no idea how I'm going to stop, I just know that I have to reach her before she goes over the edge.

She's trying to dig her fingers in but at this speed and with her gravitational pull, it's pointless. Then she flips back over, trying to get her pack off. With one hand on the straps, it rises above her in an attempt to slow down.

It doesn't slow her down much but it does close the distance between us. Snow, ice flies in my face and I keep my eyes focused on hers. They're wild, they're panicked, they're a vessel of fear.

I catch up to the pack, grabbing the strap and reach for her ice axes. I grab one and with my free hand start trying to jab it into the ice but it's impossible to get a good stick.

"Hold on!" I scream at her and my eyes fly over her head and at what lays beyond her.

Fifty feet until she's over the edge.

Forty feet.

Thirty feet.

Frantically, I try again, jabbing again and again with the axe as we slide toward our death.

Twenty feet.

Holy fuck.

We're not going to make it.

This is it.

We're going over the edge.

We're going to die.

Ten feet.

God, please…

Thwack.

My axe penetrates the ice, sinking in to the hilt, and a cry is ripped from my throat as it stops me, causing me to swing around one eighty, still holding onto the pack, both of us spinning as we're whipped around on the ice face, her body swinging up higher than me, the edge just six feet below my legs.

But Riley loses her grip on the pack.

Her hand slips away.

She screams.

Starts sliding down the ice, down me.

Reaches up wildly, fighting against her death. Her fingers rake down the length of my legs, trying to stop herself, trying to hold on.

She gets to my boot.

Her hands throttle it with all her might, wrapped around my ankle.

Half of her is hanging off the edge of the cliff, only her grip on my boot keeping her alive.

"Hang on," I tell her. I wish she wasn't wearing gloves. Gloves don't have the same grip as hands do. Gloves can slip off. We've all seen *Cliffhanger.*

I don't know why I'm thinking about this right now. I don't know why I'm thinking about anything at all. I'm just so stunned by the sheer terror of it all, I don't know what to do.

But I'm a leader. I'm a leader and my team is dying.

Tim and Jace are buried by the avalanche and I'm not there to save them.

The woman I love is dangling by a thread.

I could lose everything.

The fear is overpowering.

I don't even think I can move past it.

I can't.

"Mav," she cries out softly. "I don't think I can hold on

much longer."

The poignancy of her words brings me out of it.

Fear will find you. Better you find it first.

So I let in the fear.

I let it fuel me.

"Don't you fucking say that," I growl at her. "You're not dying, not here, not today."

"Mav," she pleads and I hate the sorrow I see in her eyes. "Mav...I..."

I swallow hard, gathering strength and I roar, "Hang on!"

I take one of my hands off of the axe so I'm holding on with just one hand now, my wrist and arm screaming in pain as I try and hold up the weight of my body and hers. I reach back into my pack with my free hand and feel around until I find another ice axe.

"Don't let go!" I yell at her, surprised at how strong my voice sounds, and then I slam the new axe into the ice right beside the current one.

Then I lift up that one and with all my strength, my muscles straining, my body pushed to the limit, the pain coursing from my wrist to my toes, I reach up and slam the next axe down, right into the ice.

We move up a few inches. Riley is pulled up with me, still hanging on for her life.

And this is how we do it.

This is how I save our lives.

Slowly, so slowly.

Inch by inch.

Axe by axe.

I climb up the near vertical slope, supported only by thin blades of metal into ice, pulling up Riley with me as I go.

My muscles are shaking, breaking.

My mouth tastes like pennies.

I can't even feel the cold anymore, that's how cold I am.

And the whole time I talk to Riley. I talk about *Friends*. And how she's more Phoebe than anyone else, but she does have a bit of batshit crazy Monica in her. She doesn't talk back much but she's listening and staying alive and she's holding on and that's all I can ask for.

It's all I can ask for.

I don't know how long it takes but we finally get to the top of the slope where the angle isn't as steep, the ridge where we were earlier is now coated in a fresh dump of snow thanks to the avalanche.

The avalanche.

I can't even think of that yet.

I wait until I get a hard stance and then I reach down and take Riley's hand, my grip firm around her wrist.

I pull her up to me and she collapses into my arms. To her credit – to our credit – we manage to keep it together, too many emotions swirling around at once.

I may have just pulled her up four hundred feet of ice using just two ice axes but two of our teammates are buried in the snow out there.

Instinct tells me we are too late now to help but our job is to search and rescue and sometimes you can just rescue one, just save one.

I saved Riley.

We get over the ridge and look down into the glacier bowl.

There's nothing but white. No sign they were ever there.

I'm spent. I'm shaking. I'm not sure how to get through this.

Riley does though. She goes into my pack and finds the device that picks up their transmitters. We always wear them if we're out as a team, that way someone else can locate you and dig you out. Like now.

The device beeps, showing us on the GPS where to go.

We're stiff at first, muscles sore and spent but we push through, running and falling and tumbling down the avalanche debris. This is dangerous in itself, but after what we just survived, I couldn't give a fuck anymore. All I care about is saving everyone else. I need to save *more*.

We reach them in the middle and begin the frantic dig to free them. I have a shovel I give to Riley and I use my hands and I can see from the determined look on her forehead that she's been here before and she doesn't want another Levi on her hands. She bounced back from almost losing her life right away. I want to be proud of her but at this moment, I can't feel anything good.

All I keep thinking is that I failed.

I failed Tim. I failed Jace.

I even failed the dead climber.

With each scoop of snow I clear out, I hear the word "failed."

I failed.

I failed.

I failed.

And then it happens.

The snow beneath the shovel starts to move.

A fist breaks through.

It's Jace.

We pull him out of the snow and he's wheezing for breath, paler than the snow and tinged with blue, but he's alive.

"I had an air pocket," he cries out, trying to breathe.

"Shhh," Riley says, putting her arms around him. "Breathe in, breathe out, we have you."

I go back to work, looking for Tim with new hope.

Riley tries to comfort Jace who seems to be going into shock. I let her do her thing, I do mine.

Maybe I didn't fail...

Maybe I…

Yellow.

Bright yellow fabric, poking through the snow.

I sink my hands down and feel along Tim's arm.

All it takes is one touch.

Just the way his arm responds to my hand.

Or the way it *doesn't.*

The stiffness.

Death is wholly inflexible.

Being covered in an avalanche is the same as having cement poured on you. Sometimes you get lucky with an air pocket, like Jace. Most times, you're encased, entombed, with nowhere to move, no place to go. You can't even move your fingers. You die, drowning in the snow, if the blast from the initial impact didn't knock you out first.

But I won't stop. I keep digging, frantic now, until I've cleared all the snow away from him.

Tim.

Tim who was working at North Ridge Search and Rescue before I got there. Tim who showed me the ropes. Tim who would go climbing with me, telling me all about his upbringing in South Korea. Tim whose favorite trail mix was pistachios, but he would never litter the shells, so he'd always have one pocket full of nuts and another pocket full of empty shells and you'd always hear him coming. We called him the squirrel and I think he liked that. He once told me that squirrels brought luck.

Tim was wrong about that one.

Tim who shouldn't have been on this mountain to begin with. I was the one who should have taken the call. I should be there where he is. He should be finding me.

"Mav," Riley whispers, tugging at my sleeve.

It takes tremendous effort to tear my eyes off of Tim's face. I look at her. Tears are streaming down her cheeks. I can't comfort her. I feel nothing but shame. Guilt. It burns everything else away.

"Mav," she says again. "We have to call in for the others. We need backup to retrieve them. Jace," she trails off as she looks over at him. He's sitting in the snow, staring at nothing, wracked by the occasional shiver. "He's in shock, Mav, we need to get him to the hospital. Now."

"I'll stay here," I tell her, looking back at Tim. There's still another dead body buried.

"You won't," she hisses at me, getting angry. "It's too dangerous. We're not losing you too."

"I'm staying here," I tell her and block her out.

"Don't do this," she says, tugging on my arm again, harder. "There's nothing you can do for him now, he's dead, okay? He's dead. And you'll be too if you don't come back with us. Please. The team needs a leader. You're the leader. They need you...*I* need you."

"Go without me," I tell her. "You can handle him yourself. You can handle anything."

I feel her silence at my back, trying to think of what to say. She wants to scream at me. She wants to hit me. But I'm not leaving.

"Fine," she says. I hear her talking to Jace and then the two of them walk off. I turn around to see them disappear around the crest and down into the trees.

I collapse to my knees in the snow.

And cry.

CHAPTER FIFTEEN

RILEY

JACE ISN'T THE ONLY ONE IN SHOCK.

It's been a day, the longest day, and it's night time and I'm at the hospital and yet it doesn't really feel like I'm here.

Jace is being treated for hypothermia and should be okay to go soon. It's about time, it's eight p.m. and everyone on the team just wants to go home and grieve.

But I'm not even sure I can grieve. I don't even feel like I'm present. I think I died a little up there on that mountain. I keep seeing myself going over the edge. I see my fingers letting go of Maverick's boot. I see myself sliding back, staring into his eyes, knowing they're the last thing I'll see and then I'm falling.

I see it so clearly that I'm not sure I'm even alive.

"You're alive," Tony says tiredly.

I must have said that out loud. I just nod, too fucked up to even be embarrassed.

All of us are in the waiting room at the ER. It's a small hospital and there are a lot of people so we're all crammed in here. Tony is sitting beside me in the chairs, Neil is pacing. Sam is here too and a few members of the volunteer squad.

Maverick is out roaming in the halls. I've tried to talk to him a few times but he's not talking. I don't think he's in shock though. I think he's feeling things too clearly.

The guilt.

And I know I'm feeling it too.

"Jace will be out in a moment," the doctor says to us as he comes into the room. "He's made a full recovery but...after what happened, well I'm sure the government will take good care of him. You know there are grief counseling services here if anyone needs one."

We nod and grunt our thanks.

Losing Tim has been a blow that I don't think anyone will recover from. We're all glad Jace is okay and alive but...

We lost a member of our family today.

Because these guys, this team, they are family.

I sigh and get up, unable to keep still. I need to wake up, need to be here.

I head over to the coffee machine and get a cup with extra sugar, then go out into the halls. At the end I see Maverick, just outside the doors in the darkness of the parking lot. Just standing there, shoulders slumped, back to me. His breath rises up into the darkness.

I know this has the chance to break us but I don't want him to break down. He stayed behind with Tim, sending me and Jace back to get help, and he knew the risks. He knew and didn't care and I feel that if I don't bring him back, we'll lose him as a leader for good. And we need him right now.

I need him. More than I've ever needed anyone.

I need his protection, his safety. I need him to take care of me and tell me everything is going to be okay.

I sip my coffee as I walk down the hall. It's hot, scalding me, tasting burnt, but I gulp down half of it because I feel like it's the thing to do, I'm a woman playing a part in a play.

The doors automatically swing open and the cold air hits me in the face but Maverick doesn't turn around.

"Want a coffee?" I ask softly.

I stop where I am, just outside of the doors, so they don't trigger automatically.

He doesn't even move.

"Mav?" Nothing. "John!" I yell.

Finally, he looks over his shoulder at me. His eyes are glazed.

It breaks my heart and leaves me frustrated all at once.

I come over to him, holding out the coffee. "Here."

He shakes his head, looks away. He pulls the beanie further down on his forehead and shoves his hands in his pocket. Everything about his stance right now screams FUCK OFF.

But I'm not gonna fuck off.

I take the coffee back and have a sip, but I don't retreat and my eyes don't leave him.

"I'm not going anywhere," I tell him.

He seems to shrug it off. "How is he?"

"He's fine. They're letting him go soon."

I watch his throat as he swallows. "Good."

"John…"

"Don't call me John," he says in a dull voice.

"Okay. Sorry. Mav."

"Don't…don't call me anything right now."

Now I get that we're grieving. I know that's what's happening. But even so, those words and his tone sting.

I put my hand on his shoulder and he shrugs it off.

"Mav," I tell him, trying to keep my voice from shaking. "Please, talk to me."

Silence.

"This wasn't your fault," I go on. "I know you want to blame yourself but…you can't. It was an accident."

"No," he says quietly, giving a shake of his head. "It wasn't an accident."

I don't even know what to say to that.

"This was a mistake," he mutters.

I know I don't know what he's talking about, but everything inside me clenches, this horrible knot in my gut that tightens at those words.

"What was a mistake?" I whisper.

"You and me. Us."

Oh God.

Oh *God.*

I open my mouth, trying to digest the pain from that hit, to find the words.

"What are you talking about?"

Please don't...please don't...not now.

He glances at me and in the sickly light of the hospital's glow, his eyes are cold. Colder than the ice that almost killed us today.

"Us, Riley. You and I...together. It was a mistake. I always knew it was but now I know for sure. In the worst possible way."

I flinch like I've been backhanded. "Mav," I tell him, my voice breaking, I try and hold myself together. "You're under a lot of stress right now. We all are. You're grieving. It's okay. But don't make rash decisions or—"

"This isn't a rash decision!" he snaps at me. "I know when I fucked up and I fucked up okay? There's a reason there are rules. It's so shit like this doesn't happen. It's so people don't fucking die!"

Oh my God.

My hand flies to my chest because it feels like my heart is breaking. "What the fuck are you saying? You're saying we're responsible for what happened to them? That's fucking nuts, Mav. That's crazy!"

"We did this!" he yells. "He's dead because of us!"

Fuck that.

Fuck *you*.

"How dare you!" I scream at him, spittle flying out. "How fucking dare you try and pin this on me! Don't you think I've been through enough already? I've been responsible for someone's death before, I won't be responsible for this one. It was an *accident* Maverick, it could have been anyone."

"And it should have been me!" he screams right back. "I should have taken that call, it should have been me on the mountain."

"And then maybe you'd be dead too, is that what you want?"

He shakes his head, walking away.

"Where are you going?!" I yell and start marching after him. I grab his arm and pull him back but he's basically a tank and I can't stop him. "You want to have a pity party and blame yourself for this, fine! But you're not blaming me. Okay? We knew what we were getting into and we chose to do it, we chose to be with each other, because we are old enough to make our own decisions. We're fucking adults, John. That is your real name, a real fucking adult name, no wonder you don't fucking answer to it."

That gets his attention.

He turns and I nearly shrink back from the simmering rage in his eyes.

"Way to kick a man when he's down," he growls.

"Kick you? I'm trying to *save* you."

"I don't need saving."

"Only me then, huh?"

He glares at me, looks away. I can't believe this is happening. I can't believe...everything is crumbling away. Everything I thought I had, it's falling through my fingers. I thought I had him.

I love you, I want to scream it at him. But I know he won't care.

"I should have said no to you from the start," he says.

"You did say no to me from the start. I wore you down."

"And I should have thought with my brains instead of my dick for one second."

Again, his words lash me. I feel like I have open wounds all over, stinging from salt. "You were thinking with more than your dick, weren't you?"

He clamps his lips together into a thin hard line.

Oh my God.

"Please tell me that meant something to you," I cry out. "Please tell me that wasn't just sex, that you care about me, that I'm something to you. What we had was…it was real. Wasn't it? Wasn't it real?"

He clears his throat. "It was never real. You knew that."

My fingers grip the edge of my jacket. I can barely breathe. Today I nearly died but this almost feels worse than that. This is a slow death, right in front of his eyes.

"This hurts. Do you know that you're hurting me?" I ask him.

"Today a man died because we were screwing each other. That's on us."

Oh fuck *no.*

No. No. No.

"Why are you being so hurtful?" I smack his arm, my hand bouncing off. "So fucking cruel? Why save my damn life just so you can fucking hurl this shit at me, huh?!"

"I've never had a team member die on my watch!"

"Not until I came around, that's what you're trying to say. Isn't it!?"

"You're jumping to conclusions," he says angrily, basically swatting me away.

"I am not. You're saying all of this. That I'm a mistake."

"You are great for the team," he says quickly. "You are not great for me."

I shake my head, trying to catch my breath. None of this feels real. None of it can be real. How can we switch from last night to this that fast? How can...

He never told you he cares about you, never said he loves you. He had said it was just for fun. He had told you that a million times but you never listen, you never listen.

I swallow hard, tears burning behind my eyes. It's all too much. And he's right. Maybe none of it was real except to me. I started sleeping with him and my emotions came out to play. I couldn't separate the physical from my heart. I fell head over heels for this man and this whole time I assumed he felt the same way.

The town's player. He told me he couldn't commit. God, did I really think that I was that special that I could change him? Did I really think I would be the one? He kept saying I was unreal...that was his way of keeping his distance. To keep me just out of the reaches of his heart.

I'm a big fucking idiot.

Suddenly I'm so drained of energy, I almost collapse right there. It wouldn't be so bad. The nurses would rush out and bring me inside to a room and maybe they'd drug me and I could dream all of this away.

"Riley," he says softly when he realizes I've been standing here and breaking silently in front of him.

I shake my head, pressing my lips together to keep from sobbing, tears running down my face.

I'm the idiot.

He's a man who lost a lot today.

I'm the girl he blames.

I should be used to this.

Love is chaos.

There is no shelter for my heart here.

"I'm going," I tell him. "I'm sorry..." I choke back a sob. "I'm just so sorry."

Then I turn and run back into the hospital, back out the front doors and all the way home.

* * *

I SLEEP for twelve hours straight.

No calls from the team come in. I know they would come regardless if anyone died or not, but they don't. God is taking a break with us for the moment.

He's not taking a break with the weather though. When I wake up, there's a huge dump of snow and it's freezing cold again. This winter just doesn't know when to quit.

I don't know when to quit either.

It's something I'm thinking of, though. Leaving.

I came all the way to North Ridge to start over. I would have gone anywhere, to be honest, and their SAR was the first to call me back. So I took the job.

But now, what kind of job is this? My boss fucking hates me it seems. He blames me and himself for the death of a team member.

And I'm in love with him. I try and tell myself I'm not, as if that will harden my heart and spare me any pain, but I'm in love with Mav, head over heels and tumbling and now I think I've hit the ground. I was airborne for too long.

It hurts. It hurts so much. It shouldn't and I wish it didn't but all I want to do is curl up in the fetal position on the floor and cry. Cry because I lost the closest person I had here in this town, cry because I lost the idea of a future here with him, as vague as that idea was. Cry because I can see his point. I can see why it's all our fault.

Shit happens. I know this so well. I've been so good at outrunning it. I left my home in Washington because I

213

thought running was the way out. I ran away from Colorado because I didn't want to face the tragedy. And now I want to run away from here, start again elsewhere.

I think about all this for hours. I don't eat, I don't shower. I lie on the ground and I think about all the *what ifs* and I think about things I should have done differently and I think about picking myself back up off the ground.

But everything seems too heavy for me to carry. I can't fathom walking back into the SAR office. I can't picture myself rescuing anyone right now because I can't even rescue myself.

That's the thing about search and rescue. We go out there and we find those who are hurt, who are lost. But if you're lost yourself, you won't be able to find anyone. You can't help anyone. You're the one who needs rescuing. And right now, I'm drowning in ice, my head barely above the surface. I'm no use to anyone until I can crawl out on my own.

That day bleeds into the next.

I wake up just after dawn, my body apparently having enough rest now.

There's that horrible moment, a fragment really, where the reality hasn't blended in yet. You're still in a dreamland, living the life from a few days before.

Then you realize the truth…

It hits you like a frying pan.

Takes your breath away.

Freezes your heart.

The truth.

This is your life now.

You don't have Maverick.

You might not even have a job.

Someone is dead.

This is your life now.

I exhale forcefully, trying to get it all out. I don't want it to pull me under anymore. I don't want to sink. It's too easy to do so.

If this is my life now, I have to make peace with it.

Accept it.

And move on.

Easier said than done.

I reach over for my phone and in the split second before I look, I have the highest hopes that Maverick has texted me. Saying he's sorry. Saying he didn't mean anything that he said. That he was lost with guilt and grief.

That he loves me.

But of course, he doesn't say that. There's nothing. Because I don't fucking know anyone in this god-forsaken town.

I sigh and check my emails, thinking perhaps he's emailed me.

But I see an email that makes my heart drop.

An email I never expected.

Oh my God.

It's from Levi's parents.

The subject line reads: **We thought you should know.**

I click the email and open it before I have a chance to chicken out and delete it. I haven't heard from them in nearly two years. Everything in me is shaking.

HELLO RILEY.

It's Pat and Art here. We're not exactly sure if this is still your email or where to reach you, or if you still care to hear from us. If not, then we're sorry but we feel we have a responsibility to you.

Levi was pulled from life support the other day. It was the hardest decision we ever had to make but it was the best one for him and everyone involved. We're sorry

things didn't end right between us and we know you should have been there. We also know you've probably tried to move on.

We just wanted you to know so you can have your own closure about Levi. We know you loved him dearly and he loved you.

Please take care and God bless you, wherever you are.

Pat and Art.

TEARS ARE STREAMING down my face.

The sorrow inside my chest is so intense, so hard, I think it might split me in two.

But I don't push it away. For Levi's sake, I let it in and I feel it. Because he deserves to be felt. So does Tim.

I let that in too and I fall back onto my bed, letting the grief climb me, consume me, turn me inside out.

There's closure in all of this.

But closure doesn't mean a door closing on pain.

You can have peace and pain at once.

The heart can weather any storm.

CHAPTER SIXTEEN

MAVERICK

"You fucked up big time. Big time."

I swallow down my beer and try and glare at Fox but I don't have a lot of anger left in me. Whatever I have is already being directed to myself, like a funnel. I don't need Fox to do it for me.

"You don't need to remind me."

"I think I do," he says, grabbing the car keys to his jeep from the hooks on the wall. "I think you might have to be reminded until you get it in your thick skull. I can't fucking believe you."

I exhale loudly and put my head into my hands. "I shouldn't have said a thing."

"Right," he says dryly. "Hurry up and finish your beer or we'll be late for dinner."

It's been a few days since the accident.

The hardest few days of my life, apart from the ones after I lost my mother.

I've had a hard time moving on.

Especially because of the things I'd said to Riley.

I just relayed everything that happened in detail to Fox.

I'm still hurt. Still mourning. Still grappling with the guilt over Tim and Jace.

I just keep thinking…if only my head was on straight. If I paid attention to my phone. If I'd just focused on my job for a second instead of Riley. In a sense I chose her over my career. My calling.

My duty.

And then I lost Tim.

I nearly lost Riley too.

And then…I lost her in a different way.

She hasn't been into work. No one has, really. Neil of all people has been coming in each day in our absence. We know we'll all pull together if there's another call but so far there hasn't been and I think everyone just needs space. Everyone is off on their own, trying to heal.

Tim's funeral is tomorrow morning. Afterward we're going to hike up Mount Ferguson and have our own prayers for him there. That's the most we've been in contact with each other, to plan that.

But I haven't texted Riley. I just can't. Not after what I said to her.

I knew how I was hurting her, I saw it on her face, her tears, I saw her broken heart and yet I kept talking. I wanted to hurt her. To push her away.

I don't know why. I want to say it's because if she hates me, if she stays away, then everyone will be better off for it. We'll be able to focus on our jobs.

But I don't think that's it. That's what I want it to be, but it's not the fucking truth.

The fucking truth is…I almost lost her.

I've lost a loved one before.

And I almost lost Riley out there.

It scared the fucking shit out of me.

So I did the stupid dumb shit that only immature morons

like myself do. I hurt her to push her away because I believed it would save me in the end.

Pure fucking selfishness.

"Look," Fox says, coming over and nudging my elbow until I look up at him. "I know you're not used to this relationship thing."

"We weren't in a relationship."

He rolls his eyes. "You're in denial but even if you want to pass it off as friends with benefits or colleagues with benefits, whatever, it was still something. She was something to you. She still is. And you're not used to that. So I get it. I get why you did the stupid shit that you did. But it's not a free pass. Now, come the fuck on before I make you."

Fox is leaner than I am but he's still packing a lot of muscle. I don't feel like getting into a fight. It always gets messy. I'm bigger, he's quicker.

And nastier.

Fucking grump.

With a loaded sigh, I finish my beer and follow him out to the jeep. Because he's feeling somewhat sorry for me, he lets me take Chewie even though she leaves dog hair all over his seats. Chewie and Shane's dog, Fletcher, get on like Donkey Kong, so she loves going to the ranch.

This dinner is a small one. Delilah and Jeanine aren't there and Rachel and Vernalee have made spaghetti instead of a roast.

Everyone wants to talk to me about what happened but no one wants to mention Tim's name. So nothing is said. My grandpa just starts the dinner by saying grace and a prayer for me and my team and the souls lost on the glacier.

But despite the sorrow in my heart, that deep pain from losing someone I was supposed to lead, I look around the dinner table at my family and realize that it's okay for me to sit in silence. It's okay for me to mourn and mope and deal with all this shit. It's okay to not be the happy-go-lucky guy for once, the man who saves the day. I can be whoever I want and they'll still love me. They'll still be there.

Riley was like that too, I tell myself. *Maybe she hadn't said she loved you but she told you she wanted John, she wanted Maverick. She wanted all of you. She wanted that from the start.*

Fuck. Sometimes, just thinking about her, the shitty things I said, what I've done, I can barely get the air in my lungs.

"I have a bone to pick with you," my grandpa says after the meal is over. He has a pipe in his hand and is throwing on a plaid shawl over his shoulders. He gestures to the door outside. "Come on."

It's cold as hell. We've been getting dumped with snow all week, ever since the accident, but even so, I grab my coat and follow him out onto the porch where he sits down on the rocker and starts lighting up his pipe.

"Cold night," I say, rather feebly.

He fixes his sharp eyes on me, glowing from the light of the pipe. "Why don't you sit your ass down, big boy."

I raise my brows but do as he says.

"You should be used to the cold in your line of work," he goes on. "That's all you do all day, go out into the cold."

"In the winter. In the summer we go out into the heat."

"Summer is never as deadly as the winter," he notes.

"Tell that to Fox."

He shrugs. "You boys and your jobs. If only your mother could see you now, see what kind of crazy things you do, the way you stick your neck out for everyone. Shane is the only one with any kind of sense."

"Shane fights fucking grizzly bears. Or at least that's how he tells it."

"She would be proud of you, no doubt," he goes on. "But she would worry. We all worry about you, John."

"You shouldn't," I say, trying to brush it off.

"What happened to your friend, it could have happened to you."

"It *should* have happened to me," I tell him. "I should have taken that call. I'm the first to respond."

"Why didn't you?"

I sigh. Too much guilt and nowhere for it to go.

"Because. I was with Riley."

My grandpa doesn't seem the least bit surprised, continues to puff on his pipe. "The heartbreaker?" he asks.

"Yeah. But… I think I broke her heart first."

He fixes his eyes on me. "Why the hell did you do that?"

I shrug, helpless, hopeless. "I don't know. I…I was *with* her. You know. In her room. When we missed the call. So right there, I was already distracted. And so when he died…I blamed us."

He's glaring at me, big bushy white brows coming together like dueling caterpillars. "I hope in God's name that you didn't tell her that."

I swallow, look away at the snow and the darkness beyond.

"You weren't raised to be that dumb," he says bitterly after a few moments.

"I was angry," I explain. "And hurt and stupid. And I know it had nothing to do with her, it's just what happened. I have to live with the guilt of losing Tim."

"So live with it if you want to, you don't have to, but certainly leave her the hell out of it."

"You don't understand," I say, even though I'm not even sure I understand at this point. "I…," God, why is this so hard for me to admit? "I got scared. I almost lost her up there too. She went down the slope, right beside me. And I went down after her. We both almost died. But I saved her. I saved her

221

first. And then we went after Tim and Jace. By then it was too late."

"You regret saving her?"

"No," I say quickly, almost horrified at the question. "God, of course not. Of course not. But it made me realize how easy it is to lose someone you love. And I thought I'd already gone through that with mom. I don't want to go through it again."

My grandfather sighs and blows smoke rings into the air. They seem to crystalize before our eyes, turning into works of art before they float away.

"You saved her because you were the closest one to her," he says after a few beats. "You saved her because you could. You saved her because you love her. And there is no shame in saving the ones you love." He pauses. "There's only shame in throwing that love away because you're afraid. Man up and grow a pair, John boy."

I give him an incredulous look. "Did you just tell me to grow a pair of balls?"

"Well there's nothing to suggest that you have them at the moment." He shrugs.

I bite back a laugh. The first laugh I've felt in days. I almost feel guilty for it, but I decide to let that guilt pass for once. It's going to take time for me to deal with all of this but at least now I know, deep down, I will deal with it.

I just wish I had Riley by my side, to help me deal.

"Listen," he says softly and when I look at him, his eyes are shining. "The one thing we can't buy, can't find, can't...*rescue*, is time. Take it from me. Time is an unstoppable force, moving us all toward the same end. Sometimes that end happens for some sooner than it happens for others. Sometimes others are left behind. But we, as those who still experience time, we have a duty to those who have gone. We have to use every second we have. Life is too fucking short to feel guilty. We all feel it, and sometimes we deserve it, but acknowledge it and move on. Don't let it hold you back. Don't sacrifice the time you have left. It's a gift that so many don't have. Believe me. It's all going to be over before you know it."

My grandfather has been around the block. He's experienced love and loss. Birth and death. He's lived through floods and storms and fires. He's seen life move on around him. He knows what he's talking about and every time he gives me advice like this, I have no choice but to take it.

He's always right.

* * *

THE NEXT MORNING is Tim's funeral.

It's brutal.

There's no other way to describe it. There are no good funerals. People cry and grieve and make threats at God. It's about paying respect, but mostly it's about giving people a venue for their grief.

So I make use of it, as does everyone else. Tears are shed. The collective sorrow is enough to make the driest eyes give in.

But it's not until later, when the team has hiked up Mount Ferguson, that we find the peace amongst the sorrow.

We're all there, except for Jace, who is on leave, and Riley.

Tony said he texted her and she never answered back.

Neil said he did the same.

I want to throttle him for that but for once he's saying it with such sincerity that I manage to be grateful that he cares.

After all, I didn't even text her.

Because I'm a motherfucking coward.

But after we pay our respects to Tim on the mountain

and start hiking back down, I know that my team is still here and they need a leader and Riley is on that team.

So I text. I call.

No response. No answer.

And so I finally show up at her house, banging on the door in my old math teacher's backyard.

No answer. No one's home. Her blinds are up too and I'm peering through her window like a peeping Tom, hoping to get a glimpse of her. But there's no sign of her anywhere. In fact, her suite looks super clean and bare and I'm starting to fear that maybe she left. Maybe she had enough. Why not? Why the fuck would she stick around after everything that happened? I mean, I pretty much blamed a death on her.

I'm such a fucking asshole.

I don't want to go home though because I don't want to deal with Fox. Maybe some cuddle time on the couch with Chewie wouldn't be a bad thing but she'll lose interest after a few moments. I can only buy her love with treats.

I don't want to go to the office either. I'll likely be alone and it will remind me too much of all we lost.

So I head to the only other place I go.

The Beartrap Pub.

CHAPTER SEVENTEEN

RILEY

"WHAT ARE YOU DRINKING?" DEL ASKS ME. FROM THE TONE OF her voice, I know she's being extra gentle, extra cautious. I have to say I appreciate it, but for once I just want things to go back to normal. Whatever normal was.

"Beer," I tell her and then as she nods and grabs one out of the fridge, plunking a bottle of Kokanee in front of me.

You know, Kokanee, the beer with the glacier on the label, the glacier where I almost died, where an avalanche buried Tim.

I stare at it for a moment and Del quickly whisks it away, putting down a Corona instead. "Sorry," she says sheepishly.

I try and give her a smile. How is she to know that a certain beer is a trigger now?

I gulp back most of the Corona and try to shrug some feeling into my shoulders.

Today was another rough day. It was Tim's funeral.

I actually went. I know I wasn't invited or maybe that's not how it works with funerals, but I went. I stayed behind in the shadows, lurking between graves like they do in the movies. I didn't feel welcome, I'm not sure why, but I didn't want to miss it either.

But while I went to the funeral to pay my respects to the man we should have been able to save but couldn't, I stayed away from the memorial hike that the team was doing. Tony first texted me about it, then Neil. I just couldn't go. It wasn't just that Maverick would be there and it would be awkward (though that was it too), it was that they'd worked with Tim for a long time and I barely knew him. It felt like I'd be intruding on a moment that I didn't earn.

With all that going on, plus feeling antsy without having been to work, I decided the pub was the best course of action. Now I know there's a chance that Maverick could come in here and honestly, I don't know what I'd do, though I'll admit I put on a dress and tights and did my makeup, just in case, just so he sees what he's missing, what he's lost.

But more than that, I need the company, I need to be out of my house and around people. I need to feel a part of this world.

"So how are you doing?" Del asks with soft eyes. "I don't mean to pry, I'm just worried about you. Rachel too. I can't imagine what you've both gone through."

I swallow and nod, hating the mention of Maverick but I play along and save face, pretending that we're still a team of two.

"I heard about Maverick," she then says. "What he did to you."

I glance at her and sigh. "How?"

"Fox," she says with a shrug. "He lives with him and Fox tells me everything."

Not everything, I think to myself.

"Hey, I'm no expert on men," she says, leaning on her elbows across the bar. It's fairly early in here still but there's a few people around. She lowers her voice. "But I've never seen

Maverick have it bad for anyone before. He had it bad for you. I heard he turned into a pile of shit for a moment there, according to his brother at least, but I know Mav. I grew up with him. The man might be many things, but he has a good heart. He really does."

I sigh and finish the rest of the beer, waving the empty bottle at her. She gets me another. "I know," I say, shoulders slumping under the weight of it all. "I can see he does. I feel it. But I think I was just thinking too much of it. You know how that is, don't you? Falling for someone who might not fall for you the same way, let alone fall for you at all."

I'm hitting a raw nerve here. She almost flinches. She turns around so her hair covers her face. "Yeah," she says, trying to sound light but I know better.

I don't want to make this about Del though. She has her own issues to sort out and I have mine. I have so many issues, I have to fucking wade through them.

As much as I want to talk about Maverick with her, hell I'll talk about anything just to have some connection with someone, the bar starts getting busier and she's in high demand. I finish the beer and am about to switch to wine when I feel a presence behind me.

My heart lurches. I don't even have to turn around to see who it is. I know. My body knows. Every single hair on my arm, at the back of my neck, is standing straight up.

Maverick.

I try and swallow, to relax, to play it cool and maybe he'll move on but there's a reason he's standing right behind me as I'm sitting at the bar and it isn't to get a drink.

"Riley," he says, clearing his throat.

I take in a deep breath through my nose and meet Del's eyes for a moment as she slings someone a drink. Her hazel eyes say *good luck.*

I slowly look over my shoulder to see Maverick standing

right there and even though I knew it was him, just seeing him in the flesh makes me want to crumble to my knees.

It's too much. He's too much. And I'm still hurting.

Come on Riley, toughen the fuck up.

I paste on a blank expression, not quite friendly, not quite mad, not quite anything. "Hey," I tell him.

My eyes catch his. I don't want to see him clearly, don't want to pick up on every nuance of his expression. The way his dark, arched brows come together, the slant of his mouth, the wariness in his eyes. He's afraid of this encounter, probably afraid that I might throw the bowl of peanuts in his face.

But even though I'm hurt, I'm no longer angry. Because when it comes down to it, I understand why he did it. I don't like it but I understand.

I'm one step closer to being a real adult.

"Can I talk to you?" he asks.

"You're talking to me right now, aren't you?"

"In private," he says, eyes darting around the room. They focus on someone and I follow his gaze. By the jukebox I see Jace along with some guys I don't know.

"I guess he's doing better," I say. "Have you talked to him?"

"No more than I've talked to you," he says, his eyes coming back to mine. "And that's why I'm here. To talk. In person. To apologize."

"Right," I say, rolling my eyes. "Where will you even begin?"

"Look," he says, his voice sharp. Then he sighs and runs a hand down his face, looking up to the ceiling. "I'm sorry. I just want to talk to you, that's all. I know you have things you need to say to me too."

"Why say anything when I could just kick you right in the balls?"

He flinches. "I deserve that. If that's what you want to do."

I give him a wry look. "I'm kidding. Kind of. But believe

me, you don't want to open that can of worms tonight. Especially when I haven't moved onto my third drink."

Mav snaps his fingers at Delilah, his face grim, and surprisingly, Del responds and slides me another beer. It's not wine, but it will do. I take it, giving her a grateful smile, and then drink nearly the whole thing in one go.

He watches me intently. "Take all the time you need."

I wipe my mouth with the back of my hand. "That's not all because of you, by the way. Or Tim."

I don't even know why I said anything but Mav is now peering at me closer. "What happened?"

I chew on my lip for a moment, wondering how much to share. But he's the only one who knows about Levi. "I got an email from Levi's parents. He's dead. They took him off life support."

He raises his brows, swallowing hard. "Riley...I am so sorry."

I nod a few times, finish the rest of the beer. "It's okay. In a sick, selfish way, it's actually good. It gave me the closure I needed. It still hurts but...at least I know that I was okay to move on. Because that's what I've been trying to do and it's been working but in the back of my head I was always afraid of being disrespectful. You know, Levi and I were never together, not like you and I were, but my heart was there and when I started to move on...move on to *you*...I felt bad. Now...I have peace. So does his family. And I know he does too."

Silence falls between us for a moment, both of us taking it in.

"Come with me," Mav says, taking my arm and pulling me off the stool.

I'm just ornery enough to pull back and tell him to keep his hands off me, but honestly, I like that he's touching me. I like that he's here. As hard as this is and how angry I am, I need this. We need this.

He leads me around the bar and toward the restrooms, taking me into a room at the end that says *Employees Only*.

"Where are we?" I ask as we step inside the dark room. He flicks on the lights.

It's the storeroom. There's a desk, computer, crates and boxes full of beer and wine, a cot in the corner with a pillow and bedspread.

"Is this where Del lives?" I ask, horrified. It's like that episode of *Riverdale* when you find out Jughead lives in the theatre projection room.

"No," he says, giving me an odd look. "She lives with her mother. This is just for when people drink too much and there's no way for them to get home."

"How many times have you slept in here?" I ask, crossing my arms and looking around.

"Way too many to count."

I smile at that and then stop myself. I shouldn't be smiling at him at all, not after every horrible thing he did. I'm *mad* at him. I should never stop being mad, no matter what he has to say. It's just that it's so easy to talk to him, so easy to slip into what's comfortable.

God, I miss this.

I don't want to lose this.

And yet it's already gone.

I slip my mask on and attempt to harden my heart. "What do you want, Mav?"

He licks his lips and takes a step toward me. I take an instinctive step back, though I know I'll hit the wall if I keep going.

"I can't tell you how sorry I am," he says, his voice low. "And I know no amount of apologizing or groveling will make up for it. That I can't erase the words I said and I certainly can't erase the way they made you feel. But, please, Riley. I am so sorry. So fucking sorry."

I swallow. My words come out thick when I say, "Is that all?"

"No." He shakes his head, takes another step toward me. "It's not all. It will never be all. Riley, I put the blame on you and that wasn't fair. It was wrong and honestly, I never meant it at all. You had nothing to do with Tim's death. Neither did I. It was just the way it went. It was luck."

"There's no such thing as luck," I say quietly. "Only timing."

"Either way, I was wrong. You need to know I didn't mean any of it. They were all lies."

"Then why say it?"

"Because...fuck. I was scared. I was hurt, I was grieving and I know it's no excuse at all but I honestly just wanted to...I don't know."

"If you don't know..."

"I didn't know what to do," he says, grabbing my hand and holding it tight. I try to pull it out of his but I can't, his grip is too strong. "No, I'm not letting go of you, not now. Not until you know I didn't mean a word. I fucked up. I panicked and fucked up and I hurt you and I'll never ever forgive myself. You and I, we were never a mistake. *Ever.* Those were more lies. When it comes to us, I don't regret a fucking thing, you hear that? Not a damn thing."

"It's too late," I whisper to him, trying to avoid his eyes. The earnest way he's searching my face, pleading. He's not on his knees but he is on the inside. He means everything he's saying. Still... "It doesn't erase the pain."

"I know."

"Mav, you knew I was vulnerable. You knew what happened with Levi, you knew I was still traumatized over what happened and you threw it in my face!"

"I'm sorry!" he cries out.

"You can be sorry all you want but it doesn't change the fact that in the face of trauma, in the tragedies that you need to be able to face, you acted like nothing more than a stupid little boy, running away from all your problems and not giving a fuck who you hurt!"

"I gave a fuck!" he yells at me, his face red. "I gave a fuck about Tim, about everyone! And most of all I gave a fuck about you! I gave a fuck about you Riley, when I didn't even know if you'd care!"

"What?!" I screech. "You –"

I'm cut off.

His lips are mashed against mine, violent as a thunderstorm and I'm caught in the updraft. His body, big and strong and unforgiving, presses against me and I'm pushed backward until my back thuds against the wall.

His hands go around my waist, into my hair.

I have a second where I think I should push him back and my hand goes to his chest to do so but then his tongue is dancing with mine, lips ravenous, taking, taking, taking, and then I'm craving him like never before.

I can't quit this man even if I tried.

I kiss him back, my mouth growing hungrier by the moment. But there's no tenderness here. Not in our mouths, our teeth clacking against each other, not in our hands that pull and squeeze and grab. Not in the way I'm being pushed against the wall, my head hitting the back of it.

Not in the way that he reaches down with his big hands and pulls up the hem of my dress and then reaches between my legs and rips a hole in the crotch of my tights.

There is so much anger and pain here, from the both of us. I know this is a mistake, I know that this isn't fixing our problems but I just want to feel him, I want him to fuck me like crazy. I want to know I have him deep physically, even if it's not in his heart.

We're not even talking. There's nothing to be said. We speak with our bodies, rough and violent and desperate.

We're so desperate.

He hoists me up against the wall and I wrap my legs around his waist and he brings his cock out of his jeans. He slams into me, hurtling deep inside, with so much force, I cry out in pain.

But then the air returns to my lungs and I grab a hold of his hair and I pull until his eyes roll back and I'm biting his neck, his collarbone, making marks, trying to draw blood, trying to create permanence.

He responds by fucking me harder, rougher. I look in his eyes and there's nothing but rage and absolution. Rage for himself, for destroying what was, absolution for what he did to me. He's trying to fuck it out of his soul, to make atones for what he did. For the things that happened beyond his control.

I know this because I feel it too. I feel it in the way Tim died, how Jace was buried, even in knowing Levi is finally gone. I feel everything and he's making me feel everything, transferring the inner pain to the physical.

And yet this pain, unlike the others, is sweet.

It's sweet because I love this man.

I still love this fucking man.

Maverick's teeth are bared as he comes and he groans loudly, a whimper that builds and deepens and it's enough to set me off.

The orgasm is abrupt, a sneaker wave that grabs you when you're not looking, then pulls you under, pummeling you with force until you can't take it anymore.

Until you've drowned.

"Oh God!" I cry out. "Fuck!" My nails dig into his skin, a

last bout of violence, and we're both riding out the wave, this powerful spinning force that has him shuddering his release into me.

We breathe for what seems like ages.

In and out.

Our chests rising. Falling.

My fingers are pressed so hard into his meaty shoulders, they're actually cramping and hurt to straighten out.

He holds me against the wall, large hands around my tiny waist, and then pulls out. I'm gently lowered but I can hardly stand.

What the fuck just happened?

That wasn't makeup sex. I don't think we made up at all. That was just…

I'm speechless. My mind and body are reeling.

And Maverick is staying by my side. He reaches for the hem of my dress and gently pulls it down off my waist. Though he's still breathing hard, his forehead sweaty, he's not going anywhere.

"I didn't mean for that to happen," he says thickly. "Just so you know."

I nod. "I know."

"But I can't leave it at that. I just can't. Riley. Please…you don't have to forgive me. But tell me you'll at least try."

I take in a deep breath, trying to avoid his pleading eyes. They look so fucking blue right now, so beautiful. I'm watching his soul.

"I'm hurt," I admit, my voice breathless, soft.

"I know."

"But I know you're hurting too. We all are."

He tucks a strand of hair behind my ear. "It's going to hurt for a while. But I don't want to hurt alone. I don't want to do anything without you. Will you at least consider coming back to the team?"

I look at him in surprise. "I never left Mav. I just needed some time. But I'm not quitting. I don't want to run anymore."

His mouth quirks up into a soft smile. "You'll stay?"

"I will. You guys need me." I added that last bit as a joke but he's nodding.

"We all need you," he says. "And I need you most of all."

We stare at each other for a few moments as those words float around us like the season's first snowfall. Then I clear my throat. "I think I need another day, but then I'll come in. I'll be ready."

"Then I will be ready too."

He picks up my hand and kisses the back of it. "I'm going to go home now. Tomorrow we'll get our heads on straight. Then we'll get back to business. I can pick you up before work."

"Okay," I say softly.

And then I watch as he walks out of the room.

I have no idea what anything means anymore.

But at least I know I'm not giving up.

That counts for a lot of things.

Sometimes that counts for everything.

CHAPTER EIGHTEEN

MAVERICK

I KNOW THAT RILEY AND I DON'T EXACTLY KNOW WHERE WE stand with each other right now, but we know where we stand when it comes to work. It's our first full day back and though we probably shouldn't go in together, I want to be there for her every step of the way. Hell, maybe I just need her to be there for me.

I pick her up at 8:30 in the morning, a little later than normal, and then we drive toward the office. The snow is finally tapering off and the breeze has the smell of spring in it again. I think this time the spring is here to stay.

We don't talk much in the truck and it's awkward and that's okay.

I'm thinking about the sex from the other night.

I'm thinking about how good it was, how good she is.

I'm thinking about all she's gone through recently, not only with Tim, with Jace, but with Levi as well.

I'm thinking about her heart and how I had it in my hands and now I don't.

I'm thinking about how we might not get back what we had.

But, fuck, I'll try. Even if she doesn't want it, I will try.

We get to the building and I'm about to pull my truck up the driveway into my parking spot but it's blocked. There's a rental car in the spot instead.

"Weird," I say to Riley as we get out of the truck and head to the door.

I open it and we both stop the moment we step inside.

There's a man standing in the middle of the room, wearing an ill-fitting brown suit, his back to us.

He turns around and smiles. I don't trust the smile. It's not threatening, but it's false. It's the smile that belongs to someone that tries too hard.

He pushes up the glasses on his nose, still smiling, beady eyes. He's like a less likable Stephen Merchant.

"Are you John Nelson?" the guy asks.

"I am," I tell him, frowning.

"And this is Riley Clarke?" he goes on, smiling at her now.

"How can I help you?" I ask him.

"Take a seat," he says, gesturing to two chairs he's arranged in the middle of the room.

"Where is everyone?" Riley asks, not moving, and I just notice that the office is entirely empty except for the three of us.

"I sent them off for a bit," the man says. He gestures to the chairs, big smile. "Please."

I fold my arms across my chest. "I'm sorry, but who are you?"

"Oh, yes, of course," he says and he comes forward, handing me a business card he gets from the leather portfolio in his hands. I notice his hands shake just a bit.

I stare at it.

William Mapother
BC Emergency Management
Human Resources.

My eyes snap back to him while Riley takes the card from me.

Oh shit.

The boss.

"Sorry to have to do it this way," he says to us. "But I got the email yesterday and there wasn't enough time to set things up. Normally we like to give you a bit of a head's up when HR is in the area."

"What's going on?" Riley asks warily.

"Please sit," he says again. "I have some questions I need to ask the two of you."

Oh fuck.

I know what this is about.

They know.

The government knows.

Someone told.

We're getting *fired*.

I look at Riley and she's as wide-eyed as I am. It takes all my resolve to slip a stone mask on, to pretend that this is something I can handle and everything is going to be fine.

We take our seats.

"So, as you can see, my name is William Mapother and like you, I work for the government of British Columbia. In fact, we've been in email contact a lot, John," he says to me. I just stare at him. I don't remember the names of anyone above me, not really. It's all bureaucrats who couldn't be further removed from what we do. They, like this fucker here, all work in an office, playing it straight from the safety of their desks. We're the ones out in the wilderness, risking our lives and breaking the rules.

Though I know it's our rule-breaking that has brought him here.

He looks to Riley. "And Riley, I believe we had a phone interview together."

She also stares at him blankly.

He clears his throat again and prattles on. "And we think North Ridge Search and Rescue is doing a fairly good job. You've answered every call you've gotten. You've saved lives. And, until recently, you minimized your own risk." Ouch. "In fact, there's talk of extending your jurisdiction over towards Cranbrook and Fernie."

Right. Of course. Which means more work for us, less people, same pay. But this isn't about that right now.

"However," William says, clearing his throat. He stands in front of us, looking down at the pad of paper in his portfolio, as if he's written everything down and he's reading a speech. Actually, I think he is. "However, it has come to our attention that there have been some complications at this office between the personnel and that complication has started to affect the work."

"What's the complication?" I ask point blank.

He gives me a quick, unsure smile. "Well, uh, this is a little awkward for me to talk about. You'll have to forgive me, I haven't been on the job all that long. I'm sort of the boy they send out to do the dirty work, if you know what I mean." He smiles at us again. Both Riley and I stare right back. His smile disappears. "Right, so. I'm sure both of you are aware of the rules we have in place to prevent fraternization. That is correct?"

I grunt my response.

He clears his throat again. "So, as it happens, the rules are in place so that the work isn't jeopardized. In the past, we have found that team members who are involved in intimate relationships can struggle to get the work done. Often, and as it is, one may sacrifice their time or lives for said team member instead of a member of the public. It is not only a distraction from the life-saving efforts at hand, it puts effort down another avenue, one not conducive to being a reliable search and rescue member."

"It would help if you said it in plain English and not reading off a damn script," I tell him.

He blinks at me in shock. "Oh. Right." He lowers the portfolio. "The TL;DR version is, having sexual relations with another colleague is a fireable offense."

"TL;DR?" I repeat.

"Too long, didn't read," Riley translates for me.

I glance at her, amazed at how composed she's being.

I look back to William. "And…?" I coax him.

"We have reason to believe that you two have been having sexual relations with each other, and as such, one of you must be fired."

And there you have it, folks.

"What makes you think that?" Riley asks. "For the record, publicly, we are just friends and co-workers. He's my boss. We are not together in a relationship."

The way she says it is so final and yet it's true. After the other night at the bar, nothing between us really changed, it just opened up a small avenue of forgiveness.

"Were you involved in a sexual relationship at the time of Tim Lee's death?"

Don't answer that, I tell Riley with my eyes and then say to William, "You never answered her question. What makes you think we were in a so-called sexual relationship?" I hate having to lie about this, it feels wrong, but I will do it to save our asses. "Do you have proof?"

"I have someone's word," he says simply. "The same person who alerted us to the problem yesterday."

"Who is the someone?" I ask even though I know.

Riley knows.

Neil!

He ignores my question. "He saw it with his own eyes.

Always suspected it, apparently, anyway, but he was at some pub, the bear trap, the other night and happened upon you two in a, um, compromising manner."

Fuck.

Fuck, fuck, *fuck*.

He was there? I don't remember seeing him at all but he must have been. Maybe he was there with Jace. He must have followed us to the back room and then seen me nailing Riley against the wall.

I don't know what to say. It comes to my word against Neil's, like I always thought it would. I almost want to point out that he screwed Riley before I got the chance but that's not going to help anything and it's just going to embarrass her. If she's not embarrassed as hell already.

I sneak a glance at her. She's absolutely still except for her hands that she's wringing together. Her features are stiff but her eyes are filled with anticipation and fear. She knows what's coming.

"So now what?" I ask William.

"Uh, well now I have to fire you."

"Both of us?" I ask.

"No," he says. "We can't afford to lose yet *another* team member."

The words are a knife to my heart and he knows it.

"I'll just have to let go of Riley. Sorry, but you're the newest member and you're the most expendable."

Riley makes a small gasping sound.

"You can't fire her," I tell him. "Because I quit."

Riley gasps even louder. "Mav! What the hell are you doing?"

"Uh, you can't quit," William says. "This is your team. The team needs you. We can't afford to lose four members in one week."

"Four?"

"Tim and Jace are gone. Now it's Riley. You're staying, John."

"Jace?" I repeat.

He nods. "He doesn't want anything to do with this team anymore. You both scarred him for life. I imagine that's why he was the first to call and complain about you."

"Jace?" I repeat, getting to my feet. "Jace is the one who tattletaled?"

William takes a nervous step back. "It's hardly called being a tattletale when you're an adult. It's called informing. Being a narc, if you will. But yes, he's the one who saw you at the bar and reported you. I think you can understand why. He blames you for what happened to him, naturally." He pauses. "Who did you think it was?"

"Neil," Riley says getting to her feet. "We thought it was Micropenis Neil."

"Micropenis Neil?" William and I repeat in unison.

"Yeah," she says, skirting over the whole micropenis thing. "It was Jace?"

"Yes," he says. "Regardless of who reported it though, we have to take these allegations seriously. And since neither of you are denying it, I'm sorry Riley but you're going to have to be let go."

"If you fire her, I quit," I tell him again, crossing my arms.

"Maverick, don't," she hisses at me.

I ignore her, keep my gaze steady on William. "I'm serious. I quit. I no longer work for the search and rescue team."

William sighs, his eyes seeking the ceiling. "John. Come on. We appreciate the heroics here but this isn't worth throwing your career away. You've been working hard for this your whole life. You just got the promotion. Think about it for a second."

I shake my head. "You have no idea what you're talking about, do you? This woman," I point at her, "is worth throwing *everything* away for. You might think that this is just some fling, that she's disposable. She isn't. She's a force of nature. She's brave and funny and gorgeous and wonderful. She's the best thing that's ever happened to me, let alone this team, and I will do whatever it takes for her to see that, and that includes losing my job. So go fucking ahead, fire her, but I'm going with her."

William looks at me, looks at Riley.

I'm breathing hard after that whole speech and Riley is staring at me with tears in her eyes. Shocked. I'm shocked too, to be honest, but I meant every word of it.

"I fucking love you, Riley Clarke," I tell her.

Her mouth drops open.

"You do?" she manages to say, her voice a whisper.

"With every part of me," I say, grabbing her by the waist and pulling her against me. I kiss her, hard, her body softening in my hands, oblivious to our audience.

When we pull apart, she's smiling so sweetly, dazed. She cups my face with her hand, I rest my forehead against hers.

"And I love you," she says.

Fuck.

They can take everything away from me right now, it doesn't matter. I've got her.

I've got her.

She loves me.

"Oh boy," William says. We both look over to him. He's looking down, pinching the bridge of his nose beneath his glasses.

I grab Riley's hand in a show of solidarity.

She squeezes it back. "And if Maverick quits, I quit too."

William sighs, shoulders slumped for a moment. Then he straightens up. "Okay, you're both fired."

"What!?" we exclaim.

"I'm sorry," he says, throwing out his arms. "I have to do

something, that's why I was sent here. You're both gone. That's it. Gather up your things."

"What's going on?" comes Tony's voice.

The three of us look to the door where Tony and Neil are standing, box of donuts and coffees in hand.

"I've had to let the two of them go," William says.

"Actually, we both quit," I tell them.

"Why?" Neil asks.

"You all know the rules," William says, sounding exasperated. "I know this is the wild west out here in this province, but we have rules and limits in place to keep people safe and in line. These two have been romantically involved and as a result, they're jeopardizing the team."

"We should be the judge of that," Neil says. I look at him, brows raised. I have no idea how this is going to go. "I'm on the team. So is Tony. Mav can't be the leader one hundred per cent of the time. He is by default, I know that, but it's not humanly possible. If he misses a call, the rest of us take it and that's the way it works. Tim was a great man and more than capable of leading. I like to think each of us can. So he took the call. It's not Maverick's responsibility to take everything on. He leads but he's a team leader and we're the team."

I exchange a glance with Riley. I wonder if she's regretting calling him Micropenis Neil. I don't think so.

"It's not just because he's the leader," William says. "I don't care if their...relationship...doesn't affect the job or not. Those are the rules."

"The rules can go fuck themselves," Tony says, biting into an éclair.

"Agreed," Neil adds. "And if they quit, I quit too."

"Ditto," Tony says through a mouthful.

"You guys," I say, "please, you don't have to do this. In fact, *don't* do this."

"You're not our boss anymore," Neil says. "Sorry, Mav. We don't have a boss."

"You have got to be kidding me," William says, slapping his portfolio against his leg. "You can't all quit. There will be no one to run this place."

"That's your problem, pal," Tony says.

William looks at all of us, shaking his head. "You don't… you can't just. Who…do you know the amount of paperwork involved in this? I have to hire another five people and get them oriented. I mean, shit."

"Yeah, or," Riley says slowly, "you could just not fire any of us and go on your merry little way."

"We won't tell a soul," I say. "Just tell your bosses that you looked into the problem and there was no problem at all. Tell them that Jace left the team and there was no issue to correct."

"No one has to know," Neil says. "We can keep secrets here. Can you?"

He purses his lips and stares at us, eyes wide behind his glasses, trying to figure out the best course of action. I don't know how long this staring contest goes on for but it's enough for Tony to finish eating his éclair and move onto another donut.

"Fine," William eventually says and we all breathe out a collective sigh of relief. He looks at his watch. "If I leave now, I can make an earlier flight back to Victoria."

Everyone is too cautious to act.

"Are you serious?" I ask, stepping out and blocking him before reaching the door. "You're not going to file anything when you get back to your office?"

He looks up at me, shoves his glasses further up on his nose. I make him nervous. Good. He nearly tore this team apart. "I'll file a report and tell them it was a false alarm. As I said, I don't care whether this affects your job or not. But I do care about the paperwork and logistical hell that this would plunge me into if you all quit. I'm the only one in my department. It would take me months to sort this station out." He pauses and nods at me. "Sorry I made you publicly declare your love. It wasn't my intention."

I move out of the way, letting him pass and go out the door.

"You publicly declared your love?" Neil asks wryly.

I sigh, running my hands down my face. "I just told the truth. We don't have to make a big deal about it."

"But it is a big deal," Riley says, coming over to me. She leans against me, arm around my waist, and grins up at Tony and Neil. "You have my permission to never let him live it down."

"You little minx," I tell her.

But I'm laughing.

Because life, for all its peaks and valleys, just got very, very good.

CHAPTER NINETEEN

RILEY

"A‍RE YOU READY?"

I look over at Maverick and shake my head. I know in this instance I'm supposed to nod and put on the brave face and say, yes, I'm ready.

But I'm not.

I take in a deep breath and look at the others.

I'm standing beside Maverick. Tony and Neil are on the other side of the river, waiting with the ropes. Sam is behind us. Hot pink pants ex-Army Sam, who is unfortunately dressed in a boring navy-blue rescue suit like the rest of us. He's the newest member of our team, no longer a volunteer.

It's April now and winter is officially over. The snow at lower elevations has melted and as a result, all the rivers are packed to the brim and overflowing.

We're situated along the Queen's River, the one that skirts along North Ridge, the one goes past Ravenswood Ranch, the one that Maverick's mother died in. We're at the end of it where the lake starts emptying out into it, a popular spot for swimmers and fisherman and tourists in the summer.

It's also a popular spot to get swept away.

And that's why we're here.

We're doing training for the spring and for the coming months, not just now when the river is swollen and raging brown from all the water run-off and melted snowpack, but in the summer when more lives will be at risk. When people put their guard down.

As part of North Ridge's Search and Rescue, you never ever stop training and now our team is really stepping it up. We're always on.

It's not that it was never run as a tight ship. Maverick has done a great job and continues to do so. But after Tim's death and Jace leaving, we all decided to put in the extra time and be extra vigilant. Because Neil was actually right. We're all in this together and we should all be at the same caliber as Maverick. Just because he's the official boss and leader, that doesn't mean he's much more than the man making the decisions. And lately, many of those decisions have been passed on to us.

It's nice, feeling like you're not just a member but part of a family and one that shares responsibilities, who decides our fate together.

So when we had a meeting last week and I told everyone that I wasn't feeling confident with my river rescue skills, we made plans to come out here and get the experience. Not just for me, but for everyone.

We're learning to rescue ourselves.

And now, here, it's my turn to go into the water. Neil just did it and so I should be able to as well. Drowning isn't something I've really thought about, especially since so much of the work I've done in the past was winter only, but now that I'm staring at the river, I have no idea how I'm going to get across alive.

"You can do it," Maverick says, his hand on my shoulder. "Trust me. Trust yourself. Trust all of us."

I nod, shake out my arms, trying to displace the nerves. "Okay."

I pick up the rope and with one hand on it, head into the water. There's a carabiner clipped from my suit's harness to the rope, so just in case I let go and the river attempts to take me away, I'm not going anywhere. It's really all about learning to go into the water, to feel the rocks beneath, read the water and adjust to it.

I take my time, though I know in a real rescue, I would be hurrying. The suits we are wearing are like thick wetsuits of Gore-Tex and we resemble a hazmat team, but even so, the water is so cold it bites into me. My lungs are airless. Everything hurts.

"You can do it," Tony calls from the other side. "Easy does it."

But the moment he says that, the river bed slopes and my feet start to slip and the water is too strong and it knocks me down. I yell and fall into the water, my hands going up, trying to grab the rope that is straining, yanking at my waist.

"Hold on," I hear someone yell but it's hard to keep my head above water. The rope is twisting and spinning every which way and it's hard to know what direction I'm facing, it's like being in an ice-cold washing machine.

Focus, I tell myself. *Don't panic. Focus. You'll be fine. Find your feet, find which way is up. Conserve your energy, get upright, get moving.*

I say these things, trying to calm myself down. It takes some time but my body starts to respond. My head and shoulders are above the water now, I'm gasping for air, I have one hand wrapped around the line and my feet are kicking behind me, just trying to keep my body in a stable position.

And then Maverick is beside me.

Rooted like a tree.

The river flows around *him*.

He's grabbing me just under the shoulders as we are taught to do and he slowly but surely takes me to a part of the river where the current isn't raging and drags me out. I try and help, of course, kicking while being as pliable as possible, but he's really doing all the work.

Now we're up on the other river bank and I'm on my knees in mud and damp grass, trying to breathe.

"You did good, kid," Mav says, kneeling beside me, one hand on my back.

I wheeze and look up at him, shivers rolling through my body. "I didn't do good. You call that good? I was practically drowning and you waltzed in there and fished me out like a bear with a salmon."

He chuckles. His smile lights up his face. He's at his most beautiful when he's outside and there are trees and mountains behind him and natural light. The sky, the earth. He's at home here in the elements. And I'm at home with him.

"Well at least Mav is up to date with his skills," Neil says to me with a smirk. I had just watched him cross the river with no problem, so I can't even say anything to shoot him down.

Then we watch as Sam goes across. Like me, he's a bit rusty, and the water sweeps him away too. But he has a lot more line, about a hundred feet's worth, so he goes where the water takes him, right into a whirlpool that's building among some fallen trees and reeds.

"Well, who wants to rescue Sam?" Mav asks us.

I shake my head, carefully getting to my feet with his help. "I think I need to play victim for today."

Tony and Neil exchange looks.

"I just got warm again," Tony says by way of explanation.

Neil sighs. "Fine."

"A little help here!" Sam yells at us from the river as he spins around and around. "I'm going to start vomiting soon."

"I'm coming!" Neil says, clipping himself onto the line and going back into the water.

"You'll get better," Mav says to me, taking my hand and squeezing it.

"I hope so," I tell him. "I have a good teacher."

I'm so tempted to kiss him right now, to do more than just hold his hand. But we've made an agreement and one that I'm sure William Mapother at HR approves of, even though we haven't heard much from him after all that.

It's no secret to the team, to the town, to anyone, that Mav and I are in a serious relationship with each other. But we also know that when it comes to the job, to the work, we're strictly professional. At North Ridge SAR, we are team members and co-workers and that's it.

Outside of work, we're everything to each other.

When we're all done at the river and finished with work for the day, the two of us head back to Maverick's place to dry off and get warm by the fire. I've been spending most of my time off with him here and Fox has gotten so used to it, he usually treats us like a piece of furniture and vice versa.

"What do you want to do for dinner?" I ask Mav after we come back from walking Chewie.

"It's a surprise," he says, smiling again. I swear all we do around each other is smile like a bunch of fools in love. Which we are. The only time we're not smiling is when we're fucking each other and that's a different kind of joy all together.

"A surprise? One of Maverick's famous dishes?"

I've had the stew, pancakes, and there's even been a mac and cheese dish so far. But I'm game for anything new.

"Kind of," he says. "We have to wait until dark though."

With spring here in full bloom, it doesn't get dark until seven p.m. now, so we sit around the house, talking with Fox and playing with Chewie until then.

"Dress warm," Mav tells me and I watch as he brings out a picnic basket from the kitchen.

"We're having a picnic?" I ask. It's been a dry, clear day but it's not all that warm either, especially at night. There's still snow and late skiing further up on the slopes.

"Maverick's famous picnic," he says, wiggling his brows. "Don't worry, baby, I'm bringing the stew too."

So I dress warm, bring some thick blankets to sit on and we get in his truck. We head all the way to the trailhead at Chairman's Peak and then use our headlamps to hike about twenty minutes up to one of the lookouts.

He quickly sets up the area, placing the blankets on a gentle slope with an unobstructed view of the town far below, then the river and the mountains on the other side. It's a clear night and the moon casts only a faint glow. The sky is an explosion of stars.

He spoons out some stew from a container, still warm and we settle down beside each other, eating and drinking wine and taking in the dark sky.

It's beyond romantic. Just us and the elements. Just us and the world.

"Hey," he says, when we've just finished eating and he's putting our bowls back inside the picnic basket. "I have a question to ask you."

But then he trails off. The most awestruck expression comes across his face, his focus beyond me, to the north.

I turn around and look to see what's stolen his attention.

I gasp loudly.

The entire sky is awash with northern lights.

I've never seen them before.

It's the most spectacular, humbling and mind-blowing sight I've ever seen.

Washes of electric green, white, even purple, glowing and moving from the tips of the mountains, stretching up in waves toward the top of the night sky. They move like flames, dancing in a supernatural element, a light show that seems wholly unreal.

I'm entranced. I feel their glow inside me, buoyant.

Magical.

"John," I whisper to him, grabbing his hand. At this altitude, in this cold air, I feel like I might float off into space and he's the only thing grounding me. "Did you know this would happen?"

"I had hoped," he whispers because it feels like anything loud might scare the lights away. "But I had no idea it would be like this."

We lapse into silence, holding onto each other, our eyes glued to the auroras as they stretch across the sky, this land, this place that has my heart.

I don't know how long we sit here in the darkness, watching them. Hours, maybe. I don't feel cold, I only feel love.

Then the lights fade away like a symphony, growing fainter and fainter until it's hard to believe they were ever there to begin with.

"That was amazing," I whisper, turning to face him, afraid to break the spell.

"Super, Natural British Columbia," he says, repeating the province's logo. He runs his fingers into my hair. "Super, Natural Riley Clarke. The way those lights made you feel, like you believed in magic again? That's how you make me feel. Every damn day."

I blink at him, feeling tears come to my eyes. I swear to God I've never been a crier but this man has a way of getting deep inside me, flattening my defenses. With him, I have none. With him, I feel everything, good and bad. The peace, the chaos. I relish it all.

"Riley," he says, his hand at the back of my neck. He stares deep into my eyes with such intensity I feel stripped bare, like he's seeing my soul and I can see his. "I know we haven't known each other that long in the grand scheme of things but I love you more than I can say…will you…will you live with me?"

I balk, break into a smile. "What? Really?"

"Yeah. Really. Not at the chalet, not with Fox. I mean, we'll buy our own place. We'll make a home together."

Every cell in my body feels like magic now, like those lights just keep on dancing, out of the sky and into my veins. I can't believe it. But something has never felt so right.

"Of course I will," I tell him, my hand at his cheek, his stubble rough against my palm. "I would love to live with you. Yes, absolutely." I kiss him. "Yes, yes, yes!"

"Unreal," he says back to me, smiling against my mouth. "But you're real, aren't you? And you're mine."

"Always," I tell him, holding him tight.

We stay like that in an embrace, our bodies entwined, our chests rising and falling as one. Shooting stars fall above our heads, satellites spin, the trees rustle with the night breeze. Super, Natural *us*.

"So when do you want to start house hunting?" I ask after a bit.

"Tomorrow if you like," he says. Then he sighs dramatically.

"What?"

He rubs at his face. "Now I owe Fox five hundred dollars."

EPILOGUE

MAVERICK

JULY

"Pay up."

I've barely stepped onto the porch, about to head into the ranch house for dinner, Riley right behind me, when Fox pulls me to the side.

I smile. "I don't know what you're talking about."

He glares at me. "You know what I'm talking about. Five hundred dollars, brother."

Riley manages to sneak her way in between us, the mediator. "Hey guys, let's discuss money matters after dinner. It's rude."

He laughs. "Like you suddenly care about being rude."

"Hey," I snap, thudding my fist into his chest which brings out a growl from him. "Be nice to the lady."

Now Riley laughs. "Oh, come on John. We both know I'm not a lady and he has a point about the rude thing. I guess it's been pretty rude the way I've been living at your house for the last while, plus the number of rude positions Fox has caught us in. When you think about it, he should be paying *us* for the sheer relief that we're finally out of his house."

I look at Fox, grinning.

He shakes his head. "Not buying it. We had a bet. You officially moved out and into your new house last week. Time to cough it up. I would have done the same for you."

I frown, pretending to think that over. "I don't know, man. I just don't know about that."

"What are you boys doing?" Grandpa appears in the door, looking over at us. "And you, dear," he adds when he sees Riley.

"Don't worry Grandpa Dick," she says with a big breezy smile. "I have them under control."

He grumbles, narrowing his eyes at us in disbelief. "Just know you can call for backup if needed, sweetheart," he says to her. He jerks his head at the house. "Will you boys come in or what? We'd all like to eat before either of you are called out for a job."

He has a point. Guilt-tripping always works. We mumble apologies and then the three of us follow him into the house.

It's the first week of July and everyone has been busy. Riley and I just moved into a two-bedroom cottage up the street from Fox. The house is small and old but we've got a lot of plans for it, which means our lives going forward will be SAR and RH—that stands for Renovation Hell. But we don't mind because it's ours and so far, the season has been pretty easy.

For us, anyway. We've had some people to rescue from the river and Riley did great. She pulled out one of them all on her own with the kind of confidence and poise that I don't know I'll ever have. Other times we've rescued people who got lost while hiking. Sometimes dementia patients disappear into the woods too. All seasons of the year, we're there to help.

But it's Fox that's in high demand. This is when I no longer think of him as an older brother and I start thinking of him as a hot shot, a smoke jumper who goes out into the kind of fires that you see wild animals fleeing at full speed. He does the impossible and this is the season where he's always called out on the line.

Today, though, he's at home. There have been some fires up north but in general it's holding steady. We all know that in a few weeks, when the rains have gone for good and the winds pick up, that's when his hell will start. Until then, he's with us.

We go inside and have a drink with everyone around the table and then Vernalee brings out the roast.

Rachel and Shane are getting married in August and so Rachel's mind has been elsewhere, preparing for the wedding. Vernalee doesn't mind picking up the reins though. She's still doing the dinners and helping them out with the Air B&B they run on the property.

Riley and Del are excited for the wedding too – they get to be bridesmaids. I can't wait to see Riley all dolled up in a formal gown, she's going to blow my fucking mind. And maybe something else.

"I'm going to make a toast," my grandfather says, easing himself up on his feet and holding out his wine glass, a knife poised to ring against it.

We all raise our glasses. Riley's free hand goes under the table and squeezes my knee. I love how she does this when we're out and about together. It's her way of telling me she's here and she's mine. Because she is. I hope she'll be mine forever.

"Here's to the hot shots," Grandpa says, looking at Fox. He looks to Shane and Rachel. "Here's to the bride and groom to be." He looks to Vernalee and my father. "Here's to those finding love at any age." Then he looks at me and Riley. "And here's to these lovebirds, these heartbreakers, North Ridge's finest, and only, search and rescue team. If you're ever lost, may you be found by them."

"Here here," we all say together, only raising our glasses because it's a large table.

But then someone goes that extra mile. Let's call her Riley. And she decides to stand up and reach across the table to clink her glass with grandpa. Which means now all of us have to do the same or we'll look like a family of chumps.

With a collective groan, the Nelson family gets up and follows her lead, everyone stretching long across the table to reach each other.

The sound of glass against glass chimes through the air.

So does laughter.

So does love.

THE END

THANK YOU FOR READING!

You can get HOT SHOT - the last book in the North Ridge Series - about Fox and Delilah NOW. Just CLICK HERE. Also keep reading for a excerpt from Hot Shot!

Want more information about the series, the author, and upcoming books? You can by:

- Signing up for my newsletter

- Joining my Facebook group (where you often have the chance to order signed books, get exclusives, win tons of books and prizes, plus meet a lot of cool readers and connect with me!):

- Follow me on Instagram (I post daily!)

- Tweet me at @metalblonde

ACKNOWLEDGMENTS

I have to admit, sometimes I don't put acknowledgements in my book. Usually because I'm on such a tight deadline that by the time I type *the end*, I can't physically type another word. Or it's because I've written so many books that it begins to feel redundant, thanking the same people over and over again and saying the same old stuff.

But you know what? People deserve to be thanked and all books deserve a little wrap-up at the end. And I'm writing this half-way through the book. Hey, it's nice to have a little break.

Maverick was an interesting book for me. I'd come up with the concept over a year ago and always planned for Maverick to be the first book in the North Ridge series. But things happened beyond my control and I decided to put Wild Card up first.

Wild Card was a hard book for me. It really was. Overly emotional stories and I just aren't working this year (hello 2017!) and I really wanted to do Shane and Rachel's story justice. I wanted to make it feel real, I wanted to have a level of respect for that couple and all that they had gone through. I ended up rewriting Wild Card three times, which rarely happens with me. THANKFULLY, when I say rewrite, I mean I just rewrote the plot. That's another plus for those like me who outline their novels, I only had to rejiggle the outline and not the actual book!

But while Wild Card and conjuring up all that angst and emotion was a challenge for me as a writer, Maverick was the opposite. Some books come easy, some books come hard (ha!), and Maverick was easy as pie from the start. Light and fluffy and sexy—it's a trifecta I'm really feeling at the moment.

Maverick, as some of you may know, was actually pushed back twice. Sorry about that. But it had nothing to do with what I was actually writing, more to do with poor planning on my behalf. I was traveling—either road-tripping down the West Coast in my egg (trailer) or traipsing through southern France and then Seattle—for most of the book. Sometimes I can travel and write with no problem (see The Play and the fact that I wrote half that monster in a van in New Zealand). Sometimes I just want to focus on my life, on the traveling, on my husband, on my friends, and not in the make-believe world of the book. It just depends.

And then the world started to go to shit (I'm hoping you're not reading this from a bunker), and that threw a wrench into my plans too. So with Maverick it was, the World 1, Karina 0.

But hey. Everything happens for a reason. I've had a year to think about this book, I'd been dwelling on it and plotting it for months, so by the time I got back home and life stabilized itself for a bit, I was ready. I was more than ready.

I won't tell you how fast I was able to write Maverick because I think that takes away some of the magic, but it was the fastest I've ever written a book. And there wasn't a moment that I was like, "Oh shit, is this even humanly possible? How can I write so much in such a short amount of time?" I didn't even think that. I just knew I would get it done. I just had this peace that told me I was going to be fine. I would do it and there was no use worrying about it. I have to tell you, that confidence doesn't happen with every book. But it happened with this one.

Of course, actually getting words down quickly doesn't mean much if the book is complete shit. And while I might be halfway down right now, I can tell you, this book isn't shit. I mean, you may think so and that's cool, but me? I LOVE IT. I love writing Maverick and Riley. They have chemistry in spades and I just want to hang out with them, look at them. Especially when I see my muses Chris Pine/Evans (with beard!) as Mav and Ireland Basinger Baldwin as Riley. Who doesn't love to picture hot people fucking? Just me?

Anyway, this book came easily to me and even caught me by surprise. I've never really written a gorgeous, sex-positive, straight-forward, man-hungry heroine like Riley before (maybe Kayla in The Play) and I had a lot of fun watching Mav trying to hold himself back from her. I have to admit, when your characters feel real, their actions will surprise you and I had no idea that Mav wouldn't give into her right away (talk about blue balls) but I'm glad he held off. It made their coupling that much more special.

So that's the story about Maverick. I had a great time writing it and I hope it provided a good, fun and sexy escape for you. And hey, that cabin scene was totally worth it, right?

Now time for the thanking. This time I have a huge list of people. How fun!

Okay, so I was in France for most of this book, so I have to thank all the authors and pals who were there. Some of you, like Melanie Harlow or Jay Crownover and Ali Hymer, were great at letting me shoot the shit about the book (mainly, do I push back the release again?!), others just influenced me by just being there and being awesome. Like KA Tucker & Anna Todd (and her bear). Colleen Hoover, Brittany Cherry, Monica James, CLo (Christina Lauren), Vi Keeland, Sarina Bowen, RK Lilley, Chris Lilley, Lexi Ryan, Alessandra Torre, Audrey Carlan, Geneva Lee, Pam Godwin and Tijan.

Then came time for the Write or Die retreat in Seattle and even though I was there to give a presentation on outlining and how I use screenwriting to plot my books, I ended up learning so much from all the authors, aspiring or not. So thank you to Rachel Hollis, SL Jennings, Dina Silver, Jen Sterling, Willow Aster, Kim Lorraine, my PR guru Jen Watson, Christine Estevez. And of course, Tarryn Fisher.

Thank you to Nina Decker for her beta skills (she's good, you guys), Mary Ruth for her wonderful teasers, Sandra for being an ear, Laura Helseth and Roxane Leblanc for quick, super-last-minute editing. Nina Grinstead for being on the ball, making me promote this dang book and keeping my life in order.

Last but never least, my husband Scott Mackenzie, who is in this writing journey with me every step of the way. And for trying to take me seriously while I poked my head in the bathroom as he was brushing his teeth and excitedly described in detail the "ropes" sex scene with Mav & Riley, whilst wearing a face mask (Ole Henriksen Hygge Hyrdaclay Detox Mask, for those wondering) and a crazy expression on my face. You're always able to see beneath the crazy and I thank you for that!

Oh and thank you Depeche Mode. As a long-time fan, your music has always influenced my writing and this time, Delta Machine and Spirit became the fuel for this book. If you can listen to "Cover Me" during the last chapter, please do so.

PS just a reminder that Hot Shot (previously titled Loose Cannon), Fox and Del's story, will be releasing in January and there should be preorder links out at all retailers by the time you read this.

PREVIEW OF HOT SHOT

CHAPTER ONE

Delilah

Love is wildfire.

I don't care what the Hallmark cards say, I don't care how many romance novels you read or the stories you hear about true love. I don't care if you watch your friends fall headfirst into love only to be lifted up by the same undertow that dragged them under. I don't care if love is all we need, love is what will save us, love will keep us alive.

In my book, love is a devastating force of nature, a raw, primal element that threatens all who dare to indulge in its flames. It's a wildfire that spreads and consumes until all that's left is a charred heart surrounded by ash and bone. There's no taming it, no fighting it back. No matter what you do, love will burn you to the ground.

Some days I'm okay. Some days even his smile will fill my heart with an immeasurable joy, like I'm being flooded with a warmth I don't know how to turn off. Some days I stand before him and I think "Do you see me now? Do you see me at all?"

And some days there isn't any wondering.

Some days I know the answer.

Today is one of those days.

The answer is no.

My name is Delilah Gordon, and all my life I have been head over heels in love with the boy next door, Fox Nelson.

And all my life I have been acutely aware that he is not in love with me.

"So," I say, trying to sound nonchalant as I wipe my hands on my jeans. "Have you seen Fox's new girlfriend?"

A strained hush falls over Riley and Rachel, my two best friends, and I steal a glance at them over my shoulder. They're exchanging a look, not sure what they're supposed to say. The only reason I'm even bringing it up is that for the last hour of our horseback ride through Ravenswood Ranch, I can tell it's been on the tip of their tongues in terms of town gossip and they've been trying hard to not bring it up.

Better to bite the bullet. Or at least try to.

"What?" I ask them when they haven't said anything. "I know you've seen her."

The horse I've been riding, Sugar, raises her head from the patch of dried grass she's munching on and gives me a dirty look. We've ended up by the shores of Willow Lake, the morning sun beating down on us, the first chance the three of us have had to hang out since the start of July. With Rachel's wedding coming up in a few weeks and Riley working for North Ridge Search and Rescue, they've been busy.

Me, I've just be running the The Bear Trap Pub. Same old, same old.

Riley gives me a bright, albeit cautious smile as she gets to her feet where she's been sitting on a log with Rachel, their horses tethered around the end. "She seems nice enough," Riley says casually, tucking her blonde hair behind her ear. "I've only met her yesterday. Mav and I dropped by Fox's and she was over…" she trails off and looks away.

I ignore the pang in my heart and my mind refuses to go there. I've trained it so well.

"I haven't seen her," Rachel says quietly, staring up at us with her haunting blue eyes. "I thought maybe Fox would have brought her by The Bear Trap by now."

"Well they've only been going out a few weeks," Riley points out. "And during two of those weeks, he was off fighting the fires. I'm sure it's nothing serious."

They're both looking at me again, with the pity in their eyes I've grown to expect.

I've never told them—or anyone—that I love Fox, that I've always been in love with my friend. But I think they know. I think everyone knows except for Fox, and thank god for that.

The last thing I need is for twenty-seven years of friendship to go down the drain. Fox thinks of me as his little sister, always has. That's never going to change.

In fact, I remember being twelve years old and at a friend's party. While their parents were upstairs watching TV, we were all downstairs in the basement and playing spin the bottle. There were about ten of us and Fox got to spin the bottle before I did.

That entire time I watched the Coke bottle make the rounds, past my friends and classmates, all I could pray for was *please, please, please let it land on me.* Let it be me. Let Fox be my first kiss.

And...it did.

The bottle stopped right in front of me, pointing directly at me like a big flashing arrow.

I couldn't even play it cool. I was already grinning like a dumb idiot.

Fox, on the other hand, looked immensely bothered by this. So much so that without even a glance at me, he reached over and spun it around again before getting to his feet and saying, "This is stupid."

Everyone rolled their eyes but didn't say anything because it was a miracle that Fox agreed to play spin the bottle anyway. He was even more quiet, moody and irritable back then than he is now.

So Fox walked away, and I was left sitting there with my legs tucked under me, feeling the weight of the world crush my chest. I laughed it off, of course, telling everyone it would have been so gross because he was like a brother.

But even though I'd known Fox since I was six years old, he was never that to me. His brothers Shane and Maverick (real name John) were but Fox had carved a fathomless place in my heart from the very beginning.

Loving Fox is all I've ever known.

"As long as he's happy," I eventually say to them. I force another smile and then look up at the sun. "It's getting hot, maybe we should head back."

Rachel gives me a small nod while I can tell Riley is fighting hard not to roll her eyes. Riley only moved to our small town of North Ridge earlier this year, and while she quickly became part of our girl gang (especially since moving in with her boyfriend Maverick), she has a hard time keeping her mouth shut about some things. Mainly, Fox's and my relationship, which she says is rife with unresolved sexual tension or UST as she often says ("There was so much UST at the bar last night, you should just bang him and get it over with").

Rachel, on the other hand, is quieter and has been through so much in her life and with Shane, that she understands. She was there with me and Fox, growing up right alongside us.

Because of that, you'd think I would have admitted to her at some point how I feel about him, but I can't bring myself to do it. I guess I'm hoping that the feelings will go away. They have to, right? Either that or I'll continue to live with it and deal with it. And by dealing with it, I mean pretending it doesn't exist. Feelings with a capital F.

It's not like I've pined away for him locked in my room either. I've dated. I've tried to fall in love. I was even engaged to a lovely man for a while, Robert, another former friend from high school. But as much as I loved Robert, I knew that marrying him would be a huge mistake and completely unfair to him. For as good, calm, kind, and patient as he was, he wasn't enough for me. The world is too big, this life too short, to want anything less than magic with someone.

Even though it was my idea to head back to the ranch, I lag behind, with Riley and Rachel ahead of me. When Sugar tries to eat the dry grass, I don't rip her head up and let her have a few mouthfuls instead. If Shane could see me now, or his father Hank, they'd give me a talking-to about spoiling the horse.

It's a gorgeous day and I take a moment to tilt my head back to the wide blue sky. Summer is in full swing, which in North Ridge is both a beautiful and dangerous time. Each year the summers get drier and hotter, increasing the risk of forest fires. Even though the town is located in the mid-south of British Columbia, near the Washington and Idaho border, the weather can be shockingly hot compared to the rest of Canada.

As such, the fire season gets increasingly longer and more intense, which means Fox's life is more and more in danger. He works from May to October as a wildland firefighter or "hot shot," one of those crazy and beautifully brave people who head out to be smack in the middle of raging forest fires. He's getting busier and busier, the job getting riskier and riskier. I try not to worry—he's been doing this for so long, I should be used to it—but I can't help it.

I've barely seen him lately either. Usually he's gone for at least two weeks at a time with a week off here and there and during those days and weeks off, we'll be hanging out, maybe at the ranch, often at the bar. But not since he last got back. He hasn't even texted me, which is odd.

I have a feeling it has something to do with his girlfriend.

God, I can barely stomach the word.

When we get back to the ranch, my ponytail sticking to the back of my neck, the horses coated with a sheen of sweat, we get their tack off their backs and take turns hosing them down outside the barn before we turn them loose.

Though I grew up on the ranch and have been riding since I was seven years old, and Rachel is now a bonafide cowgirl after getting engaged to Shane, Riley is still getting used to the whole horseback riding thing. The horse she rode, Apple Jack, is about as sweet and docile as can be and yet she's throwing her ears back and giving Riley side-eye (though "side-eye" is pretty much the only eye horses can give) until somehow Riley ends up being more soaked from the hose than the horse is.

"Of course Riley manages to turn this into a wet T-shirt competition," Shane's voice comes from behind us.

We look to the barn to see him sauntering over, a faint flush of red on his tanned cheeks. The thing about Riley is that, yes, she does happen to be wearing a very wet white T-shirt right now, but she's also a megababe with her long limbs, big boobs, long blonde hair and blue bedroom eyes. Every guy that gets within twenty feet of her immediately starts drooling.

Shane being Shane though, tries his hardest to hide it, especially around Rachel. Rachel is equally as beautiful, the Veronica to Riley's Betty, and rarely has any insecurities with Shane. I mean, the man is so hopelessly in love and devoted to her, like he's been his whole life. If I didn't adore the two of them like family, I'm pretty sure I'd be lime green with jealousy.

Riley rolls her eyes. "Good thing Mav isn't here."

"Mav?" Shane asks with a grin, tugging on the brim of his cowboy cap. "He's nothing but a pussy cat. He working today?"

She sighs and wrings out the end of her shirt while giving Apple Jack a dirty look. "If I'm here, he's working. If he's here, I'm working. I'm telling you, having the same job sometimes fucking sucks."

"Yeah but you get to see each other all the time otherwise," I remind her. "You should try my job. I just see the same damn drunks day in and day out."

"You mean us," Shane says, walking over to Rachel and

pulling her into a hug, placing a quick kiss on the top of her head.

"Do I?" I say wryly. "Because lately it's just been me, Old Timer Joe and his denture-less gal pal, my high school gym teacher who nurses his beer and sits alone in the corner crying, and a bunch of college freshmen from the city who have claimed North Ridge as some sort of craft beer haven and mountain biking nirvana. Never mind the fact that I don't serve craft beer."

"They're just trying to get in your pants," Riley says. "Delilah Does the Mountain Biking Team does have a nice ring to it."

"My point is, I barely see any of you guys anymore. The Bear Trap feels so empty without you there."

Shane and Rachel exchange a glance. "I guess we have just been so caught up with the wedding," Rachel says.

"We'll come by tonight for a drink," Shane decides. "Promise."

"I'll see if Maverick can put someone else on call," Riley offers. "Other than me." She pauses, a faux-innocent look coming across her big eyes. "Maybe he can convince Fox to come too."

With his girlfriend? I finish in my head just as Shane and Rachel look at me with those pitying eyes again.

I plaster on a smile that feels shaky at the corners. "Great."

* * *

The half hour or so before I open the bar is definitely my favorite time of the day. It's just me and the bar, no drunk customers, no eyeing the tip jar and wishing for more, no getting trapped for hours talking to the same annoying person who won't get the hint.

It's a quiet time too. I don't play any music—lord knows I

get enough of that with the jukebox later—I just enjoy the stillness and the silence, save for the small hum from the refrigerator. I've worked as a bartender here since I was twenty-years old, managed to save up and buy it from the old owner, Dwight, a few years ago and it's been mine ever since. Even though it's not the nicest bar in town or the hippest, it's the most authentic. It feels like a second-home to me and I take a great amount of pride in it.

As part of my pre-opening ritual, I polish all the wood on the booths and wipe down the chairs, bar stools, and tables. I disinfect the seats, vacuum any extra crumbs or dust. I run a dusting brush over the walls, over the paintings of bears done by local artists, the dartboard, and the neon signs I've scooped up from eBay and Craigslist.

Then I artfully scatter peanut shells on the floor. I know that seems especially redundant after all the cleaning I just did, but this is what the pub is famous for—a warm environment for the locals to drink and a place to eat peanuts served out of small copper bowls with the tradition of tossing the shells onto the floor. Of course, over time the shells get stepped on and gross so I'm always putting a fresh layer on.

I sigh when I lean against the bar and take it all in, the bright sun streaming in through the windows, illuminating the stray dust motes in the air. As much as I love running the bar, being my own boss, and having my own business, I've started wondering if it's what I'm going to be doing for the rest of my life. I'm thirty-two years old and I know I have a good thing going on here, but some days my mind wanders. There's a restlessness in me that keeps growing, carving out a hollow space and I have no idea how to fill it.

I think about a life beyond North Ridge. Growing up I was never one of those girls who wanted to shuck the small town life behind and leave for the big cities like Vancouver or Calgary. That's what Rachel did. That's what a lot of girls I knew did. They left for university with their big dreams of a career and husbands and kids and ended up living interesting lives elsewhere, only coming back to the town around Christmas time, usually with their new families in tow.

For me, I guess I was just happy living in this town. I was born here and though my dad left when I was just a baby and I was raised by my mother alone, who would later become the nanny to all the Nelson boys, I had a relatively happy childhood. Maybe it's because I grew up on the ranch and even though Hank Nelson isn't exactly the fatherly type, he was still a father figure in my life and Shane, Maverick, and Fox became my family.

Or maybe it's because Fox is here. Maybe it's him that's always held me to this town like an elastic band. No matter what I think or do, I'm always snapping back to him.

But as much as I don't want to think about it, what happens when he finally finds someone else? I've seen girlfriends come and go out of his life and it's never really affected me. Maybe because I knew they wouldn't last long— it's hard to be in a relationship with someone when he's gone for most of the year fighting fires. Either way, it was easy to just pretend they didn't exist and I continued on in my friendship with Fox like they just didn't matter. Because they didn't. Not to him.

Now though, I feel a change. Maybe it's because I haven't seen him since he's been back. Maybe it's because he's with someone new and while I haven't met her yet and have no reason to think anything more of it, I feel like things could be getting serious. Fox is the same age as me and the older the both of us get, the more likely that he's going to eventually settle down with someone.

Someone that isn't me.

A knock at the door snaps me out of my depressing

daydream with a jolt. I quickly glance at the clock on the wall. Six p.m. Right on the dot.

I give the bar a once over and then head to the door, flicking on the neon OPEN sign in the window before unlocking the door.

"I thought maybe you forgot about me," Old Joe says, holding his cowboy hat between his fingers and giving me a toothless grin.

"You? Never," I tell him, opening the door wider.

Old Joe has been here since the dawn of time and if he's ever not here at six p.m., I start to worry. The bar is closed on Sundays so I can have a day off, and I have no idea where he goes or what he does then.

He's also a pain in the ass, sometimes smoking inside or forgetting to pay for drinks, but at least the old dude keeps me on my toes.

"You're looking sad today, what's wrong?" he asks as he shuffles inside, throwing a glance over his shoulder at me before taking his place at his usual booth. I swear there's an indent from his ass in the cushion.

"I'm fine," I tell him with a big smile that's purely for show as I go behind the bar and get him his glass of whisky on the rocks. He likes to start his day off with that before moving on to beer.

"You always say you're fine, muffin," he says. "Sometimes I wonder how that can be true."

I roll my eyes and scoff as I bring the drink over to his table and plunk it down. "Hey, it's a gorgeous summer night. I'm here, you're here. It can't get much better than this."

He narrows his eyes at me suspiciously as he takes a sip of his drink. Then he visibly relaxes and shrugs. "You're right. Can't get much better than this." He pauses and looks at me with puppy dog eyes. "Maybe if I had a cigarette."

"If you go outside to smoke, you can have one," I tell him before heading back to the bar.

"Doctor says I need to cut back on cigarettes. It was either that or drinking."

"He gave you a choice?" I ask just as the door opens and Finn, Ted, and another regular come in.

Joe shrugs again. "Hell, I can't quit both."

The bar is mostly empty with a handful of the regulars until about eight o' clock when most people decide to show up for the evening, including the damn mountain biking squad that won't stop hitting on me. I go along with it, of course, because the more I do, the better they tip, and I could use a new refrigerator.

The entire time though, I'm waiting for either Shane and Rachel or Riley and Maverick to show up. I'm also wondering if Fox will, and if he does, if Julie will come.

It's about nine when the door opens and before I even glance over at it, my heart is in my throat.

It's Fox.

Alone.

My breath hitches in my chest as he shoots me a smile that seems to paralyze me from the inside out.

I haven't seen him for over two weeks and though that doesn't seem like a long time, every time he returns I feel like I'm seeing him with new eyes. It's like I fall for him all over again.

And how can I not? Fox is tall, about six-one which is good since I'm five-ten, has a lean, muscled body and is in super-human shape thanks to the strenuous physical demands of his job, and has the most gorgeous face I've ever laid eyes on. Square masculine chin and jaw, usually accented by a dark beard or large amount of scruff, brooding green eyes that are beautiful whether they are full of rage or sincerity, and full lips I've hopelessly dreamed about kissing.

Tonight he heads straight over to me, his magnetic eyes locked on mine and I give him a wide grin in return. I can never play it cool around him, even if I try.

"Hey," he says to me, as he places his large hands along the edge of the bar and leans in slightly, his eyes searching my face. "How are you?"

Am I nervous? Damn it. I'm actually nervous around him. This is new.

"Good," I tell him, trying to keep my eyes on his face and not on his arms and chest which are straining against a tight black T-shirt, showing off his tan. "I was wondering when you might show up. I heard you've been in town for a few days."

I keep smiling as I say that, not wanting him to think I'm bothered by it. I'm not even sure why I brought it up at all but my mouth just wants to babble on about something to fill the space between us.

He scratches at his beard and gives me an adorably sheepish look. "Yeah, sorry. I've just been busy. Took a few days to recover, that was a pretty wild one."

"I was watching on the news," I tell him. "They had to evacuate the whole town."

He nods. "It made things a lot of more difficult given that we didn't have as many men as we should have and we had buildings and houses to protect but somehow we did it." He pauses, giving me a soft smile that makes my knees feel weak. "I didn't think you still followed the fires, I told you to not watch that stuff. They always make it seem worse than it is."

I shrug. "I just happened to see it."

"Right. Well you know I don't want you worrying about me."

"Someone ought to," I tell him, though it suddenly occurs to me that maybe that's not my job anymore. Maybe it's Julie's.

Ask him about Julie. Ask him how she is. Ask him when they started dating. Get it over with.

But I clamp my mouth shut before I have a chance to and bring out a beer from the fridge, sliding it over to him. "Here. It's your welcome back beer. On the house."

He reaches over and takes the beer from me, his finger pressing against mine as he does so, holding on for just a little longer than he normally does. "Thank you," he says earnestly. "I have to say, I missed this place."

I laugh and pull my hand away and start polishing highball glasses with a soft cloth. It's a thing I do when I'm bored or nervous. There's certainly nothing in this bar that *needs* polishing. "You say that like you've been gone forever."

"It feels like forever sometimes," he says this with some weight to his rough voice and I glance at him. He's staring down at his beer bottle, like he's working through something. This is nothing new—Fox, for all his bravery, is always working through *something*. Sometimes I think I have an idea. Other times I can only guess. Even though I feel closest to him, there's still a lot of himself that he keeps in, choosing to wrestle with his inner demons by himself.

He clears his throat. "Sometimes I close my eyes and all I see are flames. We lost one house up there, a farmhouse, no different than the one we grew up in. We thought we had it under control but then the wind changed and someone fucked up and then the flames were on the roof, spreading down and I swear I saw faces in the window. Faces screaming for me to save them. I almost started running in until a buddy pulled me back. When I looked again, there was nothing there. The house had been evacuated days earlier."

I'm watching him, listening, a bit stunned. Fox rarely opens up about his job and he certainly doesn't do it here at the bar. Though the place is busy, no one is in earshot of us but even so, it's unlike him.

That said, I want him to continue. I want him to open up to me like this, it doesn't matter where we are.

"I can't imagine what you must go through," I tell him softly, afraid I might break the spell.

He shrugs and raises his head, his eyes meeting mine. They look pained and for the first time I'm noticing they aren't clear. They're glazed, rimmed with red. The poor guy must be exhausted, even though he's been home for a few days now. "You'd think it would get easier with time. It never does."

Why don't you quit? I want to ask. But every time I've broached the subject with him before, he ignores it. And I don't blame him. Sometimes we do a job despite the hardships, because what we get out of it is worth the risks in the end.

He slugs back the rest of his beer in one go and then taps the bottle with his fingers, his eyes fixed on mine. "Del, darling, I think I need another."

I turn around to get another beer out of the fridge.

"Listen," he goes on while my back is turned to him, "I have something I need your help with."

"Yeah what's that?" I ask, rummaging past a few bottles of Corona before I find a pale ale.

When I turn back to him about to give him his beer though, he's on his feet and waving at the door.

Maverick and Riley just walked in.

And a short woman with high cheekbones and a pixie-blonde haircut who is beaming over at us. Or should I say, beaming right at Fox.

My heart sinks.

Julie.

This must be fucking Julie.

279

And when Riley's eyes meet mine across the bar and she winces apologetically, then I know it's *definitely* her.

"Del," Fox says, clearing his throat as he looks back at me. "I want you to meet someone."

Oh fuck.

I'm frozen, wide-eyed, even as I see someone else at the end of the bar trying to signal for my attention. I can't tear my eyes away from Julie as she comes forward with Mav and Riley.

Traitors.

Not only is Julie especially petite but she's built like a bird, all delicate and dainty, wearing a white sundress, lacy sandals and bright pink lipstick. With my height and muscles thanks to my competitive swimming background, the P90X programs I work out to in the living room, and my early morning runs, she makes me look like positively Amazonian.

"This is Julie," Fox says to me and I'm noticing that now he's not meeting my eyes, though he doesn't sound like he's ashamed either.

"Hi," Julie says to me, giving me a small wave that makes the silver bracelets on her wrist rattle. "I'm Fox's girlfriend."

Girlfriend.

There. She said it.

To quote *Friends*, well isn't this kick-you-in-the-crotch, spit-on-your-neck fantastic?

"You must be Delilah," she goes on. "I've heard so much about you."

"Oh really, that's great," I say slowly, trying hard to blink. I don't think I'm blinking. I'm certainly not *breathing*.

"I just moved to North Ridge a few weeks ago," Julie goes on and she smiles sweetly at Riley over her shoulder. "Thank god for meeting Riley though, it's nice to not be the only newbie in town."

Riley's avoiding my eyes now too, which means only

Maverick is staring at me with a strained expression on his face.

Julie goes on about where she moved from and what she's doing here but honestly I'm not listening at all. I'm just trying to pretend that none of this is affecting me, none of it hurts like a knife to the heart. I've been in this position before. I've done fine.

You and Fox are just friends.

You've always been just friends.

This is normal.

But then Fox puts his arm around Julie.

Leans in close.

And I quickly turn around, fixing my attention on the customer at the end of the bar, avoiding what I'm sure is Fox kissing her, something I don't think I'm ready to handle today.

I don't see how I can handle it any day.

This is my reality now.

Forget love being wildfire.

Love is a fucking bitch.

ABOUT THE AUTHOR

Karina Halle is a former travel writer and music journalist and The New York Times, Wall Street Journal and USA Today Bestselling author of The Pact, Love, in English, The Artists Trilogy, Dirty Angels and over 20 other wild and romantic reads. She lives on an island off the coast of British Columbia with her husband and her rescue pup, where she drinks a lot of wine, hikes a lot of trails and devours a lot of books.

Halle is represented by Root Literary and is both self-published and published by Simon & Schuster and Hachette in North America and in the UK.

Hit her up on Instagram at @authorHalle, on Twitter at @MetalBlonde and on Facebook (join her reader group "Karina Halle's Anti-Heroes" for extra fun and connect with her!). You can also visit www.authorkarinahalle.com and sign up for the newsletter for news, excerpts, previews, private book signing sales and more.

ALSO BY KARINA HALLE

Contemporary Romances

Love, in English

Love, in Spanish

Where Sea Meets Sky (from Atria Books)

Racing the Sun (from Atria Books)

The Pact

The Offer

The Play

Winter Wishes

The Lie

The Debt

Smut

Heat Wave

Before I Ever Met You

Rocked Up

After All

Wild Card (North Ridge #1)

Maverick (North Ridge #2)

Hot Shot (North Ridge#3)

Bad at Love

Romantic Suspense Novels by Karina Halle

Sins and Needles (The Artists Trilogy #1)

On Every Street (An Artists Trilogy Novella #0.5)

Shooting Scars (The Artists Trilogy #2)

Bold Tricks (The Artists Trilogy #3)

Dirty Angels (Dirty Angels #1)

Dirty Deeds (Dirty Angels #2)

Dirty Promises (Dirty Angels #3)

Black Hearts (Sins Duet #1)

Dirty Souls (Sins Duet #2)

Horror Romance

Darkhouse (EIT #1)

Red Fox (EIT #2)

The Benson (EIT #2.5)

Dead Sky Morning (EIT #3)

Lying Season (EIT #4)

On Demon Wings (EIT #5)

Old Blood (EIT #5.5)

The Dex-Files (EIT #5.7)

Into the Hollow (EIT #6)

And With Madness Comes the Light (EIT #6.5)

Come Alive (EIT #7)

Ashes to Ashes (EIT #8)

Dust to Dust (EIT #9)

The Devil's Duology

Donners of the Dead

Veiled

Made in the USA
San Bernardino, CA
16 June 2019